THE JOURNALS OF ZACHARIA 1905-1985

80 YEARS OF ADVENTURE

JERRY ZIEMER

Black Rose Writing | Texas

ISBN: 978-1-68513-106-7
PUBLISHED BY BLACK ROSE WRITING
www.blackrosewriting.com

Printed in the United States of America
Suggested Retail Price (SRP) $21.95

The Journals of Zacharia 1905-1985 is printed in Garamond Premier Pro

*As a planet-friendly publisher, Black Rose Writing does its best to eliminate unnecessary waste to reduce paper usage and energy costs, while never compromising the reading experience. As a result, the final word count vs. page count may not meet common expectations.

The Journals of Zacharia 1905-1985
is dedicated to all those who think they can't.

ACKNOWLEDGEMENTS

Zacharia is indebted to the Friday morning round-table meetings run by Red Oak Writing. My coach from day-one, Michael Giorgio, with AllWriters' Workplace & Workshop, in Waukesha WI. My good friend Ralph, who kept me faithfully writing, by constantly asking what Zacharia was up to. My wonderful, diligent wife Julie, who has read every line of his journals dozens of times, loves Zacharia, cries whenever she reads of his death, and misses him dearly.

THE JOURNALS
OF ZACHARIA
1905-1985

Zacharia Valentine Zabrinski

often wondered,

was he really a

Child of God . . .

or just the biproduct

of an illicit,

passionate,

sexual encounter.

You decide.

Monday, February 14th, 1887, two-fifteen in the morning.

Valentine's Day, Copper Harbor, Michigan. U.S.A.

. . .

"Angelica, you're breathing too fast. You've got to relax."

"Mamma, I'm doing the best I can. This hurts . . . I'm afraid."

"Celeste, I need more towels."

"Mother, I'm scared. Can't I stay and hold her hand?"

"Little Fawn, you get some towels. Now!"

"Martha. Dear, dear, Martha, I know what to do. I'm going to pray."

"Forget the prayers. I need towels!"

"Mamma, this hurts . . . I can barely breathe. Am I bleeding? Help me!"

"Jake, get those lanterns closer . . ."

"Damn it!"

. . .

That's how Angelica Maria Zabrinski left this world, and how Zacharia Valentine Zabrinski entered this world.

It happened on the second floor of a weather-beaten farmhouse, three miles from town. The temperature outside was freezing, snow was swirling, and visibility was less than one-hundred feet. Inside, everyone felt numb.

Father Dominic had just arrived from town, tied up his horse and gone inside.

He found Martha, Jake, and the Indian woman named Little Fawn crying. Celeste was in a corner, hysterical. Angelica, looking like an angel wrapped in white linens, was lying on her bed.

Zacharia was next to her . . . cooing.

PROLOGUE

August - 2018

My name is Doctor Randolph Quincy Babcock. I met Zacharia back on February 14th, 1985, at his ninety-eighth birthday party.

When I met him, I had just graduated from Harvard Medical School. I was offered my residency at Portland Memorial Hospital in Maine. The front entrance was one block from the Atlantic Ocean, I could hear the pounding waves and smell the saltwater.

I'm not sure why, but something inside was telling me to wait before starting my residency. I should get to know the kinds of people I'd be serving. I should find out what life was like, as some would say, on the ten-yard line waiting to go in.

Directly across the street from the hospital was the Portland Memorial Nursing Home. They offered me free room and board, plus the amazing sum of two hundred and fifty dollars per week. All I had to do was put off my residency for six months and put in sixty hours a week getting to know the residents.

That's how I met Zacharia. I'm not sure whether it was fate, destiny, or a fluke; however, it turned out to be one of the luckiest days of my life. He was a resident at the nursing home, and I was cleaning bedpans, among other fascinating, stimulating duties.

Zacharia stood straight and tall at six feet two inches. His light blue eyes had a sparkle to them; however, his left eye was darker, I attributed it to the four-inch-long scar above the eye. He had light gray hair which he generally wore in a ponytail. He walked with a slight limp in his left leg and used a walking stick with a carved ivory top. His voice was deep and slightly on the husky side.

"Mr. Zabrinski, how does it feel to be ninety-eight years old?" That was my question. I wanted to learn.

I got an earful.

Zacharia explained that on his eighteenth birthday his dear old Aunt Martha asked him how it felt being eighteen years '*old.*' He told her to mind her own business, and said it was the only thing in his entire life he totally regretted saying. That was the day he decided to never be '*old*'. From that day forward, he was going to be *growing,* not old.

We became close friends from day one. He started calling me Dandy Randy, I didn't like it, but I never stopped him.

Zacharia never married. He fell in love once, once for eternity. He said all a man should have is one true love in his life. He thought if a man deserved more, God would have given him more than one heart. He said that was a fact. Zacharia made it to ninety-eight years, four months, and twenty days. Then he stopped growing . . . I was devastated.

I was given his journals and some letters in a leather-bound suitcase. I have no idea why I received them, but I was proud to have them. I had to place my hand on his sister Annie's Bible and promise to wait until I turned sixty to read them. I did as requested. Last month I turned sixty, and I'm finally able to read his journals. I know there's more to him than he ever let on, I'm on a quest to discover what it was. I want to tell the world who Zacharia Valentine Zabrinski was. I want to know if he found what he spent the last eighty years of his life searching for.

It may help me find me.

Dr. Randolph Quincy Babcock

1905

FEBRUARY 1905

Wednesday – 2/15 The day after my 18th birthday.

Mother told me I may have offended Aunt Martha and God at my birthday party yesterday. She said when I told Aunt Martha to *mind your own business*, she had tears in her eyes. Mother thought I should apologize to her and God. Mother also had tears in her eyes when she was talking to me. She said Aunt Martha had a lot of things to go over with me, and now since I'm 18, I should know the truth.

Mother also suggested I start writing down some things I do, both good and bad. She thought it would help me avoid repeating the bad things, and it would help me remember the good things. I love my mother. She made sense to me, so I bought a journal and I'll start writing. I can find Aunt Martha; I'll have to go searching for God.

I'll start tomorrow.

Saturday – 2/18

There was one heck of a blizzard Thursday and Friday. We got almost 2 feet of new stuff. I don't think even God could get through this; I'd bet money on it. I'll talk with Aunt Martha tomorrow when she gets home from church.

Sunday – 2/19

Aunt Martha and I talked after church today. WOW! She had some incredible things to tell me. So, I asked her . . . then who am I? Really . . . WHO AM I? She said you're Zach, the same kid you've always been.

I'm signing my name, so I never forget who I am.
Zach

Monday – 2/20
My mother died the day I was born. She died giving birth to me. Did I kill her? Why didn't I die? Where was God? I thought He was always watching; I've been told He's everyplace. Didn't He care?
Zach

Thursday – 2/23
I met Mother, Aunt Martha, who's really my grandma, and our priest yesterday. I calmed down and could think straight. Grandma threw a lot of stuff at me Sunday. She apologized and said she was sorry, then she said Uncle Jake was my grandpa.

Father Dominic got to the house just after my mother died. He said they all agreed it would be better for me if my mother's twin sister raised me. They thought, since my father was gone, it would be hard on me growing up knowing my mother died.

Right or wrong they made a pact to wait until my 18th birthday to tell me what happened. I think they were wrong. My real mother's name was Angelica. It's a beautiful name, I'm sure she was beautiful. It's the first thing that's made sense to me all week.
Zach

Sunday – 2/26
I've had some time to start thinking about everything. I love my real mother's twin sister. She's the only mother I've ever known. Her name is Celeste, I think it's a beautiful name, and I love her. I told her I'd rather not call her Mother anymore. I'd prefer to call her Mom from now on. She said she totally understood. All she ever wanted was to love me.

We talked for a long time, Mom, and me. She told me the last thing my mother said, after some crying was . . . Zacharia. Then she was gone. Mom said she looked so peaceful; mom said a lot of other things.

I'm not going to write anymore for a while. I need to . . .
Zach

MARCH 1905

Saturday – 3/11

It's been two weeks since I've written anything. I've really gotten to know my mom. She's been telling me things I never knew, I always wondered why I felt cooped up here on Lake Superior.

Now that I know about my father, it's beginning to make sense. She told me I was named after him. He was the captain of a large cargo ship, he came from Brazil, right on the Atlantic Ocean.

He was heading to Duluth for a load of iron-ore. Because of a huge storm coming in, they put into Copper Harbor. Mom said he was the handsomest man she ever saw. He was tall, strong, and had an infectious smile. She said my mother fell in love with him the moment she saw him. In the early Spring of 1886, my mother was in love.

He claimed my mother was the most beautiful woman in the world. He'd be back the next spring with the biggest diamond he could find. He was going to marry my mother. I was born on Valentine's Day that winter, he never returned.

Mom raised me the best she could. Now this information has sunk in, I think she did a great job. My mother and Mom were more than twin sisters, they were best friends.

I'm not too mad at anyone for keeping it a secret, only now I've got to find out who I am. I don't know my father, and my mother died when I was born. I have to find out more about them. I also have to find God. I have to ask Him where He was the morning I was born.

Zach

Monday – 3/13

I asked Mom why I've been calling Grandma and Grandpa my Aunt and Uncle all my life. She explained it was all part of Father Dominic's plan. He told them since my father disappeared and my mother died, I'd always be part of a small family. He went on to tell them, from his experiences, the best priests come from small families.

Father Dominic asked Grandma how she'd like to have her grandson become a priest. Mom said Grandma was all smiles and Grandpa frowned. Then he explained, if I call them Aunt and Uncle, they wouldn't seem quite as close as if I call them Grandma and Grandpa, and it would be easier for me to leave them to become a priest.

Mom said Father Dominic could tell if I was priest material by my 18th birthday. If I was priest material they'd keep everything a secret. If I wasn't, they'd tell me the truth after my 18th birthday. Mom said Grandpa stormed out of the room, cussing.

I suppose I should be mad at Father Dominic, but he probably thought he was doing God's work. I can't fault him for that. What makes me furious is the fact he'd have kept it a secret from me if I was priest material. Seems a devious thing for a priest to do, at least to me. He can work it out with God when his time comes.

I may never understand my life.

Zach

Wednesday – 3/15

I spent a lot of time with Grandma today after chores. I've let the place go these past few weeks. We could run out of wood soon, plus the horses have been neglected. Old Black Eye was glad to see me today, I wiped her down good. I could tell she was happy.

Grandma told me much about my mother. She said Mother was small, delicate, and beautiful. Grandma said being pregnant was hard on my mother, before anyone could tell she was pregnant Mother started hiding in the house. She stayed there from early November until the day I was born.

They told the neighbors Mother died from the influenza that was going around. Grandma said Mother was ashamed of being pregnant and not married. Mother thought she was a disgrace to Grandma and Grandpa. Grandpa thought the captain of a boat from a faraway place committed an evil act.

After they buried my mother, Grandpa went into hiding for five weeks. He had an old log cabin out in the woods, and he stayed there. I remember the place, Grandpa used to take me there and teach me things about being a man.

He showed me how to put my finger on a cut and stop the bleeding. He explained how God created my little body with a heart which pumped blood to every inch of me. He taught me how to skin and field dress a 10-point buck, and save the meat, so we'd have venison all year.

He explained how to tell if the soil was right for planting and when the proper time to harvest was, he never got it wrong. He taught me how to talk to chickens, so they laid larger eggs.

I loved my grandpa, the only problem is, I thought he was Uncle Jake. I wish I would have known. He died when I was 15.

Zach

Sunday – 3/19

I went to see Father Dominic today. I was looking for some help in understanding everything he did. He knew my grandpa quite well and said to overlook how Grandpa felt. Father said Grandpa was a good man, he was just hurt at the time.

Father Dominic said he made up the whole story. He told everyone I came to my grandparents' house as a one-month old baby, and Celeste was adopting me. Supposedly, Grandmother's sister Alma, who lived in Detroit brought me here. He said, Alma's daughter supposedly had a baby out of wedlock, went insane and killed herself.

Father admitted it was a crazy story. He apologized but he felt it was best for everybody. Celeste was told to raise me as her own son. She did a great job and I love her as a mother. I'm not sure how I feel about Father Dominic.

Zach

Tuesday – 3/21

I have to talk with Grandma and find out if Grandpa thought I was the product of an evil act. I also need to find out if my mother was ashamed of me. I couldn't sleep last night.

Zach

Wednesday – 3/22

Today was filled with chores. Taking care of the horses and putting new shoes on Old Black Eye. Then cleaning the cistern, fixing the southern wall of the outhouse, and getting rid of a months' worth of ashes. I told Grandma we'd talk tomorrow.

Zach

Thursday – 3/23

I had a nice talk with Grandma today. I'm upset with the fact Grandpa thought I was the product of an evil act. I feel bad, but I can't get it out of my mind.

Grandma tried to reassure me he loved me. The last thing in the world he'd want is for me to think otherwise. At first he did think my father had committed an evil act, but Grandma reminded me that my mother had just died, Grandpa was furious with the world, and my father.

Grandma said he was hiding from the world in his cabin. He thought the story about me coming from Detroit was baloney. He said he'd go along with it, until I turned 18. Grandma said he came home every Saturday afternoon for the 5 weeks. He'd get the horses ready and on Sunday morning we'd all go off to church; maybe he's watching me.

I'm not sure about God.

Zach

Saturday – 3/25

Mom's mad at me. She can't understand why I question everything, I tried to explain my mixed-up feelings. All this knowledge thrown at me right after my birthday. Maybe they should have waited until I was 21. Maybe they never should have said anything. I thought I was happy before. I thought God was in our church and He helped anybody who needed help. Where was He when I was born?

Mom said my mother loved me unconditionally. She said my mother would have her and Grandma talk to her belly so I could hear them. She could never get Grandpa to talk to her belly, so she hung around him, so I'd hear his voice. Mother loved Zacharia and always believed he'd come back for her. Mom said his name was the last thing that came out of my mother's mouth.

Zach

Monday – 3/27

After church yesterday, Mom and I went to the family cemetery, behind the farmhouse. We stood over my mother's marker. All it said was, Here Lies Angelica, A Good Woman, Gone Too Soon, 1887. I had seen the marker before, but I never thought about it, I never asked who she was, there was never a reason to.

I asked Mom why she never married anyone. She said we'd talk about it later. We went back to the house and had hot chocolate with Grandma. A nice afternoon.

Zach

Friday – 3/31

Mom came out to help me with the horses this afternoon. She said she misses working with them, I think she wanted to talk. The horses know her voice and the minute they heard her they started whinnying. Old Black Eye knocked over her water bucket she was so happy. Mom and I had a good laugh.

Then she started crying. Mom said she felt terribly guilty. On the night Mom thinks my mother was involved with Zacharia the three of them were supposed to go into town. There was a dance to celebrate the coming of summer. Mom said she came down with a fever the night before and wasn't able to go. She thinks they were intimate because she wasn't there. She blamed herself.

When my mother died Mom could hardly contain herself. She said she was screaming and crying so much Grandma kicked her out of the room. Grandma had the Indian lady Little Fawn helping her, but there was nothing they could do. My mother was gone.

That's when Father Dominic came upstairs. He's the one who thought up the idea about Mother's cousin in Detroit and the one-month old baby. He thought it would protect my mother's reputation. They all agreed it sounded crazy, only there wasn't much time to think about it. Mom was hysterical, Grandpa was irrational, Little Fawn was crying, and Grandma was the only person who could think straight. Father Dominic and Grandma agreed.

When we were cleaning up the last of the horses' waste, Mom hugged me. She said I saved her life. She said if it wasn't for me and the idea of raising me as her son, she may have killed herself. She had lost her best friend. She was devastated.

Zach

APRIL 1905

Wednesday – 4/12

We had another snowstorm last night. I wonder what the weather's like down where my dad came from. It's probably hot and sunny. Someday I'm going to find out.

I'm beginning to understand what went on 18 years ago.

Mother fell in love with the captain of a large ship and got pregnant . . . not my fault.

I was too large for my mother's small body, and she died when I was born . . . not my fault.

Grandpa hid for five weeks . . . not my fault.

Father Dominic worked out the crazy plan about where I came from . . . certainly not my fault.

Mom agreed to raise me as her son . . . not my fault, but I was lucky.

I don't think any of this was my fault. I guess I should believe Mom and get on with my life.

Zach

Sunday – 4/30

Mom put together a pre-graduation party for me today. According to all the papers, tests, and books our teacher Ms. Bagley has, I've learned everything I need to get my high school diploma.

I have to get down to the city of Marquette, Michigan on Friday May 19th, to take the actual tests. Ms. Bagley doesn't think I'll have any problem.

I'll see.

Zach

MAY 1905

Thursday – 5/11

I came home from working at the dock this afternoon with a black eye, a busted-up lip, and a slight limp. Mom was furious. Since my birthday, some stuff about my background got out. Emil called my mother a whore. I told him to go suck eggs.

All hell broke loose. My best friend Pete, who had no idea what was going on, came to my side. Dock workers can be pretty tough, only I'm no shrimp, and Pete's almost my size. Well it didn't last long. The boss came out trying to figure out what the hell was happening.

No one got fired. Emil walked away cussing. Pete's fine, he didn't have to do anything. Mom's upset because people are talking about me. Maybe it'll be a good thing to get it all out in the open.

Time will tell.

Zach

Friday – 5/12

I'm due in Marquette next Friday for my big test. My face is clearing up, but I have a little limp. Emil hit me below the knee with an oar. He found it laying on the ground next to him after he fell when I hit him with a right jab to the nose. He says I broke it. Couldn't have happened to a nicer guy. I don't know why, but lately Emil's always trying to get under my skin. Maybe it goes back to all the fights we had in fifth grade. All I know is he's a creep.

I told my boss I was taking off next Wednesday to try to get my high school diploma. I said I'd be off for about a week. He told me not to come back. I thanked him for being so considerate, spit on the ground, and walked away. About a dozen guys were clapping and cheering. Pete and I went out for a few beers. I won't tell Mom.

Zach

Tuesday – 5/16

I leave tomorrow for Marquette. I'm worried and excited all at the same time. The weather should be fine for traveling, yesterday would have been perfect. I'll take a boat from here down to Marquette.

Pete says I'm stupid for leaving such a great job at the dock. I try to explain to him I want more than a job at the dock. He doesn't seem to understand. He's been my best friend since second grade, I told him when I'm rich and famous I'll bring him to work with me. Ha, Ha.

Zach

Thursday – 5/18

Arrived in Marquette yesterday. Had an incredible boat trip, the waves weren't too high, and we had a northwest wind at our back. Got a ride in a 1904 Oldsmobile curved-dash runabout motor car. It's made here in Michigan, down in Lansing.

It has 7 horsepower. Old Black Eye better look out, 7 horses under one bonnet. I was amazed by the experience, the wind blowing in my hair, sitting so high off the ground, I was thrilled. I asked what type of industry this was, and the driver said it's called engineering.

I take my test tomorrow. I studied all the way here, and I'll study all night. I'm nervous, a little. Hope God's on my side this time. I think He cares.

Who knows?

Zach

Friday – 5/19

Man was that a test!

The building I took it in was incredible. 4 stories tall and there must be a hundred classrooms. It's called Longyear Hall, it looks like a castle. I believe I did OK. There were some areas I wasn't too familiar with; however I think I did great when it came to explaining why I wanted to get my diploma. I told the teachers, I wanted to go on to college. To get a degree in engineering. I think they liked it.

They had me come back after supper for another interview. They wanted to know more about our schoolhouse in Copper Harbor and Ms. Bagley. They asked me if I could come back Monday morning at 10. I overheard one of the teachers say something about out in the middle of no place. After seeing Marquette, I agree with her.

Zach

Sunday – 5/21

They gave me a room in a huge home across the street. There must be at least 12 bedrooms. It's incredible, they called it a dorm and there are some other guys staying here. Since I wasn't planning on staying an extra 3 days, they gave me some spending money and told me to look around town.

This afternoon I stopped at an ice cream parlor called The 4 M's. It stands for Mighty Merry Marquette Michigan; I had the best strawberry ice cream I've ever had. 4 guys were sitting at a table about 20 feet from me, it looked as though they were having a fun time. One fella glanced over at me, and I heard him say something to the other guys, about a hick.

They all laughed. Leaving, I walked over and asked what was so funny, I told them I was from Copper Harbor. One of the fellas about my size, looked up and told me to mind my own business. When I get home, I'll have to ask Ms. Bagley what hick means.

Zach

Monday – 5/22

Went back to Longyear Hall at 9:30 this morning. I had a hard time sleeping last night. I met with the same 3 teachers. The head teacher, Mr. Beacon, told me to relax, everything would be fine. I smiled and thanked him.

I passed the exam and I'll get my diploma. I was thrilled. It's the first time in a week I could breathe. They said if I wanted to be accepted into engineering school I'd better read up on some things. They gave me 4 used books about engineering and suggested I do a lot of studying. I'll have to take a placement test at the University of Michigan down near Detroit.

I thought, no problem, until I opened one of the books an hour ago. It looked Greek to me.

Zach

Friday – 5/26

I came home over land instead of a boat, I wanted an adventure, and I had the chance. I was footloose and fancy free. I felt as if I was on top of the world, actually, Copper Harbor is on top of the world, or so it seems to me.

I did it all on 20 dollars. Mom was proud of me, for supper she put together a graduation party. Mom, Grandma, me, and Pete, we had a great time. Pete still can't understand why I want to leave. He thinks I don't love my mom, and I'm running away. He's crazy. I love my mom more than anyone else in the world, and I don't run away from anything.

Zach

Monday – 5/29

I started reading those 4 books on engineering. Wow! Talk about some tuff stuff. I love it. I'm going to do it. I'm going to become an engineer.

I tried to get my old job by the docks back, I'll need money for school. No dice. The creep Emil's related to the boss, and Emil doesn't like me much. I don't like him either. There seems to be more snickering and whispering going on when I'm around than there was last winter. Pete says he's heard some stuff, he won't talk about it. He says I should ignore it.

How can I ignore something I don't even know? I asked Mom if she knew anything. She said she doesn't go into town much. She's only 38 and I think she's pretty. I told her she's foolish not to go into town, she laughed and gave me a kiss.

Zach

JUNE 1905

Sunday – 6/4

Maybe it is time to leave this place. Maybe we are in the middle of no place. Maybe I am a hick as those guys thought. When Ms. Bagley told me what a hick was, I was mad, now I'm not sure, maybe they're right.

Mom's 38, she's pretty, at least I think so, and she won't go into town much. Grandma's got to be at least 60 and the farm is tough on her. Why do we stay here?

Zach

Thursday – 6/8

When I went to see Father Dominic a week ago the Bishop from Detroit was there. Father Dominic told me to wait out in the parlor for a while. I waited for at least half an hour before Father came out, he had some interesting news for me.

Grandpa had sent a package to the Bishop in Detroit. Inside was an unopened letter along with a note explaining the letter could not be opened until the day after my 18th birthday. In the letter Grandpa explained the entire event of my birth, and all who participated in, what Grandpa called, the Great Hoax.

Grandpa also included some things only he and Father Dominic knew about. Things he had told Grandpa on one of their hunting trips. Somehow it included Emil and his grandpa Walter. That's as much as Father Dominic would tell me.

Zach

Sunday – 6/11

Mom, Grandma, and I had a long talk today. I'm going to be an engineer, a damn good one. Grandma's only 57, and she says she's still full of life. Mom's 38 and she takes after Grandma. I'm 18 and I don't have a clue who I take after.

Grandma would love to sell the farm; she says she can't wait to get on with her life. Mom's fed up with this area. So, the 3 of us made a plan. Grandma's going to sell the farm and the 3 of us will move to Detroit. Mom and Grandma will buy a house, and they'll start fresh in Detroit. I'll start college. I'm excited, but first I've got some things to finish here in Copper Harbor.

Zach

Wednesday – 6/14

I went to see my old boss today. I shook his hand, told him he was a jerk and when I had enough money, I'd buy his company, fire him, and make Pete the boss. The boss laughed and said I should get lost. Then I looked up Emil, he was in a tavern drinking. I told him he was worse than a jerk and I think he's an illegitimate bastard. He took a swing at me and fell over, he mumbled something about getting even with me if it's the last thing he ever does.

I walked away laughing.

Zach

Friday – 6/16

I went to see Father Dominic again today. I went to confession, actually we both went to confession. Me to him and him to me. I think he's a good man and a good priest, even after what he did.

Father said watching me grow up was one of the highlights of his life. He also said I would have loved my mother. He said her union with my father, even though they weren't married, was an act of love. He wanted me to promise I'd never quit looking for God.

I promised.

Zach

Friday – 6/23

Grandma's having second thoughts, she had a dream last night, she said Grandpa came to her in the same clothes he wore at their wedding. He asked her if she was having second thoughts about being together until death do they part. He told her he held up his end of the deal and asked if she was going to hold up her end. He told her what goes around, comes around. She said she woke up sweating and scared.

The neighbor down the road has offered to buy 140 of the 160 acres. He told her she could keep the 20 acres with the house, barn, and family cemetery. He offered her an amazing deal and said it would be all cash. It puts me in a pickle, only it would be a great deal for Grandma. I never thought she wanted to leave anyway, mom's staying hush-hush about the whole idea. I'm 18 and ought to get on with my life.

Zach

Monday – 6/26

Grandma prayed a lot yesterday, and the 3 of us talked a long time. Grandma and Mom decided to stay here. Grandma's getting an incredible deal on the farm and she's going to buy 2 of those Oldsmobiles I told her about, one for her and one for Mom. She's also going to buy the general store over on Gratiot Avenue. Mom can run the store and drive to town in an Oldsmobile. Grandma says I should stay here and study until next spring. I think I'd go crazy sitting around here for almost a year.

Zach

Tuesday – 6/27

I sent a letter to Mr. Beacon down at Longyear Hall. I was wondering if he knew of any job I could get around there. A job that might have something to do with engineering.

Zach

Thursday – 6/29

Went into town with Mom today to take a look at the general store Grandma wants to buy. It seems to be in a great location, right on main street. I think Grandma's plan is excellent for the 2 of them. I believe, now since everything's figured out, Mom can get on with her life, I hope she finds a man.

The sale of the farm is going along quickly. Mr. Doberman already gave Grandma a down payment. He wants to get the fields ready for some planting, he thinks, with my help, he can still get in a crop of corn. He says I know the land the best, one thing I do know is the land, don't seem I know much else right now.

Zach

JULY 1905

Saturday – 7/1
Helped Mr. Doberman at the cabin today. When I stayed there a while ago, I swept it out real nice. Not Mr. Doberman, we had buckets of hot water, and we scrubbed the place down till it was too nice, at least for me. I left there feeling pretty sad. Gramps and I spent many hours, even days out in the cabin. Those were the best days; I felt all that was lost.

Felt pretty down all day today. Things have changed so much, half the time my brain's spinning. I wonder what my dad was like, or my mother, sometimes I even wonder what I'm like.

Zach

Monday – 7/3
Tomorrow's the Big Day. A big parade on Gratiot Ave., all the kids decorating their bikes, I did that for about 5 years. Fireworks after sundown. Lots of fun, I guess. My hearts not into it this year. Pete wants me to help him work on the float for his uncle's blacksmith shop. He says it'll get me in a better mood, I told him I want to leave town, he wasn't very happy to hear that.

I hope Mr. Beacon got my letter. Maybe I should go there even if he doesn't have anything. What do I have to lose? I can't be any more confused there than I am here.

Zach

Tuesday – 7/4
I helped Pete today and it turned out to be more fun than I expected. We were heading to the parade when Emil and I crossed paths. He said

something about my father, and I called him an SOB. We almost got into it again. Pete's uncle grabbed me by my arm and pulled me away. I'm glad he did, Mom sure would have been disappointed if I got a black eye on the Fourth of July.

I saw Mom walking and talking with Mr. Klein this afternoon. He's got a farm about 4 miles from us. A nice farm. His wife died about 6 years ago, I believe from pneumonia. Seeing him and Mom talking made me feel good, not as down as I was on Saturday.

Grandma wants me to look into those Oldsmobiles. I told her when I got to Marquette, I'd find out about them. She wants them long before the snow comes. She said she might send me to Marquette next week. She'll give me 30 dollars for the trip, I got excited. Maybe things are looking up.

Maybe it's God.

Zach

Thursday – 7/6

Grandma doesn't waste any time. When she makes up her mind, it's off to the races. She gave me 30 dollars and I'll be out of here Saturday. She wants 2 of those cars, she said the bank told her she can wire money anyplace in the world. I thought about the place in Brazil where my father sailed from. I didn't say anything to her.

Mom was walking and talking with Mr. Klein at the parade. Grandma sold 140 acres, and I'm going to college. I'll go talk to Father Dominic tomorrow before I leave. I'll get the name of the Bishop in Marquette and talk to him when I'm there. I'd like to see what else he knows about Grandpa's letter.

Zach

Saturday – 7/8

A lucky break for me. Pete had 2 weeks of time off coming, so he came with me. I found Mr. Beacon at Longyear Hall, and they have a spare room Pete, and I can use for a few days. Pete's surprised at the size of Marquette, and he loved the ride in the Oldsmobile. Maybe he'll understand me now.

When Grandma heard Pete was coming she gave me another 30 dollars. Grandma's excited, I wonder what Grandpa would think.

Zach

Sunday – 7/9

Today Pete and I went to the 4 M's and had some great ice cream. I had the deepest chocolate I've ever tasted. Pete had the strawberry, he agrees with me, best ever. We ran into a couple of guys I met back in May, I told them when I found out what hick meant I was pretty mad.

One guy said they didn't mean anything, and said he was sorry. One of the other guys laughed and said something about if the shoe fits. I guess I don't understand the language down here. Maybe I am a hick. So, what if Pete and I are hicks, I think we're pretty nice guys, and what the hell was he talking about, if the shoe fits. Why else would I wear them?

Mr. Beacon said if I can get here by September 1st, he can get me a part time job helping seventh grade math students. He called it a teacher's aide; he says it'd be good experience for me before going to college.

I'm thrilled and Pete's confused. He finished 8th grade with Ms. Bagley and works at the docks and his uncles' blacksmith shop. He never understood why I wanted to get a high school diploma. Maybe someday he'll come around. I know he has the brains, in a lot of things he's smarter than me.

Tomorrow we go looking for Oldsmobiles. Grandma likes the idea of a curved dash runabout. She thinks it sounds neat. She kept reminding me she can wire money anyplace.

Zach

Monday – 7/10

The only person around here who handles Oldsmobiles is the local blacksmith. His name is Herbert Brickman. He said we should call him Herb. He bought one in 1901, the first year they came out. Herb says few people want one, they think they're too noisy and they smell. Herb thinks the people are nuts, he says it's the way of the future. I agree.

Herb doesn't believe I can come up with the money. Herb spends more time with Pete than me. Pete's uncle is a blacksmith, so they talk the same language. It sounds foreign to me. Pete and Herb did most of the talking. I stood around looking dumb. I guess.

Herb said he still has 5 1903 Oldsmobiles and 2 1904's. I think he has more out behind his shop. Herb wants 650 dollars for the 1904's and 595 dollars for the used 1903's. I told Herb I'd talk with Grandma and get back to him tomorrow. Pete and I took a ride on the trolley car on Front Street. That was new for both of us. Neat.

Zach

Tuesday – 7/11

I talked with Grandma this morning on the telephone, she was amazed to hear my voice. It took a while for the banker to convince her it was me on the phone. She said the decision about the Oldsmobiles was up to Pete and me. I think she has more faith in Pete than me, he's used to working on things. She thinks I'm just smart.

We met with Herb after lunch at the 4 M's. Pete and Herb spent about 2 hours going over how Oldsmobiles work. How you start them, what can go wrong, how to change a tire, all kinds of stuff. I tried to pay attention. Pete kept getting me involved. I figure if I want to go into engineering, I'd better learn about how cars work.

Then came the money talk. Herb says he has a lot of people who want to buy what he has. In 2 days, I never saw anybody else there. He said since yesterday he had 6 people make an offer. He wants 25 dollars more per automobile then yesterday.

I told him I wasn't a hick and if the shoe fits wear it. I didn't know what it meant, but it sounded good the other day. Herb said OK if I can get the money to his bank tomorrow morning, he'll honor the price he gave me yesterday. Pete grinned.

I saw Mr. Beacon, and told him I'd love the job and can be there by September 1st. I explained how our automobile shopping went and he was excited for us. He said Herb's a nice guy, he's just always looking for an extra dollar.

Today was a good day.

Zach

Wednesday – 7/12

Grandma had the money sent to Herb's bank first thing this morning. She sure is anxious. Grandma's gotten much livelier since selling the 140 acres. She's enjoying life. Makes me happy. Pete and I went back to Herb, he said we could pick up the Oldsmobiles on Friday morning. He wants to take Pete out tomorrow driving and show him all the particulars. Whatever that means.

Grandma bought the 2 1904's. She said the last thing she wanted was last year's model. While Pete's with Herb tomorrow I'm going to look up Bishop Eis. I want to find out if he knows anymore about when I was born.

Zach

Dear Zacharia: Friday, February 14th, 1903

If you're reading this letter, I guess I've passed away. You may have noticed; I've been having a harder time breathing lately. Our doctor told me my lungs are decaying. I don't know why, and I hope I'm here for your 18th birthday, but if not -

How many times I wanted to tell you I was your grandfather. Every time you said Uncle Jake, I had to bite my tongue. I had to honor my promise to Grandma and Father Dominic, as crazy as I thought the idea was. I'm hoping this letter gets to you after the letter I sent to Father Dominic. I hope he's still alive.

I want some time to pass between his letter and yours. It may give you some time to process what went on the day you were born. I'd like to tell you some things I think you should know.

First off, I hated your father, until you were two days old. I loved you, how could I hate the man who created you? I know God had a plan and I thank Him every day for you, even if I had to be your Uncle Jake, instead of Grandpa.

Second, since I'm apparently gone, I want you to keep an eye on Grandma, she can be feisty. She may try to do some crazy things. Love her and protect her. If she sells the farm, make sure she has a good life.

Third, you have the greatest woman on earth as your mother. Love her, no matter what. She gave her life for you and your mother. I believe you saved her life also.

Fourth, beware of Emil. He comes from an unstable family. They were always trying to harm your Grandmother. I never knew what it was about, and Grandma would never tell me. All I know is she was afraid of them. She said it went back to when she was 16.

Fifth, always know I loved you unconditionally. And I counted down the days until your 18th birthday so I could tell you the truth, and finally be called - Gramps.

Sixth, always love God. Never give up on Him.

Love, Grandpa Jake

PS: See you later.

Friday – 7/14

After reading Grandpa's letter yesterday, I was depressed all day. I never left my room. Bishop Eis told me he was waiting until August 14th to get me the letter, but since I was here, he thought it would be alright to give it to me now. I agreed with him.

Pete brought me some food around three o'clock. He tried to cheer me up. I think it was a miracle he was with me. I feel much better today. With luck we'll get the Oldsmobiles tomorrow morning at 10, then we'll head home. I'll show Mom the letter from Grandpa when I get home. I'm curious as to what she'll think.

I love Grandpa Jake.

Zach

Sunday – 7/16

I think Pete's mad at me. Today he called me Zacharia. He's called me Zach ever since 2nd grade. I guess I goofed things up yesterday morning. I got involved with Mr. Beacon at the school. We talked about what I'll be doing in September when I start my job. All of a sudden the morning dragged on till after noon.

Yesterday we didn't get to Herb's place to pick up the Oldsmobiles until 2, and he was working on wheels for someone's wagon. By the time he got around to helping us it was 4. We lost the room at Longyear Hall, so Herb let us stay at his place. He's a pretty nice guy. He didn't charge us anything and his wife made us a super supper.

Today we drove, if that's what you call it, to Ishpeming. The trip was only supposed to take us a couple of hours. We left Herb's place at 11, right after church. We didn't get here till 5. We traveled 6 hours instead of 2. Mostly my fault. I seem to have trouble getting this darn thing to go in the direction I want.

I went off the road more than I want to remember. Twice we had to find a farmer to use his horses to pull me back onto the road.

Cost Money! No fun!

Zach

Monday – 7/17

We made it to Nestoria today, we're staying with Pete's aunt and uncle, and their 4 kids. They're all amazed at the Oldsmobiles, we had to give them all a ride. Pete's cousin fell out when Pete was driving. He was only going about 4 miles an hour and his cousin stood up and waved when Pete turned. The whole family laughed, they're a pretty tough group.

I only went off the road twice today, and both times we were able to get it back on the road. Pete says I'll master driving by the time we get home, I'm still not sure. I think Pete could drive his Oldsmobile across the water, he's so good at it.

We had another home cooked meal by Pete's aunt tonight, really great. His cousins were lots of fun to be around, especially Sally. She's 17 and I think she's cute. Pete let me take her for a ride. I did pretty well until I almost backed into the door out by the cow barn. Sally laughed and squeezed my hand; I liked it. I might try to stop here on my way to Longyear Hall next month.

Zach

Tuesday – 7/18

We're in Baraga. Today went pretty smooth, only one real hiccup, and it wasn't my fault. Pete rode over a pothole that did something with the gravity fed carburetor. We had all the tools to fix it and we were back on the road in an hour.

Pete says we could drive farther every day, but I don't want to. We'll be home by Saturday, and I want to enjoy the trip. If I'm going to show Mom and Grandma how to drive these things, I want to have a lot of experience. Pete says when I leave for school, he can help Mom and Grandma. They'd be in better hands with him, but I won't tell them that.

Zach

Wednesday – 7/19

The trip today was good. We got to Houghton. We could have gone farther, but this is such a neat city we decided to stop early and check it out. I'm getting the hang of having the thing go where I want it to go.

While we were eating supper downtown, someone tried to steal Pete's Oldsmobile. Our waiter came over to our table and said some guy was trying to start it. Lucky for us the guy had no idea what to do. When Pete caught him, the guy looked at Pete and took a punch at him. Then all hell broke loose. Pete and the guy went at it for a couple minutes.

Fortunately, a cop was walking by and broke the whole thing up. The cop knew the jerk and arrested him. The other guys in the restaurant started laughing, they knew the guy and apologized for him. Nobody likes him, and they felt sorry for us, so they bought our supper and spent some time showing us around town.

Oh, yeah, Pete's fine except for a sore right fist. He says, "You ought to see the other guy."

Zach

Thursday – 7/20

Stopped in Red Jacket for lunch today. We had a flat tire this morning. Herb thought we'd have at least one a day. Pete had me change everything, he said it'd be good experience. Someday someone's going to make the whole mess a lot easier. Maybe when I get to engineering school, I can work on it. Today's the first time I thought about engineering school in what seems like months.

After leaving Red Jacket it started raining. Things got miserable, we put on our rain gear which helped a little. The road got muddy and slippery, seeing in front of us became almost impossible. After a while Pete spotted a farmer who came running down the pathway to his house, waving at us to pull in.

Pete couldn't wait to get out of the rain, so we pulled in. Arthur, the farmer, treated us to some hot coffee and apple pie. Art's a widower and he saw us coming in the rain and figured we could use a break. It turned out Art had some blacksmith work done by Pete's uncle Paul.

Art and his wife Anna had gone to Copper Harbor to look into buying the general store on Gratiot Avenue 6 years ago. Their carriage broke a wheel and needed to be fixed. I told Art my grandma had just bought the store. Art brought out a bottle of fine whisky to celebrate.

We're staying the night.

Zach

Friday – 7/21

We left Art right after breakfast, we shook hands and said we'd meet again. Art's got to be at least 40, so who knows what will happen, however it sure was nice meeting him.

We made it to Eagle River around lunch time, so we stopped and had a soda and a sandwich. We had planned on staying there but we still had a lot of daylight, so we decided to head to Eagle Harbor. Grandpa has a distant cousin living here so we're staying with him and his wife.

It took him a while to realize who I was, but he sure remembers Grandma Martha. He and Grandma used to dance together at all the family weddings. He said he really liked Grandma. Maybe that's why he and Grandpa became distant.

Tomorrow. Home at last.

Zach

Saturday – 7/22

What a home coming. Will write more later.

Zach

Monday – 7/24

My spirits were lifted, and I was thrilled when we got home Saturday. It was a long trip, and I was pretty tired. Pete did fine, he seems to have more stamina than I have, probably from working at his uncle's blacksmith shop.

Mom and Grandma are thrilled. Pete took Mom and I took Grandma for a ride yesterday. This time Pete followed me. We went into town past the general store and up and down Gratiot Ave. Captain Willey was walking on the side, and I honked at him. I think he tripped over his own feet. Grandma was laughing so hard she started choking.

Tomorrow I'll ask Mr. Doberman if it would be ok if I spend a week out at Grandpa's cabin. I'll offer to clean it up nice and catch some fresh trout for him and his wife. Pete wants me to come down to the docks after work with the Oldsmobile. I think he wants to show it off; I passed for now.

I need some rest a lot has happened since my birthday.
Zach

Thursday 7/27

Yesterday was fine until around 6 last night, it scared the dickens out of me. I spent some time wondering if God was mad at me because my mother died. The cabin started shaking, the coffee pot slipped off the wood burner and Grandpa's 10-point buck fell off the wall. I ran outside to see what was going on but by then the shaking was done.

I had Old Black Eye tied up at the hitching post. I was going to get her ready for the night, only she had broken loose and took off. I found her by the creek drinking. We walked back to the cabin, but I had to do a lot of talking to her, so she'd follow me. I was shaking myself; I had a hard time sleeping.

I was at the house this morning and Mom told me there was an earthquake in Red Jacket last night around 6. Everybody Mr. Klein and her, met at church last night, had the dickens scared out of them. No one was hurt, at least up here, but there were a lot of trips to the outhouses. Some people in town blamed the Oldsmobiles for shaking things up. At least God wasn't mad at me.

Maybe He's mad at everybody.

Zach

Monday – 7/31

I may have heard God talking to me last night. I was at the cabin around midnight with a perfectly clear sky. I asked Him why so many crazy things were going on in my life. I thought it was a normal question. I think Grandma asks that question a lot. A shooting star flew across the sky and two words came to mind. Trust Me. That was it. Trust Me. Could it have been Him?

Zach

AUGUST 1905

Thursday – 8/3

I'm done at the cabin as of today, I may never go back, time will tell. I have this month left to teach Mom and Grandma how to use these Oldsmobiles before I leave for Longyear Hall. Mr. Klein has been coming around the house on and off and I'm thrilled about it. Mom's smiling more often. I imagine my mother would be pleased.

This weekend is the Summer picnic and dance in town. We may be in the middle of no place, but we know how to celebrate Summer. I've been trying to figure out how to get Sally up here for the dance, but it's so darn far. I wonder if I'll ever see her again. She sure was pretty, and I liked it when she squeezed my hand. I've never kissed a girl, but I'd never tell Pete.

Zach

Monday – 8/7

Old Black Eye had to be put down Saturday. She was over 20 years old and had a bad limp in her right leg. I think it came from the earthquake ordeal. Mom's doing pretty good with the Oldsmobile, Grandma won't even try hers. I'm putting a hold on my college adventure, at least for a year. I think it's the right thing to do, for now. I think Mom and Grandma need my help for a while.

Since Grandma won't drive her Oldsmobile, I'll drive it. I'll get in touch with Mr. Beacon at Longyear and tell him what's going on and apologize.

Zach

Thursday – 8/24

The farmhouse is looking much better. I painted the entire outside white with deep, deep, deep red trim. Mr. Klein says it looks great. He told Grandma if she ever wants to sell the place, she should tell him. Grandma told Mr. Klein to kiss her behind. Mom choked; it was neat.

Got a new horse. Named her Little Fawn, in honor of the Indian lady who helped me get born. Grandma cried. I see Pete every couple of days. He stops in at the store to visit. I spend about 6 hours a day, 6 days a week helping Mom there. It helps with my math skills, and I make money. Pete keeps harping on me to try to get my old job at the dock back, however I won't go near anyplace Emil's at.

I never did show anybody the letter from Grandpa. I figured why upset them. I did ask Grandma about Emil's family background. She turned white as a ghost, put her arms around herself and walked out the room. She did smile an hour later when I mentioned Grandpa's distant cousin over in Eagle Harbor and dancing. She twirled around the kitchen humming. She's been acting strange lately, Mom won't admit it, but I notice things.

I think now God's helping all 3 of us. I think it's about time. He's a little overdue.

Zach

SEPTEMBER 1905

Friday – 9/1

I was supposed to be at Longyear Hall today, starting my new adventure. Mr. Beacon certainly understood my predicament, he said if things change, I should get ahold of him. I think he likes me. I think he's smart as a whip and he's no hick. I tease Pete about being a hick every once in a while, he doesn't like it. He loves working on the Oldsmobiles, wants Grandma to sell him one, no way that'll happen.

Mr. Doberman wants me to help him get the crops in when the time comes. He thinks I should know the exact time because of what Grandpa taught me. I wish Grandpa were here now. I'm glad I decided to stay here, only there are some nights I wonder. Where would I be? What would I be learning? Those thoughts get me down.

Damn good thing I love Mom and Grandma.

Zach

Monday – 9/11

Up, down, up, down, I should be called the seesaw kid.

Mr. Doberman and I worked out some dates for harvesting. Grandpa taught me how the weather here on top of the world is so much different than by Iron Mountain. Because of all the water around us we don't get a frost until early October. Mr. Doberman's fields are in terrific shape.

Pete was trying to figure out how to use a gas motor instead of a steam engine. He darn near started his uncle's blacksmith shop on fire with the gasoline. He heard Emil's spreading some rumor about Grandma and what happened 40 years ago. Emil's an SOB.

In my spare time I've been reading those engineering books, I find them fascinating. Ms. Bagley's still teaching at the school. When she heard I wasn't going to Marquette she asked me to help her out once in a while.

I've been going to church more often. Grandma's happy about it, she said my mother would be pleased.

Zach

Saturday – 9/16

I crossed paths with Emil this morning at the café in town. I'm beginning to hate him. Grandma says I shouldn't hate anybody, but that's a hard suggestion to follow. I asked him about the rumor I heard he was spreading, and he laughed. Then I took my chair and hit him over the head with it.

I think I'm in trouble.

Our constable made me drive him out to our place and explain to Mom what I'd done. Mom was really mad at me. The constable told her Emil wasn't going to press charges, and I'd better stay away from Emil. Mom wants me to write an apology to Emil, I told her to suck eggs. Now I can't work at the store for a week. No paycheck . . . Crap.

I'm not sure what's going on, but all the while Grandma was giggling behind Mom's back. Grandma clapped when Mom wasn't looking. I'm supposed to be at Longyear Hall helping kids with math, and on my way to Michigan University. However, I'm in Copper Harbor in trouble with the law and Mom, helping kids in our dinky schoolhouse.

What gives?

Zach

Thursday – 9/28

We finally got all the crops in for Mr. Doberman. The week turned out to be excellent for harvesting. Everything worked out perfectly, almost as if Grandpa had done it. Mr. Doberman wants to hire me; he wants to put me in charge of all his crops. He says I can work miracles with the land. He never had any kids and I think he looks at me almost like a son.

If I want, he and his wife will put me up in their home. I'm not ready to leave Grandma right now, Mom I'm not so sure of. We haven't been talking much since the chair incident. It's funny, when Mom's not around, Grandma kisses me on the cheek and smiles. Grandma has been acting funny lately, so I smile back.

Pete stopped by earlier in the week. He was amused when he heard about the chair and Emil. Pete's uncle is looking into selling Oldsmobiles and is wondering if I'd like to sell them for him. Be in charge of Mr. Doberman's crops, sell Oldsmobiles, work at Mom's store after she's not mad at me, help in the dinky schoolhouse or go to Michigan University.

I wonder what God wants me to do.

Zach

OCTOBER 1905

Sunday – 10/1

Went to church with Mom and Grandma. Father Dominic and I had a nice talk after mass. I guess he and Grandma talk a lot. She goes to church a lot more than I do. Grandma seems to have a superb relationship with God. I don't know if I even have a relationship with Him. I love Him, I just don't know if that makes a relationship.

Mom and Mr. Klein sure have been spending a lot of time together lately. I've never seen them kiss, however they sure do enjoy holding hands. I don't think Grandma's so happy about it. Yesterday I heard Mom and Grandma talking about how Mom may as well live at his place, considering all the time they spend together. I'd be in a pickle if Mom moved out.

I start working at the store again tomorrow. Mom says she forgives me for telling her to suck eggs. I think she misses my help. She's getting pretty good at driving her Oldsmobile, she nicknamed it Black Eye, after our old horse.

Zach

Wednesday 10/11

I spent today helping Ms. Bagley at the schoolhouse. It amazes me how much good she does for the kids. She's been teaching here almost 30 years. She asked me if I could take over for her.

Her back's giving her trouble and she has to go to Marquette to see a chiropractor. She's certain I could do the job. I don't know what to do. I think the idea of being a teacher's aide would be an excellent experience for me. It might look nice when I apply at the University.

Zach

Sunday - 10/15

Spent all weekend working with Pete on the area he almost burned down. He thinks I should pass on the teacher's aide thing. I think he might be jealous of my wanting to go on to school. I know he has the brains, I guess he's happy here. I wish I could be happy here.

I wonder what my father was like. Was he smart? Was he handsome? Was he strong? Would he have been satisfied to be in one place? Would he have been able to stay here?

Someday I'm going to find out.

Zach

Tuesday – 10/17

My minds made up. I'm going to accept the job from Ms. Bagley. I start tomorrow. I told her I'd work until she gets back, but not a day after May 18th. She's thrilled. It takes a lot off her mind, and mine.

Grandma's thrilled and Mom's upset. What else is new? I told Mom she should hire Emil to replace me at the store. She threw a potato at me. I told Mom and Grandma I was going to apply at the University next spring. I suggested to Mom that she should marry Mr. Klein. He could sell his house, and they should buy Grandma's place, now Grandma likes the idea.

Pete and Mr. Doberman tell me they're amused watching everything that's going on with me. Pete says I'm a numbskull. I like him, so whatever he says doesn't bother me.

Zach

Saturday – 10/28

Mom's been having a hard time getting to the store. Too much snow for the Oldsmobile, so we put it in the barn, and it's back to the horse. Her new horse Little Fawn is good at pulling the carriage, so Mom won't have any trouble getting to town this winter.

Grandma sold the Oldsmobile I've been using to Pete's uncle. She said it was a deal she couldn't pass up. He gave her 50 dollars more than she paid for it. I told her it didn't bother me, so she bought me a horse. The kids at school get a kick out of it, from an Oldsmobile to a horse. Pete laughs. I've named the horse Freckles, actually the kids at school came up with the name. Freckles has 19 spots from his nose to his eyes. The kids counted.

Pete's uncle is going to start selling Oldsmobiles next spring. He's been corresponding with the factory and has an agreement to represent them for Michigan's entire upper peninsula. All he has to do is guarantee he'll open up shops in Houghton, Ironwood, Iron Mountain, and Marquette by May 1st, 1907. That gives them 18 months. Pete says, 'no problem.' His uncle also had to send them a big chunk of money. Pete's more excited than I've ever seen him.

I'm excited for him, but I feel as if I'm not getting anywhere. What do I do? I teach kids to read and write, and they don't want to be in school anyway?

Oh, heck.

Zach

NOVEMBER 1905

Wednesday – 11/15

Snow, snow, and more snow, good thing we've got the horses. Mom's doing great at the store. She's hired help, and now has 4 people working for her. Grandma doesn't get out much anymore, she always seems happy though. She likes to dance around the kitchen and give me kisses on the cheek. I like it, but I do get concerned about her.

Mom told Mr. Klein what I said about getting married. He dropped down on one knee and proposed right on the spot. Mom had already decided she'd love to marry him but was totally surprised at his reaction. She told him he'd have to clear it with me. I seem to get myself into these pickles pretty easy, maybe I enjoy it, who knows. Mr. Klein's coming here Saturday night to 'talk' with me.

I heard Emil got into a fight at the docks and was thrown into jail for a week. One of my students, his cousin Patrick, told me Emil's a jerk. He said whenever Emil comes to a family get together, he always ends up fighting with someone. Patrick said Emil's Grandpa is even worse. I take his word on it. I haven't seen Emil since the chair incident.

Can't wait for Saturday night.

Zach

Saturday – 11/18

Mom's getting married.

Mr. Klein was nervous, and I was all smiles. I'm thrilled for them. He said a few years after his wife died, he started noticing Mom and wanted to ask her out, but he thought Grandpa would get mad at him. After Grandpa died some of the things he'd heard about Grandma concerned him. When he met Grandma on the Fourth of July, he discovered how nice she was. That's when he started seeing Mom.

All I said was, if he loved Mom, he could wait 6 months to marry her. Their wedding date is Saturday May 19th. The day after school's out.

The day I become a free man.

Zach

Thursday – 11/30

Thanksgiving Day 1905.

I'm thankful, but I'm still not sure who I am. Don't know my mother. Don't know my father. Thought my grandma was my aunt. Thought my grandpa was my uncle. Thought my mom was my mother. I wonder what the rest of my life will be like.

Zach

DECEMBER 1905

Sunday – 12/3

Had a nice visit with Father Dominic today. He tried to explain how my always wondering who I am makes sense. He said it would be a normal question for anyone in my situation.

Father Dominic explained how my mother was an indoor person. Her and Grandma never missed a Sunday mass, and they often came during the week. Mother was incredibly religious and when she found out she was pregnant she was horrified. She stopped going to church for fear someone would notice.

He knows she loved my father. He said she was so excited to have his baby and show him when he came back the next spring. Father says I'm the product of 2 people who made a loving union. He said I should quit beating myself up over it. I agreed.

But can I?

Zach

Tuesday – 12/12

School's been closed the past 2 days. We got 20 inches of heavy snow. It started Sunday after church and didn't stop till Monday night. I've been shoveling and I hooked up the goofy snowplow Grandpa made. It connects to the horse, and if I'm lucky the horse can pull it, with a lot of help from me.

Pete came to the house with the Oldsmobile today. His uncle made some chains they could put over the back tires, so he'd get a good grip in the snow. Then they took off the front wheels and mounted old sleigh runners on the front end. It's the strangest looking thing I ever saw.

He took me for a ride. I couldn't believe how smooth it ran, it felt smoother than with all the tires on. Pete's going to go places. When I get my engineering degree and put it together with his ingenuity, we'll make a great team.

Look out world.

Zach

Friday – 12/22

The house looks great, Grandma and Mom have it decorated beautifully. Mom got some incredible deals on ornaments through her store. I've never seen so many sparkling things hanging on a Christmas tree. Mr. Klein is here almost every day; I'm getting to like him. I can tell he loves Mom.

Schools going well, the kids are coming around to accepting me. Some of them call me 'Zach the hack.' They mean it in a friendly way, they think it sounds cute. It's been a long time since I thought about anything being cute. Maybe working with the kids has been good for me.

I'm glad Mom talked me into keeping a journal. Once in a while I look back and marvel at everything that's happened in 10 months.

Zach

Monday – 12/25

Christmas 1905. Copper Harbor, Michigan. Mom, Grandma, Mr. Klein, Pete for 2 hours, Father Dominic for an hour, Mr. Doberman for half an hour. What more could I want? I feel great. No matter what's going on in my life, Christmas will always be my favorite time of year.

Merry Christmas!

Zach

Sunday – 12/31

Met Emil after church this morning. He accused me of giving him a skull fracture with the chair back in September. He wants the constable to lock me up. He said he filed charges and I'll be behind bars by Tuesday. He claims he's been having headaches ever since and can't see straight. I told him he never did see straight.

Mom started crying, Father Dominic tried to talk with Emil, to no avail. Pete wanted to step out back with him and settle the matter right then and there. Mr. Klein told Emil to go to hell. Grandma stepped in and told Emil to shut up or she was going to spill the beans about his grandpa. Emil asked what the hell she was talking about, and Grandma said, *"go ask the old bastard!"* Emil took off and the rest of us all gasped.

Thank God for GRANDMA!

Zach

1906

JANUARY 1906

Monday – New Year's Day 1906.

Last night was one heck of a night. Pete's uncle shot off fireworks by the Lake, Pete was here until after midnight, and Mr. Klein spent the night. I let him use my room, I slept on the couch. Father Dominic stopped by around 10.

Grandma danced and hummed around the kitchen for what had to be 3 hours. I don't have any idea what she knows regarding Emil's grandpa, but it sure shut Emil up. Mom has no idea either, and Father Dominic grins when I ask him. Something about the sacredness of confession.

Grandma and Mr. Klein worked out a price for the 20 acres and house. When Mom and Mr. Klein get married, he'll buy the place. All Mom has to do is promise to bury Grandma next to Grandpa. It made Mom cry. Me too, a little, I didn't want them to see me.

Today was a lazy day. It got into the 30's and the sun was out all day. A perfect winter day. Pete and I took his contraption out for a spin on the ice. He let me drive for a while. I wasn't sure if the ice was thick enough. He guaranteed it was. He was wrong, but we were right next to shore, so we got his uncles horses and pulled the contraption out.

It's hard to believe they're going to sell Oldsmobiles all over Upper Michigan. Pete say's I'm making a mistake going to college. He wants me to work with him, not for him, with him. It sounded nice. I'm not sure what to do.

Zach

Friday – 1/5

Half the kids are out of school with the flu, and the other half don't want to be there. Ms. Bagley never told me what to do in a situation like this, so I decided to play games. First, we played musical chairs which the girls liked, but the boys' thought was dumb, I agreed with them.

Then we had gunny sack races across the room. I timed them and the boys were having a blast until Kathrin won by 3 seconds. By then there was only an hour left, so we worked on our multiplication tables. It's the sort of day a teacher wants to forget. Good experience for me, I guess.

Emil's cousin Patrick told me Emil's hotter than a hornet. Emil's grandpa whipped Emil with a belt, then Emil gave his grandpa a black eye. His cousin's glad he lives on the other side of town.

Zach

Sunday – 1/14

We couldn't get to church today, way too much snow, it started Friday afternoon. I let the kids leave school early. When it was all said and done, we had 6 inches Friday, 12 inches Saturday and 4 inches today. Grandpa taught me a lot about the weather, and I could tell by the clouds we were in for a big one. Thanks Gramps.

Once it stopped around noon, I spent the rest of the day moving snow around. I moved the chickens into the barn, so they'd be easier to get to. I've got Mom's Oldsmobile covered with blankets trying to keep as much stuff off of it as I can. I can't wait till spring.

Mom put together a nice service right here at home. Ever since Mother died, Grandma has a small chapel area set up in the parlor. I think it was better than going to church, at least for me. Mom made a venison stew for supper and Grandma made a terrific pumpkin pie for dessert. Thanks to the snow I had a great day. I'll miss this kind of day when I'm gone.

When I'm gone . . . sounds funny.

Zach

Friday – 1/26

There's going to be a big dance in town tomorrow. Every winter the town plans a mid-winter dance. Everybody around the area is invited, even kids. It hasn't snowed in 4 days, so things are fine for getting around.

I saw Pete after school today, he said he'd come out and pick us all up with his Oldsmobile. Mom said she was going with Mr. Klein in his buggy. She thought Pete's contraption would scare the horse. Grandma's excited, she can't wait to ride in Pete's contraption. I sure am having a hard time figuring out Grandma lately.

Zach

Sunday – 1/28

I was too . . . something yesterday to write anything.

The dance started out fantastic. The band was incredible, I think they knew every song anybody requested. Mom and Mr. Klein never missed a dance. Grandma and I danced 3 times, she even got Pete to dance once. He owes her a lot for buying those Oldsmobiles.

By around 10 most of the kids had gone home. Then Emil's grandfather showed up. He was drunk. Again . . . or still. Emil wasn't with him. I thought it was odd. I figured they had a fight. Well, Emil's grandfather started cussing, and running up and down the dance floor. He tried to grab Grandma and dance with her. He called her 'pretty little lady,' and said something about 40 years ago.

I jumped up, but Pete was there before me. I think the old man was lucky. Pete had him by the arm, and was pulling him away, when Grandma hit him over the head with a bottle of champagne. She told him to get the hell out of there or she'd tell everybody about 40 years ago. Everything was over before half the crowd knew what was happening.

We didn't contact the constable; Pete's uncle took the old man home. The band played for another hour. Grandma said, what goes around, comes around, and then she danced a few more dances. Mom was horrified, Grandma smiled, and Mr. Klein scratched his head. I have no idea what it was all about. I didn't know Grandma 40 years ago.

Zach

Wednesday – 1/31

Emil's cousin Patrick came to school today and told me Emil's grandpa has been sent away for observation. He said Emil was crying when he told him. I don't know if I should hate Emil or feel sorry for him.

Zach

FEBRUARY 1906

Saturday – 2/10

Winter at the top of the world. I'm not sure why the past winters haven't bothered me so much, but this one sure has. It seems I'm always confused about something. A year ago, I didn't have a care in the world. Now I'm full of them.

I like the idea of being an engineer, I also like the idea of making money and selling Oldsmobiles. I'm pretty sure I don't want to stay as a teacher's aide past May 18th. I sure don't want to stay up here and tend Mr. Doberman's fields. I can rule that out.

I wonder what my father would do if he were me. Would he up and pull out? Is that what he did? Did he up and never come back? Was he a coward? Someday, I'm going to find out.

Zach

Wednesday – 2/14

My birthday. It feels as if I've aged 10 years in one year. Maybe I'm 28.

Mom and Grandma had a great party for me today. Grandma had ordered 6 new books on engineering, the kind I'll be studying at the University. She had them wrapped up separately, and hidden all over the house, like Easter eggs. It was fun.

Mom and Mr. Klein gave me a new pair of insulated boots and an incredibly warm winter coat. They came from Macy's out of New York. Mom can order from them at her store. Pete gave me a beautiful wooden sign he hand carved and put gold leaf in the letters. It reads, Decide! He was grinning when I opened it up.

Mr. Doberman sent over a bushel of carrots, a bushel of potato's, 3 dozen ears of corn and some winter squash. I think he hopes I'll work for him. Father Dominic stopped at the house and gave me a rosary which had been blessed by Bishop Baraga 40 years ago in Marquette. He said it would help me make decisions easier. I can use all the help I can get.

Zach

Sunday – 2/18

Went to church with Grandma, Mom, and Mr. Klein this morning. Mr. Klein picked us up with his new carriage. It was made by the Studebaker Wagon Company out of South Bend, Indiana. It's a beauty. Mr. Klein doesn't have a lot of faith in vehicles with gas motors. He says they smell. I'm not sure where he stands when one of his horses lets loose with a load, however he's marrying Mom, so I keep quiet.

After church we took Father Dominic out for a nice dinner, to a new restaurant in town on Gratiot Ave. Pete's uncle is the owner. He brought in a chef who studied in New York as a partner. Pete was stunned when he found out about the whole thing.

Apparently, his uncle has been saving a lot of money over the last 30 years. I guess after what happened with my grandpa, and his breathing problems 3 years ago, Pete's uncle decided it was time for him to live it up. That's why he wants to sell Oldsmobiles and he's starting a new restaurant. He never married and Pete's his only relative.

Now Pete has more reasons for me to hang around. He's convinced with my brains and his smarts, as he calls it, we'd make a great team. He's probably right, only I have my own plans.

I think.

Zach

Thursday – 2/22

Patrick said Emil's grandfather was sent to Detroit. They have no idea how long he'll be there, and Emil was acting nicer. He said Emil mentioned something about trying to get his high school diploma after Ms. Bagley comes back. He told Patrick if he was ever going to get the best of me, he figures he'll need more education.

I didn't particularly want to hear about it, and I don't think Patrick wanted to tell me, but he figured I ought to know. Maybe Emil's blowing smoke, trying to make himself look good to his relatives. Time will tell.

Zach

MARCH 1906

Saturday – 3/10

The sun was shining today, it almost felt like spring. Mom's making plans for the wedding, and every day she gets more excited. Grandma's pretty excited also. She said she can't wait to sell the house and move to Marquette with me. She thinks I'm going to teach school at Longyear Hall. She said with all the books she gave me I should be a super teacher.

Grandma says with all the money she gets for the farm she can buy a house and we can both live in it. Now I'm totally confused, but I'm used to that. Mom told me not to worry about it, she'll straighten Grandma out. I think it's something to be concerned about. Before she left Ms. Bagley gave me a book about ageing and forgetfulness, it sounded similar to Grandma.

Pete's uncle ordered 4 new Oldsmobiles today, they should be here on April 1st. He thinks April fool's day is the perfect day to get delivery. They only have 13 months left to get those 4 locations for selling Oldsmobiles. Pete still says, 'no problem, relax.' I guess it's not my money. I do like Pete, and I wish the best for both of them.

Why do I always feel as if I'm outside looking in?

Zach

Sunday – 3/18

Two months till school's out and Mom and Mr. Klein get married. I think Mom has Grandma coming around to living at the farm with them. She's been changing a lot of the furniture around, so Grandma has 3 private rooms for herself. They moved all the stuff where Grandma prays in the parlor, up to one of the bedrooms and Grandma's happy now. When I mentioned school the other day, she wished me good luck.

Church today was pretty nice, except Emil was there. I've never seen him within 6 blocks of church before. Wonder what gives? Is he trying to find God? I guess God loves everybody.

Maybe even Emil.

Zach

Monday – 3/26

Pete won. The past few weeks at school have been all I want. Maybe I'm not cut out for school, either as a student or a teacher's aide. I never want to step inside a classroom after May 18th.

Pete and I talked a lot this weekend. I committed to working with him, his uncle, and Oldsmobiles. He's thrilled. All I ever call his uncle is Pete's uncle, now he wants me to call him by his name, Paul.

The 2 of them have come up with the name, Paul, and Pete Autos. They call it PAPA'S Oldsmobile Company, and they're ready to go. Paul's the sole owner and Pete's the president. I'm excited about the whole idea. They want me to open the location in Marquette, since I'm pretty familiar with the area, and some of the folks there. I'll head there on June 1st.

Zach

APRIL 1906

Sunday – 4/1

Went to church with Mom and Grandma today. Mr. Klein's under the weather. Mom's tired of me calling him Mr. Klein all the time, she wants me to call him by his name, Frank. Sounds fine to me.

Pete and I worked every night last week on the Oldsmobile. He's taught me more than I ever would have imagined. If I'm going to sell them, I've got to know them. I'm finally excited about the future. Pete and I are going places.

Patrick told me Emil's studying like crazy. When I'm done as an aide this spring, Emil will try to get my job with Ms. Bagley. I'm perplexed by all of it, but I guess what ever will be, will be.

Zach

Thursday – 4/12

The kids are getting antsy. The weather's turning better and none of them want to be here. I think they're getting tired of me as their aide. Ms. Bagley had 30 years of practice with the spring jitters. I don't quite know what to do with them. I think it's smart that I'm going with Pete and Paul. I think Oldsmobiles are easier to work with than kids.

Zach

Sunday – 4/22

Mom's crying tonight. I told her I still had questions about who I am. Now she's mad at me. I can't help it. Mom thinks I'm nervous about my future. I said why shouldn't I be.

Zach

Saturday – 4/28

I had a nice talk with Frank, this afternoon. He tried to put my mind at rest. He's pretty sure what I've been told about my birth is right. He knew my grandpa pretty well. He said Grandpa was an incredibly good man. I showed him Grandpa's letter and he smiled. He believes it will be good for me to get away to Marquette.

I agree!!

Zach

MAY 1906

Saturday – 5/5

Two weeks until school's out and Mom gets married. I can't wait. I've been going over things with Pete about selling Oldsmobiles and what the plan should be. Paul ordered 20 more Oldsmobiles from the factory, 5 for each location. They should get here by the middle of June. I'll have some to sell right from the beginning.

Patrick said his cousin Emil's studying every night after working at the dock. Emil's grandfather is still gone and should be home by July. Patrick told Emil what I'm doing. He said first Emil started laughing then he started cussing. Patrick thinks I should be worried. Someday I'm going to find out about Emil and his family. What did we ever do to them?

Mom and I are back on civil grounds. I told her after she gets married, I'm going to stop writing in this thing. She cries too easy. When I leave here after the wedding, I'm going to stop in Nestoria and look up Pete's cousin Sally. Are all women so moody?

Zach

Tuesday – 5/8

Pete, Paul, and I had a good meeting today. Pete and I will go to Marquette together, and meet with Herb Brinkman. Paul has most of the groundwork finalized with him. Pete and I have to sign some papers. Paul bought out Herb's part of the Oldsmobile deal. Herb wants to retire to Florida. From my perspective, I don't totally trust Herb. Never did, but this is their company. I'm along for the ride.

Zach

Saturday – 5/12

One week to go. I told the kids at school Wednesday would be the last day of school for them. They love me now, no more, 'Zach the hack.'

Mom looks beautiful in her wedding dress. As usual I've been way to concerned about myself the past few weeks. I haven't paid enough attention to her. This week will be devoted to Mom, Grandma, and the wedding.

Her store has been doing amazing. Most of her employees are great, but she caught Patrick's younger sister stealing. I'm glad I'm leaving, the last thing I need to get involved with is some problem with Emil's family. I'll deal with Emil when I'm on my own.

Grandma looks terrific in her new dress. Maybe the crazy old man took a liking to Grandma 40 years ago. Who knows?

Zach

Tuesday – 5/15

Pete and I have both Oldsmobiles running and looking great. We're using them in the wedding Saturday. I'll drive Mom and Frank; I think they'll look outstanding in the Oldsmobile. Pete will drive Grandma and Father Dominic. Father's nervous but I told him Pete's great with the Oldsmobile. I'll be glad when all the festivities are over.

Tomorrow's the last day of school. The kids are antsy, so I did recess 4 times today. Patrick told me to have a safe summer, he puzzled me a little, I told him I intend to. Ms. Bagley came home on Saturday, and she has the OK to teach next year if she wants to. She told me she wasn't sure yet. She almost begged me to stay another year. NOT going to happen.

I went to church after school today. I stood outside and prayed everything will turn out fine this Saturday.

Zach

Thursday – 5/17

What a relief. School's over. The kids are gone. It's 65 and sunny outside. Things are looking up. Grandma's getting nervous about the wedding and selling the house. Mom and Frank keep trying to calm her down, only Grandma cries a lot.

I told Grandma to trust God and she laughed. She's been acting strange, she never laughed about Him before. We went out to the graves of Grandpa and Mother after supper and sat on the bench for quite a while. She hummed a lot; we said 2 prayers and sang Amazing Grace together. I've spent some nice times with Grandma, but this time was one of the best.

I asked her about Emil's grandfather again. She didn't get all excited this time. She said she didn't remember too much. I reminded her she was probably around 17 at the time. She said they went to school together, she thought he had a crush on her. She couldn't remember if she liked him or not. She said his name was Walter.

She said her father hated Walter's whole family. It had something to do with barns. Grandma was starting to get tired. I mentioned Walter sounded like a nice friend, and Grandma started crying and humming again. Then she kissed me on the cheek and said she loved my mother.

We went back in the house.

Zach

45

Friday – 5/18

Tomorrow's the day. Frank told me Grandma has been wonderful to him all day today. He said she kissed him and was excited about the wedding and selling the house. He didn't know what I said to Grandma, but he was incredibly thankful. I told him I'd send him the bill. We both shook hands and laughed. I'll be glad to get to Marquette.

Tomorrow's the big day. I'm excited for everybody.

Zach

Sunday – 5/20

Yesterday's over. I couldn't have wanted any more for Mom. She looked absolutely gorgeous.

I walked Mom down the aisle. Frank walked Mrs. Klein back.

Now both of my mothers are gone. I feel sad. Don't want to write much more right now.

I'm sure Grandpa Jake was thrilled.

Zach

Wednesday – 5/23

Mom and Frank came back from a 2 day honeymoon. They both have a lot of things to do. Mom looks radiant and Frank's all smiles. They make a nice couple. They both, at different times, tried to talk me into staying here in Copper Harbor. Not a chance.

I said I was leaving this Saturday, along with Pete, to get to Marquette. I've got my life to get started, they both understand. I told them I love Grandma and both of them, and I'll always remember where my home is. Mom cried. I'll never understand women.

Zach

Friday – 5/25

I'm all set. Pete will be here at 10 tomorrow morning. I think he's more excited than I am. He's been wanting to work with me since grade school.

He says we'll be terrific together. I hope he's right. Paul has lots of money wrapped up in this adventure.

Pete said the new restaurant is doing great, and the partner from New York pretty much runs it. Paul can spend time on the 4 Oldsmobile locations. That was one of the things I was worried about. Since Paul spent all the money on the Oldsmobiles, I wanted to be sure he had the time to spend with us.

Pete says it's up to me and him. His uncle's a great blacksmith and saved up a lot of money, only he's not very business savvy. Now's a fine time to tell me. I thought Paul was a good businessman. I'm not worried though. Pete and I should do fine. We're not hicks.

Zach

Saturday – 5/26

Mom and Frank were at the house at 8 this morning. They've been staying at Frank's place until I left. Mom made a huge breakfast, and some sandwiches for Pete and me to take along. They act similar to the kids I had in school this year, a lot of laughing. Nice to see.

Pete and I left at Noon. We did some crying, kissing, and hugging. I reminded Mom I was only about an 8-hour drive away, if the roads were good, or a 4-hour boat trip, if the water's good. Once we get our offices up and running, we'll get telephones, and we can talk once in a while. I told Mom and Grandma it wouldn't even seem as though I was gone. They both cried.

This adventure's slowly starting to sink in. Hope I'm up for the task.

Maybe God's finally watching out for me.

Zach

Tuesday – 5/29

We got to Marquette today around noon. We met Herb at the 4 M's Restaurant for lunch. The state of Michigan began registering cars toward the end of last year. Now there's a lot more paperwork to do. Herb calls it political crap. Surprisingly, Pete called it the price of doing business. He might be smarter than I thought.

We found a nice location right near the trolley main office. Herb says we can steal customers from the trolley if we play our cards right. He might be smarter than I thought also. I felt like asking, hey what about me, what can I offer? Then Pete looked at me and asked what time it was. I guess I'm needed after all.

Zach

Thursday – 5/31

We signed a 1-year lease on the office space, so we have 1 of the 4 locations nailed down. Across the alley is a building with room for a lot of cars. It belongs to the trolley company, and they leased it to us. The trolley manager told us the future's on the outskirts of town. Pete and I agree, but we're working with a budget, so this location's fine. For now.

I've got 2 bathrooms to clean, floors to scrub, windows to clean, and an office to organize, plus I have to buy a suit. I've got to have everything ready by Monday morning at 10 AM so I can open the office up to the public. I'm going to become an official representative of the Oldsmobile Motor Company.

God help us all.

Zach

JUNE 1906

Dear Mrs. Klein, 06/08/1906

Mom, I love you. I thought this would be a neat way to address you since you're married. Don't worry, I won't do it again. You're always Mom to me!

This has been quite a week. Plenty of things to get ready plus I had to get a new suit, actually I had to get a suit, I've never had one before. We have this neat office with 2 desks, a couple of bathrooms, one for me and one for clients.

That's what I'm supposed to call customers, not like at your store. Here they are clients, pretty fancy, hey?

I put a sign in the window looking for someone I can train about Oldsmobiles. A guy named Michael stopped in on Wednesday. He seems pretty smart. He graduated from high school, and Mr. Beacon gave him a good recommendation.

Pete says I should hire him part time, around 20 hours a week and pay him 20 cents per hour. I did, and he starts next Monday. It'll be nice to have someone else around here. He can do the bathrooms and windows, Ha, Ha!

It sure was great of Frank to buy the first Oldsmobile. Pete was jealous. Since I have the first location Paul put most of the Oldsmobiles right here, until they get the other 3 shops set up. My goal is to sell all of them by the end of the month. I think I can do it. I'm pretty good at working with the clients, and we're getting more every day.

It's only Friday the 8th and I already have five guys interested. I took one guy out for a ride on Wednesday, and he was thrilled. He loved the wind in his hair. He said his old horse could never do that, and his horse makes messes all over the place. He gave me a 200-dollar deposit and is going to the bank tomorrow for the rest of the money.

I did have one set back the other day. On Thursday morning I came to work and found 2 of the cars had their tires deflated. Someone let the air out of the tires. There was a note in one window saying, long live the trolley. I suppose we may be stepping on somebody's toes. I told the local police and they're keeping an eye out for trouble.

Got to go, it's almost 8 and I haven't had supper, plus that guy will be here tomorrow around noon, hopefully to get his Oldsmobile. I'm not supposed to call them cars, I'm supposed to call them Oldsmobiles. After all I'm an official Oldsmobile representative. It says so right on my business card.

Love to both of you!

Zach

PS: Give Grandma a great big kiss from me!!!!!

JULY 1906

Dear Mom, 07/01/1906

I love you!

Things here are going fantastic. 4 of the 5 guys I talked about last month, bought an Oldsmobile. Plus Michael and I, sold 7 more in June. It means with Frank's car, those 4, and the next 7, we've sold 12 Oldsmobiles in one month. I had hoped to sell all of them. It may have been wishful thinking. Pete and Paul left here this morning dumbfounded.

They both like Michael. The kid, I call him kid even though he's just a little younger than me, is good with cars, and people. I think if he plays his cards right, he could go places with Oldsmobile, but what do I know.

Pete opened the 2ⁿᵈ location in Iron Mountain. Paul was going to, only he decided he'd prefer to be up in Houghton, closer to home. Pete says it's got 3 great windows right on Main Street. Pete and I talk on the phone at least every other day. It keeps both of us charged up.

Paul said he talked with the Oldsmobile corporate office in Lansing. Since we're doing so well, and he's paid so much to start up the deal, they'll ship the next 50 cars up here, at no upfront cost to him. All we have to do is pay the freight charges as the cars come in. Their only stipulation is we wire them the money within 3 days of selling a car.

Paul's thrilled with how things are going. Me too! He mentioned corporate loves the name of our company, PAPA'S Oldsmobile Company. I thought it may have been a 'hick' type of name, but what do I know.

I did have another setback. Monday, when I got to work, I noticed 2 more cars with flat tires. This time they were cut with a knife. I notified the police right away. They did a great job and found out a 30-year-old guy who used to work for the trolley company, had gone to the hospital Sunday morning, with a large cut on his hand.

They found him and he confessed. I met with him on Tuesday. He explained how he was laid off from the trolley company, and he figured it had something to do with these new cars on the streets. The police said he has something called Mongolism. He's a very nice guy. I believe he was scared, so I didn't press charges and Michael taught him how to fix the tires. We're going to hire him part time to do all our cleaning, running errands, etc.

Well, I guess that's it for now. I sure do miss all of you. Maybe I write too much about what's going on here, but it's so exciting. I think I made the right decision to go with Paul and Pete. At least for now.

Grandma – I LOVE You, this much *---*
Love to You and Frank,
Zach

Dear Mom, 07/29/1906
Love You!

Thanks for the nice letter. I Hope things are going better for Grandma. It sounds like she took a nasty fall out by Grandpa's grave. You mentioned she seems more forgetful now. I thought she was getting forgetful before I left. I know she's feisty, and I agree with what the Doctor told you.

By the way, you mentioned Emil's grandpa Walter never came back from Detroit, and he died there. How did it affect Grandma? I never could figure out their relationship, could you? Oh, well.

Things here are going along so smoothly I can hardly believe it. Michael and the new 30-year-old guy Charles, are doing great. Charles keeps the Oldsmobiles so sparkling our clients are fascinated by the paint jobs. It turns out almost everybody in town knows Charles and they're all thrilled I hired him after the trolley company fired him. I think Charles brings in more clients than Michael or me.

We're having trouble with the trolley company. They claim they had no idea how we were going to use their building when we signed the lease. I met with some of their big wigs and attempted to re-explain what we're doing. They're seeing if they can break our lease. Paul hired an attorney.

One of these days I'm coming home to see all of you, only for now I've got to get dinner and get to bed. Tomorrow's going to be another great day at PAPA'S Oldsmobile Company. I hope.

Love to the 3 of you! Give Grandma a big kiss from me.
Zach

AUGUST 1906

Dear Mom, 08/19/1906

Did you say Frank's thinking about having gasoline pumps put in at the store? I know I was teasing him about the idea a while ago. I never thought he'd do it. I think it's fantastic. You made my day, which is saying a lot right now.

As I told you last month the trolley company's trying to get us out of here and Paul hired an attorney to fight them. I met with our attorney yesterday in an attempt to figure out how to convince the trolley people we're not a threat to them. Our attorney's wondering if we can get some bigwig from Oldsmobile up here to state our case.

Pete and I like the idea. Paul's hesitant. I think he feels he should be able to handle it on his own. I guess, as Pete told me a while ago, his uncle's a great blacksmith just not the best businessman. I happen to think Paul's both, that's because he had all the money, and I respect him a lot.

Charles is incredible, everybody loves him. He stutters a little, sometimes he seems more like a kid than a 30-year-old guy. He has a constant grin on his face and would do anything for anybody. He's almost too trusting. I'm sure glad I hired him. He's fun to be around, and he keeps the cars glowing, day and night. He even talked me into putting up some lights on the Oldsmobiles at night.

I'm trying to forget all about the trolley people and their attorney. Paul has to deal with them. I'm only concerned about the PAPA'S dealership right here in Marquette. Michael, Charles, and I can sell Oldsmobiles anyplace they put us.

I sent a letter to Pete's cousin Sally, over in Nestoria back in June, telling her I'd like to come over and visit in August. I got a letter back 2 weeks ago saying GREAT. I'm heading over there next Saturday. It's about a 40-mile trip each way. I should get there by 10 in the morning. I'm thinking about taking Charles, he'd love it. I'm getting pretty excited. Got to go.

By the way, I've been going to church on Sundays. Went this morning with Michael to his church. I'm not real picky, I think God's in all of them.

Love,

Zach

PS – PS – PS – Give Grandma a great big, huge, kiss and hug from me.

SEPTEMBER 1906

Saturday – 9/1

What a past 3 months, it's been a whirlwind. I hope I haven't neglected my inner spirit by not writing in this journal. I know Mom wanted me to keep a journal, but I've been having more fun living my life and writing letters home to Mom every month or so.

Writing to myself seems odd, isn't life about living in the present? Why on earth do I want to look back at yesterday? I want to look forward to tomorrow! I'm having an incredible time right here in Marquette.

When I was back home writing in the journals made some sense to me. I could keep track of what was going on. Now when I look back at some of my writing, I sounded so confused. I questioned everything. I sound as if I was lost sometimes.

The last thing I feel here in Marquette is lost. I feel like I belong right here, right now.

I love back home, and I love everybody there, except Emil. I miss back home and all the folks. I'll go back home from time to time to visit and be happy, but I could never GO back home. I like it here. Hopefully, I'll enjoy it wherever I am from now on.

Zach

Sunday - 9/16

Things here are going great guns. The 2 guys I hired are turning out to be a godsend. Michael's amazing with clients and the Oldsmobiles. Charles is so much fun to be around. He acts so silly sometimes, and then a minute later, he's so serious it makes me laugh.

We've had some trouble with the trolley people. Paul has everything under control. I think he may have bribed the president of the trolley company, cause now the guy's driving around in a brand-new Oldsmobile, and it didn't come from my inventory.

Had lunch the other day with Michael and Charles at the 4-M's Restaurant. I ran into those guys from last summer. I asked them if they remembered the hick from up north. It turns out the fella who told me 'if the shoe fits' works at the trolley company. I think I may convince him to buy an Oldsmobile.

Maybe writing in this thing once in a while, and reading past entries, will be good for me after all. Maybe it'll keep me grounded. Keep me from getting too big for my britches. As Mom would say.

Zach

Sunday – 9/30

Things around here are getting interesting. I'm not sure what's going on and Pete doesn't want to talk about it. All I know is Paul was called to Lansing to meet with Oldsmobile management. Pete says he heard Paul talking on the phone with them, something about money. Then he said he'd be there as soon as he could.

Pete's doing better at his location in Iron Mountain. I'm still out selling him; I think it's because Marquette's a bigger city. I think I'm going to drive over by Pete next week and surprise him. Michael and Charles can run this place for a few days, heck I think Michael could run this place.

I believe the things I've done here are working out pretty darn well. Paul and Pete both seem happy with how it's going. I enjoy it. I like working with Michael and Charles. I've got a neat apartment and I can see Lake Superior. The pace every day is stimulating, to say the least.

Everything about it should have me thrilled, however, now winter's coming and sales are slowing down. I'm starting to question things again. Reading in my journals started me thinking about my mother and father again.

I imagine anyone who's been raised in a complete family would never understand my questions. They never wake up in the middle of the night wondering who their mother and father were. What part of the world was their father from? That stuff may not matter to some guys.

It does to me.

Zach

OCTOBER 1906

Dear Mom, 10/14/1906

I'm sorry I haven't written you since August. Things here have been busy. I had a wonderful time with Pete's cousin Sally. I did take Charles along, what a hoot that was. I'm glad I had him with me cause on the way home I had a flat tire in the dark. He had it fixed in fifteen minutes.

Everybody there liked Charles. With his smile and laugh, he's hard not to like. He and Michael are working out nicely, they're worth every dollar they make. Don't tell them if you ever see them.

I don't know if I ever told you about my apartment. It's on the 2ⁿᵈ floor of an old Victorian house which was converted into 4 apartments. It has 2 bedrooms, a small kitchen, a huge bathroom, living room and an outside front porch. From the porch I can see Lake Superior. Makes me think of my father.

I miss all of you, especially Grandma. I miss you also, only you're married now so you've got Frank. Grandma doesn't have a guy, or does she? I wouldn't be surprised if she found a guy. Maybe Emil has an older uncle. Ha, Ha.

There are some goofy things going on here with Paul and the trolley folks. I deal with the trolley people, and we decide on something and then 3 days later it's all changed because of something Paul does. Oh well, he has the money, not me.

I'm coming home for a visit. I'll be there Friday the 26ᵗʰ and leave to come back here on Monday. Warn Grandma, I'm looking for those big kisses. Maybe I'll bring Charles, he and Grandma would make a perfect couple.

Love,
Zach
P.S. I did kiss Sally, out behind their barn. The sun was going down, it was romantic.

NOVEMBER 1906

Sunday – 11/4

Spent last weekend with Mom, Grandma and Frank back home in Copper Harbor. Sounds funny when I write it – back home. Had a good time, how nice to feel Grandma's kisses again. I missed them.

Mom looked great, all smiles ear to ear. She seemed to glow, and Frank, he looks great. She says the store is doing well. The problem with Emil's cousin stealing has been resolved. She apologized, and Mom accepted it. Mom takes more time off since she married Frank, I don't blame her.

Grandma spends lots of time out by Grandpa's marker, she said she prays a lot. I went with her after church on Sunday and spent half an hour with her there. I casually asked about Walter, Emil's grandfather. This time she stood up, danced, and started humming. She had some tears running down her cheek. I was completely dumbfounded so I changed the topic, started talking about Oldsmobiles. They seem to be the only thing I know much about right now.

I had lunch with Ms. Bagley on Saturday. She decided to stay teaching one more year, then she said she'll retire. Emil's about ready to take his high school graduation exam. Ms. Bagley thinks he won't have any problem. Emil told her he'd like to be her substitute teacher anytime she want's off. She said he's turning out to a very nice guy since his grandpa died.

I DON'T TRUST HIM ANY FARTHER THAN I COULD THROW HIM.

That's a fact!

Zach

Sunday – 11/25

Thursday is Thanksgiving. I'm giving both Michael and Charles a 4-day paid weekend off. They're thrilled. They both invited me over to their parents' home for dinner. I'm trying to decide if I should go see Sally for Thanksgiving, over by one of them, or home.

Seems to me ever since Pete gave me the sign which reads Decide, I've been pretty good at deciding, only this one's tougher. I don't want to come across as being too fond of Sally, but I do enjoy being with her. I think she likes me a lot, at least Pete told me she did.

If I settled down here, I would certainly get to know her better. Do I want to stay in Marquette forever? That's what I keep wondering. What about the pounding waves and the smell of saltwater I used to think about? What about my father?

Whatever was going on with Paul and the Oldsmobile folks must have been settled. Pete hasn't said anything about it, and they keep sending us more cars, although now it's cash on delivery. I guess Paul has quite a nest-egg built up, lucky guy. He says he has plenty of money right here in the bank.

I'm going to see Sally for Thanksgiving . . . but alone.

Zach

DECEMBER 1906

Sunday – 12/2

Went to see Sally for Thanksgiving and I totally surprised her. Not smart on my part. How can I have 2 guys working for me, sell Oldsmobiles pretty darn well, get the money to the corporate office in Lansing when they need it, make payroll, pay the rent for the shop and my apartment, on and on and on, and then screw up seeing Sally.

I got there and she had a 'friend' there for dinner with the family. She introduced me to him as a friend of her cousin Pete. He seemed like a swell guy, I even liked him, still, I sure felt awkward.

Sally and I talked after dinner and her 'friend' had gone home. She was flattered I'd come all the way to see her. She said now she's older, she's starting to think about getting married, and what sort of guy she likes. She said we've known each other for 16 months and asked if I was I serious about her.

She asked a lot of stuff. Oldsmobiles don't ask questions. She asked if I'd come there for Christmas. I told her I had to go home if I could make it. She was disappointed, she's even cuter when she pouts. I sure don't want to get married yet. I'll never understand women, but I sure enjoy her.

Zach

Sunday – 12/16

Next week is Christmas, one of my favorite times of the year. Business has dried up. Makes sense, horses do better in 10 inches of snow than Oldsmobiles. We haven't had anyone in the showroom for 2 weeks, other than the fella who works at the trolley company.

He came in pretending he was interested in a new Oldsmobile and was talking with Michael. Charles saw him from the back room and called me over to warn me about him. Before I could get out to the showroom the guy took out a wrench and started smashing the glass and lights in one of our prettiest cars in the room.

Michael and I tried to subdue him. He was incredibly strong and mad as hell. He got away, took off down the street, and never saw Charles. The police arrested him last week, we were able to tell them who it was thanks to Charles. He's in jail for now, and we have to go to court January 18th to testify against him. Charles is worried, he thinks the guy will beat him up.

I'm closing the shop on Friday and won't open it up until Monday, January 7th. We'll all get a nice 2-week vacation. I'm paying both of them, they're thrilled. I'm heading home for Christmas, a few days up there, then down to spend New Year's Eve with Pete. He's got a girlfriend in Iron Mountain. Says he can't go home; she wants him to stay there.

Women. Phooey!

Zach

1907

JANUARY 1907

Thursday - 1/3

Well that was one hell of an experience. I had a fine time back home with the family over the Christmas Holiday. Seeing Mom, Grandma and Frank is always nice. I didn't get to see Pete as planned because a snowstorm was coming. I believe I was the only person in Upper Michigan who could tell what was coming.

All the credit goes to Grandpa, he taught me well. We had 3 days of nice sun, cold and nice, then clouds started coming in from the west. The wind started changing directions for a couple of days and I knew we were in for it.

I stopped at Sally's place for New Year's Eve, pretty interesting to say the least. Her family thinks I make a lot of money. I think they want her and I to get together, I mean 'together.' Her brother happened to be going to his friends' place so I could use his bedroom, which I thought was nice. Sally's a pretty girl, with her long wavy red hair. She has a nicer figure than I've ever seen, I could say she's a knock-out.

Well, I could never tell Pete this, but about 2 in the morning she came into my room and asked if I loved her. She started taking off her night gown and climbing into bed with me. She said she loved me. Well, I like girls, but I got scared. I'm not ready to get married.

For a brief second, I thought of my mother and father and how I was conceived. I sat up, put my clothes on, and sat on the edge of the bed. Sally was puzzled. I explained about my father and mother, she said she understood. I think she was insulted, but I was flattered.

I like Sally, only I don't think I'll be stopping there again. It's a New Year's Eve I'll never forget.

Zach

Dear Mom, 01/05/1907

Things here are slow, I mean SLOW.

I had a great time with all of you over Christmas. It felt good to be back home for the holidays! I don't think I've ever eaten anything as tasty as Grandmas' pies. Maybe someday I'll have a wife who can cook as swell as Grandma. Who knows?

I think the present from you and Frank is incredible. If I ever get to Lansing and have to meet with the Oldsmobile people, I'll look like a million dollars. It's interesting all the things you can get since you bought the store.

I told you I was heading to see Pete and spend New Year's Eve with him and his new girlfriend. Well I had a change of plans along the way. I remember a lot of the things Grandpa taught me about the weather and I noticed changes in the clouds and the wind direction. When I got to Houghton, I headed toward Baraga.

I decided to head over to Nestoria to visit with Sally. I wanted to avoid the snowstorm I knew was coming. I was welcomed with open arms. I think they think I'm a big wig with Oldsmobile, that's what they call me anyway. They wanted me to spend New Year's Eve with them.

They're a nice family, strange but nice. They've got a nice size farm. I think they have 35 cattle, lots of chickens, and 6 nice horses. Maybe I'll sell them an Oldsmobile someday. I spent New Year's Eve with them and headed out first thing Tuesday morning. I beat the storm home by 6 hours, thanks to Grandpa's teaching me.

Her family thought I was crazy for leaving so early. I wanted to get out of there and get back to my place. Well, as I said it's slow here, but I guess it's to be expected. Who wants to buy a car in the middle of winter?

Give Grandma a kiss, give Frank a hug, and have Frank give you a kiss from me.

Love,

Zach.

P.S. I like Sally a lot, I'm just not sure I want to settle down right now.

P.P.S. After I got settled in my apartment, I put on some warm clothes and stood on my front porch in the snow and watched the waves on Lake Superior crashing onto the beach. I thought of my mother and father.

Wednesday - 1/16

Friday's the big day in court. Charles is nervous about seeing the fella who broke all the glass in the new Oldsmobile. He's certain the guy will beat him up when he sees him someday. I'll try to keep Charles out of court if I can.

Last week we had 3 guys come in with problems with their Oldsmobiles. They forgot to put the mixture of calcium chloride and water into the radiators. They blew out the core plugs in their engines.

They were ticked with us until Charles talked to them. They wouldn't pay any attention to Michael or me, however they listened to Charles. He does have a calming effect sometimes. Charles taught himself how to replace the plugs and by Friday evening everything should be finished.

Talked to Pete on Saturday, sounds as if he and his girlfriend Samantha, he calls her Sammy, are getting pretty tight. He asked about my visit with Sally. I told him I thought she was a little forward and he howled. He said he should have warned me, only he thought it would be a good experience for me. I told him he was lucky he was over in Iron Mountain, or I'd punch him.

Charles offered to letter some signs for the showroom. He says he's pretty good with lettering brush. He did some showcards for the trolley company, so I'll give him a try next month. He's a man of many talents.

Pete mentioned something about his uncle Paul and the restaurant up in Copper Harbor. I guess the partner isn't as experienced a chef as he said he was. Pete said they had to close after New Year's Eve, and they may not open till June, if they even open up again. His money problems must be pretty bad.

Zach

Saturday – 1/19

We had our day in court, without Charles. They fined the guy 4 week's pay, plus all the expenses for court, and the cost to fix all the broken glass. It seems the guy has a reputation for being a hot head, however he happens to be the best mechanic the trolley company has. I'm glad I've got Charles. Hope I can keep him.

I'm getting tired of winter. I wonder if they have Oldsmobile shops in Florida.

Zach

FEBRUARY 1907

Saturday – 2/2

I'm in another one of my pickles. There's no money flow. Paul's having trouble with his restaurant, so he's strapped for cash. Pete's saving every penny he can get for his wedding. I can hardly believe it. Pete told me he and Sammy are getting married July 20th.

I have enough money for 6 months of my personal expenses, rent, food, etc. I'm not sure how I'm going to keep Michael and Charles going for the next 3 months. I'm pretty sure by mid-May we'll have people coming through the showroom again. I hope.

Charles did paint some neat showcards for the showroom. I tried to give him some money, only he wouldn't take any. He said it was fun, how can I lay him off? Michael brings in lunch for the 3 of us every day, he says his mom has plenty of food, how can I lay him off?

I guess my only option is to go to the bank on Monday and see if PAPA'S Oldsmobile Company can borrow some money. I think Paul's signature should have some power behind it. Maybe I even have some influence with my name. Who knows? What do I have to lose? I haven't been in a pickle for quite a while. It's fun . . . a challenge.

Confidence and a good attitude, that's what I need to show the banker on Monday. I'll go to church on Sunday and ask God for His help.

As a backup.

Zach

Monday – 2/4

Those guys are tough. Paul's been having trouble with the bank, and they're upset with him. They said it was funny to them that we had to start paying cash for the Oldsmobiles. Maybe Lansing was too anxious to get their vehicles up here and didn't check deep enough into Paul's background.

The bankers said they could understand my predicament. What they want is a list of everything we have, and how much we owe anybody. Then they need a list of who owes us money and how much. Then they want an idea of how much we think we might sell in the next 4 months. They want all the figures by next Monday. If they like what they see, they said I could sign for a small loan.

Zach

Tuesday – 2/5

I think Michael knows how things are going. He asked if there was anything he could do to help out. I told him to have his mother bake a nice 20th birthday cake for me.

Zach

Friday – 2/8

We've got all the figures ready for the bankers. Looks like we have well over 7,000 dollars in assets. I think the bankers should be thrilled. I'm certain the bank will come through once they see the figures.

Michael came up with the idea of a Mid-Winter Inventory Reduction Sale. He suggested marking up the Oldsmobiles 10 percent and giving a 15 percent discount if someone buys one by the end of February. I love the discount idea, only I'm going to do a straight 5 percent discount. If Paul approves. Charles is going to paint 6 showcards we can put up around town to promote it.

We'll start the sale Monday when I get back from the bank.

Zach

Monday – 2/11

The bankers were quite surprised at the figures, and they liked Michael's idea of the Mid-Winter sale. Michael's going places in this world, I'm sure of it. The bank is going to give us a 500 dollar credit extension I can tap into as we need. It's twice as much as I'll need so I can sleep well this week. I have to go back on Friday and sign all the paperwork.

We started the mid-winter sale today and 2 people already came in because of the signs Charles made.

Zach

Thursday – 2/14

My 20th birthday, how time flies. We sold the 8th Oldsmobile today, 2 more to go. The sale has been fantastic, the city has been fantastic, I love it. We took a one third down payment on each of the Oldsmobiles and offered to give back 95 percent if the client changes their mind before the end of March. The other 5 percent will be for our expenses. No one had a problem.

We had a birthday lunch at the shop and Michael's mother made a fantastic cake. It read Happy 20th Birthday Zach. There was also a shape of one of our Oldsmobiles on it. Charles played his harmonica and sang happy birthday. He never ceases to amaze me, quite a guy.

The head banker stopped by right as I was getting ready to cut the cake. He wished me a happy 20th birthday. We shook hands and I thanked him. He reminded me about meeting at the bank tomorrow. I smiled and said I wouldn't miss it for all the world. I told him we may not need any money after all, but I'd like to sign the papers for the future.

Zach

Friday – 2/15

I guess I'm screwed. I'm only 20. I'm not old enough. The banker thought I was 28. Apparently last year on my birthday I told Pete I felt as if I were 28. Pete told Paul I felt like 28, so Paul told the bank I was 28. Yesterday when the banker saw my cake and it said 20, he was shocked. He didn't say anything in the showroom with clients there.

I'm too young to sign any damn papers.

The bank got ahold of Paul, they told him he had to get somebody who was GROWN UP to sign the papers. He has to get it done by next Friday.

I'M NOT GROWN UP ENOUGH!

My bubble's busted. My head's spinning. I talked with Paul this afternoon. I had a hard time keeping my composure. He said I was doing a fantastic job in Marquette. He said it didn't change anything, I just can't sign any financial papers.

Paul doesn't know me though. The bank said I wasn't grown up enough. What the hell am I then? I don't have a father or mother. I killed her, and my father ran away. Maybe I should go sleep with Sally, maybe then I'd be grown up enough for the banker.

DAMN IT!

Zach

Sunday – 2/17

I've got to control myself. None of this is my fault, absolutely none of this. So, what if I did say I felt as if I aged 10 years in a year. I never said I was 28. That's Paul's fault. So, what if I'm only 20. I've done a damn good job here. Doesn't it count for something?

Why should I stay some place where they think I'm not grown up enough?

Zach

Friday – 2/22

Interesting week. Michael's father Todd is a lawyer in town, he's been a lawyer here for almost 25 years, and he's fairly well off. When he heard about the problem, he wanted to meet with me. Me, the kid who's not GROWN UP. We had a nice meeting on Tuesday. Michael, his dad, and me, I gave Charles the day off.

It seems Todd has enjoyed hearing about PAPA'S from Michael. He'd like to be a part of it. The bankers love Todd, I love his wife's cake, even though it's what brought down the whole thing. Todd and Paul have been in contact and Todd's buying into PAPA'S. Michael's thrilled.

Todd wants me to stay on and run the place. He says I've done an outstanding job, that's a direct quote from him. I'm flattered. I promised to stay until the snow melts. Todd gave me a brand-new Oldsmobile, and 5,000 dollars, it comes to almost 5 years pay.

Todd says I earned it by getting this location up and running. He's thrilled and I'm thrilled. I may not be grown up, but I ain't no hick either. Todd bought a 1/2 ownership into the PAPA'S, so now it's Paul and Todd. Pete's still the president, only now he has 2 bosses. He's not too thrilled about it.

I've heard via the grapevine Todd's worth over 3 million dollars. It seems to have to do with logging and mining. He wanted Michael to work some place for a year or 2, to see what working was like. Smart man, I've got to learn something from him.

Once again, I'm not sure what to do. I like the car thing. I sure know about the weather and farming. I was going to go to college. Mom's got a nice store; I could open a gas station – oh – wait a minute – I'm not GROWN UP ENOUGH!

Zach

Dear Mom, 2/24/1907

I had a swell birthday party at the shop. Michael's mother made a great cake. Charles played his harmonica and sang happy birthday. The guy never ceases to amaze me, you and Grandma would love him. Grandma and Charles would make an incredible couple, just not a married couple.

Things here are still slow, money's pretty tight. It's also tight with Pete and Paul. Oldsmobile sales in winter in Upper Michigan are turning out to be non-existent. I think next winter Pete ought to convert some of the Oldsmobiles to the thing he made with the chains over the back tires and the sleigh runners on the front end. The strangest looking thing I ever saw, but it worked.

Things at the shop have changed a little, Michael's father Todd, has bought into the company. Todd's a lawyer here in Marquette. He's been a lawyer for almost 25 years. He also believes cars are the future.

I've got a lot of time off coming, so I might come up to Copper Harbor after the snow leaves, or I may go to Lansing to the Oldsmobile factory, or maybe even Florida. I'll keep you posted.

I Love You and Grandma a bunch,
Zacharia

MARCH 1907

Saturday – 3/2
We sold all 10 of the Oldsmobiles last month. Everyone's thrilled. I'm not sure if I have any emotions right now. I get by day to day. That grown up thing took the wind out of my sails.

In a month or 2, when the weather clears and the snow is gone, maybe I'll pay a visit to Pete and his wife-to-be. Then again, maybe I'll go to Lansing, or maybe even Florida. I've got a new car and 5,000 dollars. I'm a big wig, I'm just not grown up . . . yet.

Zach

Saturday – 3/30
The sun came out today. Finally! We had about a dozen folks come through the place this week looking at Oldsmobiles. I don't have much enthusiasm anymore, but I treat the people fine. I think. Michael and Charles keep trying to convince me to stay around here, to no avail. I've got to leave. They don't understand it, they never could.

Todd has been great to me. I've told him everything that's happened to me since my 18th birthday. I think he understands my need to, as he calls it, Find Myself. I think it's a good term, it makes sense to me.

Monday, Todd's sending me over to Ironwood to meet with his friend and help him out for a while. They have a shop rented for the 4th dealership. It needed to be opened by May 1st in order to keep the folks at Lansing happy, and keep PAPA'S working. I told him I'd stay there for a month, and it would be my last act as an official Oldsmobile representative. I think Todd's sad. Monday is April 1st. April fool's day, pretty ironic.

Zach

JUNE 1907

Saturday – 6/1

Ironwood is set up and running. We sold the first Oldsmobile on Friday April 19th. Wally, Todd's friend, was thrilled. He wanted me to stay and help him out for a few months. Not going to happen. Why does everybody want me to stay here? Well, Todd understands why I'm leaving.

Left there on Saturday May 18th and drove over to see Sally. I think she thought I was going to propose when she saw me. She gave me a big kiss before I could say anything. When I told Sally I was leaving for parts unknown, she slapped me. She said she hated me and started crying.

Boy she's a knock-out, even when she's mad, I almost changed my mind. I did get her calmed down. I told her I thought she was beautiful, that helped. I told her she'd find a husband no problem, after all she's only 19. I think. I don't know how old anybody is anymore.

Tomorrow I head over to see Pete. I've got to tell him I won't be around for his wedding in July. He's going to be mad at me. This is going to be one of the hardest things I've got to do. I can hear him already. He'll call me a traitor; he'll say it was supposed to be him and me conquering the world together. Then I'll remind him, he's the one getting married, not me.

Zach

Monday – 6/3
As I thought, he's MAD.
Zach

Tuesday – 6/4

He's still mad. Hick, he called me a hick. I knew he'd be mad. I don't blame him. He can't possibly understand me. I can't even understand me, how could he? He'll get over it. He has Samantha, or Sammy, as he calls her.

I told him I was leaving without going up to Copper Harbor and he accused me of running away again. Like he said a couple years ago. He doesn't understand, if I go home, I may never leave. I've got to 'find myself,' as Todd said.

Zach

Dear Mom, 6/15/1907

I love You, and Grandma, more than anything on earth!

Sorry I haven't written sooner. Things have been sort of goofy lately. In my last letter I told you I had a lot of time off coming, which was misleading. I quit. I've been telling you; money has been tight at all of our locations. Some of it's because Paul had to start paying cash for the cars. I can call them cars now since I don't work there anymore.

Well, back in early February I went to the bank, and asked about a loan to help us get through the next few months. Everything was going along smoothly, they approved a 500-dollar credit extension, all I had to do was sign some papers. Well, I got to the bank the next day and the banker told me I was too young to sign papers. Paul had told the banker I was 28 years old. When he found out I was only 20, he almost passed out. So, I decided I didn't want to be around there any longer.

Todd tried everything to get me to stay. He's amazed at how I took the place from nothing to what it's become. I told him it was all thanks to Michael and Charles. Todd said it was one of the most important ingredients in a good leader – getting the right people behind him. I was flattered. However, I'm not staying.

Todd gave me a new Oldsmobile and some money. He said if I'm ever looking for a job, or need a reference, to contact him. He's apparently quite a successful attorney in Marquette. He's worth a fortune and has plenty of contacts all over the state.

Well, here's the tough part, I'm not coming home right away, it'd be too emotional. I stopped and saw Pete; told him I was going to miss his wedding. He's incredibly mad at me. That's the way it is, he'll get over it, I hope. I'm fed up with everything.

EVERYTHING EXCEPT YOU AND GRANDMA.

I still think about my mother and father every once in a while. Actually, more than once in a while. So, I'm taking a trip. I'm not sure to where, but I'll keep you all posted. I'm trying not to be selfish. I just need to get away.

Don't ever forget – I LOVE You and Grandma. I'll be fine, try not to worry too much.

Love,

Zach

P.S. I will be back home, have patience.

DECEMBER 1907

Dear Mom, 12/25/1907

Christmas in the City of New York. WOW. That's all I can say.

You and Frank HAVE to come here someday, it's incredible. There are more cars here on any street than you'll see in Copper Harbor in a year, and more folks in my apartment building than in the entire city of Copper Harbor. And the harbor here, well you have to see it to believe it.

The Statue of Liberty and Ellis Island leave you breathless. Well at least me. Folks who live here seem to take them for granted. Sometimes somebody walks past me, while I'm looking up at something, and they'll say, "welcome to New York, stranger." Thanks' to all the clothes you bought me, at least I don't look like a hick.

I feel at home here, all the people, all the hustle and bustle. It's neat, however I think I said the same thing when I first moved to Marquette. I wonder if that's the way it'll be for me from now on. Maybe with my father never coming back, and my mother dying when I was born, I'll never be able to settle down in one place.

NOW – don't go crying. I love Copper Harbor. It'll always be my hometown and you're always my Mom. Will every place I go from now on feel like home and never really be home? Am I meant to wander and never settle down? These would seem like crazy questions to most people, but not to me. Sorry.

I was walking through Central Park back in November, you should see it. You wouldn't believe it. It's 840 acres. It's 5 times as big as Grandma and Grandpa's farm was. Some of the local folks think the city wasted its money. I think someday they'll understand how important a park is. City folks, who can understand them?

This year for New Year's Eve they plan on dropping a ball from a flagpole on one of the buildings downtown. It's the first time they're doing it, and I'm here. It'll be held by a cable and at exactly midnight it will start its way down. I saw it the other day. It's about 5 feet in diameter and weighs about 700 pounds. It's loaded with light bulbs which will be lit. It's crazy. This is a crazy town.

This weekend, a group of young ladies who sew clothes for a living are going on strike. They want their rent lowered. Can you believe it. There are about 400 of them and they convinced almost 10,000 of us to withhold our rent until the rent's lowered. Hope it works, the landlords are ticked off, hope I don't get kicked out of my apartment.

I moved in on August 1st and signed a 10-month lease. I told them I was 28, Ha, Ha. Next May I'll be 21. Holy cow, 21, finally. I'm starting to grow up. Maybe. My place is a tiny apartment, they call it a studio, not much bigger than our chicken coup, but I'm right down the street from a fairly new restaurant called Lombardi's Pizza. I love the place! It's really neat, and the pizza's great.

After I left Pete, I headed to Chicago and spent July 4th there. That was neat. I think they had about 1,000 times more fireworks than we have up in Copper Harbor. I sold the Oldsmobile to a dealer there and caught the train to New York. Someday I'll tell you all about the train trip. Quite an experience, to say the least. You meet some real strange folks on a long train ride.

DON'T worry about me, I'm fine. I have to find myself, as Todd said.

I LOVE YOU AND GRANDMA!!!

Zach

P.S. Mom, on the first Sunday of every month at exactly 2 pm, your time, I'm going to call you at your store.

1908

MAY 1908

Dear Mom, 5/23/1908

Living here in New York City is incredible. I don't think I've ever been outside when there haven't been hundreds of people around, even at 3 in the morning. The only time I saw people up in Copper Harbor at 3 in the morning was to milk cows.

When you and Frank get here, if I'm back, I'll show you around. You're probably wondering what I mean by if I'm back.

Well, I've been here 10 months, and I feel it's time to get on with my life – so I've signed on as a ship hand on the Lusitania. It comes out of England, from the city Liverpool. It's a brand-new ship, and first got to New York last September. It makes trips back and forth. I'll be working in the dining area.

When I met with the captain, I told him some things about my dad. I said I wanted to learn all about ships, and I was pretty good at reading the stars. When he heard I grew up in Copper Harbor, on Lake Superior, he was impressed. I think it made me a shoo-in. I didn't say anything about PAPA'S. Why would he care? Besides, I try to forget about that.

The 5 phone calls home have been wonderful. However, they'll stop for a while. I'm scheduled to get on the ship Monday. I believe we set out for Liverpool Wednesday. There won't be any phones within a 25-mile area.

I'm still speechless about you having a baby. As I said on the phone, I think it's great. I'm sure Frank will be an excellent father. I already know you're an excellent mother. Think I can call the kid my little brother or sister when he or she comes?

I love you, and don't worry about me. I'll be fine. I'm hoping to possibly find out something about my dad. Maybe someone will have heard of the SS Onoko.

Love,

Zach

JUNE 1908

Dear Mom, 6/10/1908

I'm writing this laying on my bunk bed, in this room for 8 guys. 2 other fellas are doing the same thing I'm doing, only they're writing their girlfriends. 5 of the fellas are out walking around the ship. Believe me it's a BIG ship, I could walk for hours and never go over the same spot. It's much different than my place back in Marquette, or the apartment in New York. I don't miss either of them, though. However, I do miss Copper Harbor every once in a while.

There are 4 bunk beds in the room, luckily, I got one of the top bunks. I think it's because I'm one of the older guys in the room. Right now, it's 7 at night, at least where we are now, some place out in the middle of the Atlantic Ocean. I work the lunch meal, so I don't show up until 9 in the morning, then I work till 5.

The hours seem funny, however we have almost 2,000 passengers and almost 400 crew members. There's a lot of mouths to feed. I was assigned to put away anything the dishwashers wash. I was hoping to be a server, they say it comes with seniority.

The trip from New York to Liverpool was rough in areas. On the 3rd day out, it was so rough some folks had cups of coffee spill. They were pretty upset, although we have an incredible Maitre D, his name is Vernon, he kept everybody calm. He's a short guy with a weird mustache, an English accent, and a ponytail. He must be about 50.

I think about all of you every day. I hope you don't worry about me too much. I'm beginning to think I must have a great deal of my father in me. Now that I'm finally on my own, I don't worry too much about anything. I think I can handle any problems thrown at me. I'm confident my dad felt the same way. I realize my mother was different than him, still she must have been trusting. I believe it's an important asset, trust.

I sometimes wonder, if the banker in Marquette, would have been more trusting, maybe I'd still be there. I'm happy here though. I don't think I could have found myself in Marquette. I hope I'm headed for more than running an Oldsmobile shop in Marquette. Sounds like a strange thing for a guy who put's dishes away for a living to say, yet I believe it. A fella has to start some place, and I seem to be pretty good at it.

I was talking with Vernon, the Maitre D, this morning about what I'll be doing when we head back to Liverpool. He's the only person on ship I told about PAPA'S. I even gave him one of my old cards. He was amazed I hadn't told anyone else.

He's moving me up to be a waiter in one of the smaller dining rooms. He said it has 10 tables and I'll be in charge of 5 of them. I'll be working with a man from France named Andre. I met with him after lunch today. He's scary. Vernon says he's all talk, and not to worry. I'll make twice the money with the tips. Vernon said all tips are under the table. I said, if the shoe fits. He loved it.

Love you all,

Zach

P.S. Give Grandma a great big kiss from me and remind her I love her. I hope she remembers me!

SEPTEMBER 1908

Dear Mom, 9/21/1908

It was wonderful to hear your voice. I was thrilled you got my postcard. So, you're expecting the baby this Friday. I guess, by the time you get this letter, I'll have a baby sister or brother. CONGRATULATIONS to you and Frank, also to Grandma. I wish I could have been there, on the other hand, it is Frank's event.

I've been a waiter now for 14 weeks, and I enjoy it. Working with Andre has been a real experience. He's a nut for neatness and cleanliness. He'll even measure my sleeve length from the tip of my sport coat to the tip on my shirt cuff.

If their different, he makes me readjust them. My shoes, if one's shinier than the other, I have to make them the same. My hair, well that's another story.

I have to report to him one half hour before the shift starts, so he can go over everything with me. Then I have to memorize the entire menu, how everything was prepared, and the dessert menu. The good thing is every night we only have 3 entrees, and 2 dessert choices. Very often I get the same patrons, that's what I'm supposed to call them. I have to remember their names, and any other pertinent information.

Andre's a nice guy beneath it all. He tries to be gruff, but after dealing with some of the clients at PAPA'S, he's pretty easy to deal with. I'm learning a lot about being nice even when it's tough. Maybe it will help when I see Emil again. You mentioned Emil was trying to get a union going in Copper Harbor. I thought one of his uncles owned the dock up there. I imagine it causes a stir in the family. Oh, well.

I told Andre I liked his name. He told me if you get 10 Frenchmen together and ask for Andre, at least 5 guys will come over. He said if you get 100 Frenchmen together, and ask for Zacharia, you probably won't have anyone come over. He likes my name. I think it's why he requested me.

I'm still in the same room with 7 other guys. Now I'm on the 4 to midnight shift, so I show up for work at 3:30 in the afternoon. Sleeping with all the different shifts gets hard sometimes. I think after I'm here awhile, I'm going to suggest everybody in a room has the same shift. Sometimes the easiest things to fix seem so hard for others to understand. I think I learned that from Charles at PAPA'S.

Well, CONGRATULATIONS, again on my baby sister or brother, I hope all went well.

LOVE, to you All, and the Baby.
Zach

NOVEMBER 1908

Dear Mom, Thanksgiving Day, 1908
You should see the dining room. I'm not sure you could ever imagine how spectacular it is. There's nothing like this in all of Upper Michigan, maybe even

the whole state. The Cunard Company sure knows elegance. That's the company who owns the ship.

Hope everything with all of you is great and you had a good Thanksgiving. I hope my little sister's behaving better than I did when I was 2 months old. I thought of you, Grandma and Grandpa, and all the fantastic Thanksgiving meals we had together at the farm. I miss all of you!

We're some place in the middle of the Atlantic Ocean. I think we're heading to New York. No, I know we're heading to New York, just kidding. Although us guys always test each other, half the time we don't know for sure. I guess, how can I find myself, like Todd wants, if I don't even know where I'm going?

I thought you'd get a kick out of this note paper and envelope. We're allowed to write one note a week for free, otherwise we can buy them. I'm going to buy a dozen.

Love,
Zach
P.S. Don't forget about me!

DECEMBER 1908

Dear Mom, 12/25/1908
I'm in Liverpool, England, on Christmas Day. Who would have thought? A guy from Copper Harbor in Liverpool for Christmas. I found a church called St. Peter's near the ship and went to their service this morning. It was Beautiful. The singing, the pageantry, and the decorations were incredible.

The church was built in 1788. The outside's nothing stupendous, however the inside was incredible. The church members were as friendly as anyone in Copper Harbor. They have an accent though, and it takes some getting used to. One guy who I room with on the ship went with me. He wound up crying at the end of the service. He said it reminded him of back home too much. When we get back to New York, he's going to quit, and go home. I'll miss him.

I imagine Christmas with a baby has to be a huge change for all of you. I'll bet you're having a ball. I can picture Grandma rocking her. I can also picture Grandma giving her a kiss on the cheek, I miss them. I think about all of you a lot, especially when I'm trying to fall asleep, while 4 guys are playing poker in our little bunk room.

Being a waiter is coming along nicely. Andre has turned out to be a ball to work with. He doesn't check me over as much anymore, but he sure likes saying Zacharia. He has a way of putting a French twist on how he pronounces it. He'll call me over to him, saying "Zacharia, over here!" with his French accent, and he gets all the patrons laughing. My role is to smile, stroll over to him and say, "yes, my lord, how can I be of assistance?"

Then Andre goes into 1 of the 6 skits he's prepared. I have to practice each one until it's perfect. Each one lasts 2 or 3 minutes. They're hilarious. Everybody laughs, then we both bow down, and we usually get a round of applause. The whole scene is reserved for once a night – unless the patrons want an encore. Those are the nights Andre glows.

I haven't mentioned, or even thought about God for a while. I guess going to church this morning must have reminded me about Him. Thank God for the nice reminder. After church, my buddy and I went to a nice English café and had tea and trifles. Ours was soaked in brandy and covered with whipped cream. How quaint is that?

A bunch of us guys from the ship went into town for supper today. We wanted to see the town decorated for Christmas. We decided to explore, you know how much I like to explore. We stopped at this little bar. They call them pubs here in Liverpool. Well, somebody must have stepped on some local fellas' foot. The local fella called us a bunch of foreigners and said we ought to go back home. I told him, as I like to say, "if the shoe fits."

He took a swing at me, and thanks to my times with Emil, I managed to duck his left jab and I landed a right hook on his nose. He started bleeding, took the Lord's name in vain, picked up a chair and was about to clobber me with it, when an officer, they call them Bobby's in Liverpool, came in. Needless to say, we were escorted out of the pub, and asked not to come back.

My buddies were all laughing. We found another pub, and I didn't have to buy a drink all night. Now, laying here in my bunk on Christmas night, writing you this letter, I feel guilty. I'm pretty sure you would have been mad at me. I'll go back to the pub Sunday and apologize to the owner. If the jerk is there, I'll ask how his nose is, and buy him a beer. I think if I'm going to find myself, I've got a lot to learn.

Mom, I Love You, Grandma, and the Baby.
Merry Christmas!
Zach

P.S. Mom – I love you, don't ever forget that!! Maybe I never should have been told about my mother and father. Don't worry about me. I'll be fine wherever I am.

P.S. P.S. I'll try and call you at the store whenever I get the chance and I'm in New York!

LOVE

Zach

6 YEARS LATER

1915

JANUARY 1915

Sunday -1/31

I quit the Lusitania yesterday. I'll be 28 in 2 weeks and it's time for me to get on with my life. Captain Dow, tried to talk me into staying with him. He mentioned he was looking into taking over a different ship. I was flattered, but I told him I'd be 28 in a few weeks, and I had to get on with my life. Over the years I've let him in on some of my life, and I think he understands. He said if I ever needed anything, I should get in touch with him.

I mentioned my father Zacharia and the Great Lakes boat the SS Onoko to him last November. He said he'd heard about a Captain named Zacharia, who had spent a couple of years on the Great Lakes. He said he heard the fellow was from some place in South America, and he was on a mission.

That's all he could remember. When he gets back to England, he'll do more inquiring. I look forward to possibly hearing more about my father. At least I've found someone who may know something. That's more than I ever learned up in Copper Harbor, things are looking up, finally!

I got a nice apartment up on the east side of Central Park. It's right on Madison Avenue and 65th Street. I could have gone back where I was, only I wanted more peace and quiet for a while. I did a smart thing transferring all my money to a bank here in New York. Between what I had and the money I made on the boat in 7 years I'm up to 10,000 dollars. Tips and bonuses were good.

I'll call Mom on my birthday and see how things are going with them. I'm finally feeling pretty damn nice about myself and where I'm heading. I think I'll look up Lisa and see what happened to that group of sewing ladies, who started the rent strike. I've been curious about unions, ever since I heard Emil was starting one in Copper Harbor. Good old Copper Harbor, I look forward to going back home.

Life is good!

Zach

FEBRUARY 1915

Sunday – 2/14 My 28th - Birthday

Who do you think you are? Those were her exact words.

I've been asking myself that question for 10 years.

Zach

Monday – 2/15

She hung up on me. Mom's furious. I guess I don't blame her. I probably would have done the same thing. I'll try again tomorrow.

Zach

Tuesday – 2/16

I'll wait till tomorrow to call her. I'm not sure why I thought she'd be happy to hear my voice. She hasn't seen me since Christmas 1906. 8 years and 2 months ago.

Holly CRAP!

Zach

Wednesday – 2/17

She didn't hang up, but she wouldn't say my name. I told her I understood, and I didn't blame her. I told her I've never stopped loving her. I said I'd call again on Sunday after church. Maybe she'll calm down by then.

Zach

Sunday – 2/21

We talked a little today.

Mom's had 7 days to digest my lack of contact for 6 years. I tried again to explain how I've been searching for something, and I don't even know what it is.

How all the time on the Lusitania was so good for me. How I worked my way up from putting dishes away to being the First Junior 3rd Engineer. How it was such an accomplishment for me. How I could have been promoted to an even higher rank. How I left the Lusitania because I turned 28 and was the age the banker up in Marquette thought I was.

I tried to explain it all to Mom, but when I was done, she cried.

She said she thought I was dead.

Zach

Tuesday – 2/23

We talked for a while today, she was a little calmer. I told her I'd come home for a few weeks in June. My sister's name is Annie Maria Klein, named after my mother. She's 6 years old, and her birthday's September 25th. I can't wait to see her. Mom says she looks like my mother, only her hair is black, like Frank's.

I think Mom's getting better. I haven't told her Captain Dow said he may know something about my father. I can wait with that for a while.

Zach

APRIL 1915

Thursday – 4/1 April Fool's Day, 1915.

I thought today would be an interesting day to call Pete. He thought it was an April Fool's Day trick, so he hung up on me. I called him back and the first thing he said was "Okay, who is this really?" I mentioned Ms. Bagley and PAPA'S. Then he said, "Holy shit, it is you!"

We talked for almost an hour. He wasn't mad. He said there wasn't anything I could do that would surprise him anymore. I guess he knows me better than I do. I've been lucky to have him as a friend. Maybe he's been a gift from God all along. Maybe I should thank them both.

He and Samantha have 3 kids already. It blows my mind – 3 kids, and I've yet to be with a woman. Is something wrong with me? That's a dumb question, of course there's something wrong with me – I just haven't figured it out yet.

He wanted me to be the Godfather to the 1st kid, a baby boy he named Zak. The problem was he had no idea where I was, so he chose Michael, the guy I hired in Marquette. I was flattered. I knew Michael was good right from the start. Pete said Charles played his harmonica and sang Happy Birthday at Zak's 1st birthday. My 2 guys from Marquette, that made me feel pretty damn proud.

Told Pete I'd be back in June for a week or 2. It's always nice to hear his voice, been a long, long, time. Maybe that'll be my legacy. Here and gone, and here and gone again.

Zach

MAY 1915

Dear Mom, 5/09/1915
Good grief!
I don't know if you've heard the news yet. The Lusitania was torpedoed by a German U-Boat last Friday. Almost 1,200 people died. All my friends who were in the crew may have died. I'm stunned! Things here in New York are hot. Almost everybody wants us to go beat the crap of the Germans. I'm in a daze.

I'm glad I called you back in February, at least you know I wasn't on the ship. Maybe I should have been. Maybe I could have saved someone's life. I think I may have nightmares about this for a long time. The only reason I left is because I was turning 28. Now I feel like a heel.

I said I'd be home in June, now I have to wait a little longer. You know I'm fine for now, so don't worry about me. I'd like to come home for Annie's birthday in September. She'll be 7 years old, and I'd love to be there for her birthday. I want to give her a HUGE hug and kiss. It'll be great to see everybody again.

Never forget – I LOVE You, Grandma and Annie!! That's a fact!
Zach

AUGUST 1915

Dear Sis,
I can't wait to get home to see you. Oh, yeah, I look forward to seeing your mom and dad also. Tell them HI from me.

New York is exciting. I think you'd like it here. Maybe someday I can show you around, after you're older. I have lots of friends here in the BIG City, and they all wish you a Happy Birthday.

You've probably met my good friend Pete's son Zak. I think you're both about the same age. I'm sure you're both nice kids and get along fine.

I had a neat time working on the ship Lusitania. I was on it almost 8 years. Lots of fun. You should have your mom keep these notecards from the ship, someday they'll be worth a lot of money. Money you could use when you go to college.

I hope Grandma keeps kissing you as much as she used to do to me. I always had fun, only they could get messy!!

Tell your mom and dad I should be home by you on either Monday the 20th of September or Tuesday. I'm looking forward to being back in Copper Harbor. It's been a long, long, long time, I hope I remember it.

Love,
Your big brother,
Zach
P.S. Give your mom and Grandma a kiss from me!!!

Saturday – 8/28

Called Pete this morning and told him I'd be back home around the 20th of September. He sounded excited. He has 3 kids, a wife, and he's excited because I'm coming home for a week or 2. It made me feel good. He said they have room for me in their place. I'm used to my own space, so I'll find a nice hotel in Iron Mountain.

He mentioned something about a huge change at PAPA'S and he can't wait to tell me all about it. Then he mentioned Michael has some news he thinks I'll be surprised at. Sounds as if it's going to be quite the trip home. Annie is the one I'm looking forward to meeting, my little Sister.

I realize Annie isn't my sister, she's really my cousin, but I'm not saying anything about it. To me she's my little sister, and I'm her big brother, we have some of the same blood lines. That's good enough for me, and nobody better dispute it.

Zach

Sunday – 8/29

3 weeks ago I decided I'd better start thinking about the rest of my life. I've got more than enough money, so I'm not pressed for cash. I went to a couple of car dealers to look around, but after my time at PAPA'S, I think anyplace else would be anticlimactic. Went to the docks to check them out, all I thought about was Emil. I got goose bumps, so I left.

Then I remembered the OLD banker up in Marquette, the one who said I was too young, not GROWN UP enough, so I decided the banking industry sounded interesting. I figured, what do I have to lose. I did a lot of checking around the city and was told The First Trust Company of New York was where to start. So off I went. What a greenhorn I was, but maybe that helped.

This past Monday was either my incredibly lucky day or God was on my side. A banker in an amazing 3-piece suit must have taken a liking to me when he saw me. After talking for almost half an hour about my background, and I told him everything, again, what did I have to lose, he asked me to sit for a few minutes. Well I sat for at least half an hour, was about to get up and leave, when this big, brawny, fellow comes over to me.

He introduced himself as Max Marquis. He said he was the man to see. The Main Man. He was dressed like a million dollars. His black shoes looked like tiny mirrors. My first reaction was to get up and high tail it out of there, then I figured, again, what did I have to lose?

Apparently when he heard I was on the Lusitania for almost 8 years, he wanted to meet me. And when he heard I worked with a French waiter for a few years, well then he said he HAD to meet me. He said they were in the process of putting together a 500-million-dollar loan to France and Britain! Something to help them with their war efforts.

I know I gulped. I told him I was a hick from Upper Michigan, and he laughed. He asked if being from Michigan I was a hunter. How could I lie? I said I sure was. I told him I was pretty damn good at it. I told him I could track a rabbit on concrete, again, what did I have to lose?

Well, I have no idea how or why this all happened. I had stopped by to check out the company, and now Max has hired me on, as what he called, a personal assistant. He already has 5 assistants, and he added me to the group. He said he likes even numbers.

My head's spinning, as it was on my 18th birthday, only this is better. I start tomorrow. I'll train for 2 weeks, then Max is giving me as much paid time off as I need to go home. Max said his wife told him I should go and, "Visit with the folks, and meet his little sister."

I believe God may be on my side. No, this time He WAS on my side!

Zach

P.S. I forgot to even ask what the pay is!

OCTOBER 1915

Sunday – 10/10

I MISS back home!!!

Got back to New York late last night. I'm pretty beat. Start work tomorrow at The First Trust Company. Have no idea what I'll be doing. I've got to rest my body, and my soul.

Zach

Sunday – 10/17

First week at The Trust was pretty boring. Nothing like starting PAPA'S. Opening the Marquette dealership was exciting now that I look back. Hiring Michael and Charles, fighting the trolley company, that was some pretty neat stuff. The Trust is stuffy. I've got to change it if I can.

My little sister Annie is fabulous! What a birthday party Mom threw, there had to be over 60 people. I knew everybody who was over 10. I was gone longer than I thought. All the PAPA'S dealerships had someone there to celebrate. Annie looked wonderful. If she takes after my mother, well then, my mother was beautiful. My father was no fool. Hope I'm not either.

Mom and Frank are doing fine. The store has its ups and downs. The bank crash of '07 hurt business for a while. Mom had to let a few people go, one of them was Emil's cousin. Mom told her it had nothing to do with stealing. I guess the gal knew and understood. Sales were way down, and Mom had let 2 others go before she let the gal go.

It seems it was all Emil needed to start something. He's been trying to get the fellas who work at the dock to boycott Mom's store. Once a jackass always a jackass. Mom said Emil should go suck eggs. I laughed at that one, like the old days. I wonder about Emil sometimes, can't quite figure out what his problem is.

Grandma's the same, loves to kiss, sing, and dance. Her and I spent a few times out at the graves talking about Grandpa. She sure does miss him, she said she can't wait to see him again. When I told her about Max and his company she kept asking how a man could have so much money. I told her his wife is pretty darn good at spending it, so he has to make it.

Spent 2 days with Pete, Samantha and their 3 kids. Had a great time. Zak is quite the little man, he's over 6 years old, or I should say he's 6 and growing. Michael's father Todd bought out Pete's uncle a few years ago. Paul retired to some place in Mexico. Surprised the heck out of Pete.

Todd now owns PAPA'S. He gave Pete and Michael each 20 percent, Charles 5 percent and he put 5 percent in my name. Pretty much floored me. I tried to get Pete to take it, but he refused. I told him I was financially set and had this amazing new job, only he kept refusing. It looks as though

PAPA'S is going crazy with sales. Oldsmobiles are turning out to be the best car around for the price.

Todd told Michael and Pete that when he's ready to sell the other half of PAPA'S, they'll be the first guys he offers it to. He promised it'll be a price they couldn't refuse. Michael married Pete's cousin Sally 3 years ago, blew my mind. First time I heard about it. Go figure. Life will never cease to amaze me, and I'm only 28. Should I have stayed up in Copper Harbor back in '07?

I don't think so, but it sure is nice to go HOME!

Zach

Sunday – 10/31

Max is sending me and 3 other personal assistants to Europe, for a couple months. He wants to know exactly what's going on over there. He knows there's a war going on. He understands why a lot of Americans want us to get involved, but he also knows a lot of Americans want us to stay out of it. So he's sending us to find out what the folks over there want. It turns out his great-grandfather on his father's side was from France, and his great-grandfather on his mother's side was from Germany. Now they're at war with each other, that puts Max in a bind.

I asked, "why me," he said, "If you can track a rabbit on concrete, you can keep an eye on the other guys." He said, for some reason, he trusted my intuition better than most. I thanked him. He suggested I look around to see if any of my friends from the Lusitania survived. If they have, he wants to hire them.

He's a damn good man. No matter what some of those other rich guys say!

Zach

1916

JANUARY 1916

Tuesday – 1/25

We haven't been here long, and I already miss the USA.

War can seem like the end of the world. Your enemy is always trying to destroy you, and all you're trying to do is make it to the next day.

That's what a French General told me a few days after we got to France. Zach

MARCH 1916

Saturday – 3/4

It's nice to be back in New York!

England and France are both in a pickle. Money's tight, spirits are low, and too many lives are being lost.

The Allied forces need money, only I think they need manpower even more. The USA is supposed to be neutral, only I don't know how we can stay neutral. The German U-Boats are sinking ships left and right, they sunk the Lusitania. They claim the Lusitania had weapons on board, maybe they did, maybe they didn't. Was it a reason to kill 1,200 civilians? That's my question.

I heard rumors about The First Trust Company of New York. Some good and some bad. How they stand to profit from the war, or possibly lose a fortune. I'm not sure the issue should be money. I believe the issue should be freedom. All I know from what I saw, is England and France are in a jam. We can help them keep their independence.

It seems, from talking to folks over there, if Germany were to win the war, they'd never stop with France and England. The people asked, what about Spain, Portugal, Norway, Sweden, Ireland, Finland, Belgium, Netherlands, and Italy, who's already joined with England and France? The people worry all those countries could fall like dominoes.

Then I ask myself, what about the USA? I believe joining with the Allies is our only choice. I've seen the destruction that's been created. I realize more will come, but without our intervention, I fear far worse may happen. We were sent there to look things over. It seems we're either on the side of the Allies or Germany. I'd pick the Allies in a heartbeat. All 4 of us feel the same way.

Zach

Sunday – 3/5

Max was extremely satisfied with our report about Europe. He says he doesn't want to go to war, only he doesn't know how we can avoid it. It sounds like, from what I hear, our entire banking system would take a huge hit. He figures it isn't all about money, but I'd hate to be around him if England and France lose.

No one here wants Germany to win, and if they say they do, they get run out of town. Or worse. Times like this I miss Copper Harbor. It's only been 6 months since I've been there, although it feels closer to 6 years. I wonder if we go to war, how it'll affect back home? Why war? Emil and I fight, and we don't know why. The Allies and Germany fight. I wonder if the soldiers know why. I don't understand any of this.

Zach

Sunday – 3/26

While I was in England I looked for any survivors from the Lusitania. I found one of my old bunk mates. He was still shook up about the tragedy. He said they had been warned about the German U-Boats and how they were torpedoing ships. He was so happy to get close to home, when all of a sudden, BAM. Hell on water broke out.

I asked about Andre, the waiter. Andre died on the ship. The last time my friend saw him he was swearing in French and doing one of his skits, while dishes were falling all over the place. I asked about the Maitre-D Vernon. He had taken his wife and 6 kids with him, on the last trip back to New York, the same one I was on. My friend said Vernon didn't tell anyone for fear they might make him stay in Liverpool.

Vernon wanted to protect his family from the war. He told my friend he rented a house on Staten Island 6 months earlier and was promised a job as a waiter in some restaurant on the Island. I've got to find him. Captain Dow resigned from the Lusitania in March last year, that's all my friend knew about him. I've got to try to find him also. He's the only person who's ever heard of my father and the SS Onoko.

Zach

JUNE 1916

Sunday – 6/11

I found Vernon, he was working in a nice family restaurant on Staten Island, as the head waiter. It took me 3 days of searching, and it was worth every day. He was amazed to see me. He still says I'm handsome.

He told me he left England with his wife and 6 kids to come to America. He'd been meeting people on the Lusitania all those years and hearing how terrific America was. He said he had to bring his family, but 2 of his sons stayed back to join the war effort. His wife cried, but they had to think about their younger kids, and the world they'd grow up in.

I reminded Max, that he said if I found anybody I worked with on the Lusitania, I should let him know. I introduced the 2 of them, and Max was thrilled. Max thinks Vernon is a true Englishman, and he was pleased to hear how much Vernon loves America.

Max gave Vernon a job on Jekyll Island as a waiter. He told me if Vernon plays his cards right, he could work his way up to being the Maitre-D at 1 of the restaurants there. Vernon and I went there last month to check it out.

I heard about Jekyll Island a few times from the other personal assistants. They told me it's the richest, most exclusive, most inaccessible club in the world. After seeing it I believe it. Vernon was stunned. Max offered to put his family up on the Island. Vernon and his family will have their own house to live in; Vernon says his wife will be thrilled.

So was I.

Zach

JULY 1916

Dear Mom, Tuesday, July 4th, 1916

I'm in Albany, New York for the 4th of July. Max sent me up here to meet with some bankers on Friday, so I thought I'd come up a little early to see how Albany decorated for the 4th. Me in Albany, the state capital, talking with bankers. Why don't you tell the banker in Marquette, the one who thought I wasn't old enough?

Max seems to trust me a lot. I was in England and France with 3 other personal assistants of Max's over the holidays. He wanted our opinion on how things are going over there, before he decides if they should pump a lot of money into the war. I told him it was terrible over there, but the people are trying to keep their spirits up as much as possible.

I am going to ask Max how I can join the war effort. After being in Europe, I feel I've got to try to help any way I can. Max knows people and I think he could be a big help to me. Whatever you do, DON'T WORRY ABOUT ME. I figure, with how I got off the Lusitania before the torpedo hit it, I must have a pretty darn good guardian angel.

LOVE, to all of you!!

P.S. Give Grandma and Annie a hug from me.

Zach

OCTOBER 1916

Sunday – 10/29

I had a long talk with Max yesterday. He's been having me help with President Wilson's re-election campaign. I've been going to various community organizations, like the Chambers of Commerce, and whichever civic groups I think would help. It's been pretty good for me. I think it'll help if I stay in the New York area, and I see no reason not to, at least for now.

EXCEPT, I want to get involved with the war. I want to help the French people. I'm not sure why, but I fell in love with their culture, even though it was war time. Their pride in their country is phenomenal. I hope to bring some of it back here after the war's over. It will be over someday!

Wilson's election is a week from this Tuesday and I'm pretty sure he's a shoo-in. That is, if the shoe fits. I told Max after the election I'll need his help in joining our armed forces, and I'd like his suggestions. I think he was both happy and sad at the same time. He said he was proud of me, and he'd also miss me. I still don't understand why, but that's what he said. Maybe he's got a thing for Michigan. Who knows?

I know Mom would worry about me, but she has Frank, Annie, and Grandma. Max said there's talk about starting a draft if the USA does get involved. He totally agrees if Germany were to win, it would be catastrophic for the entire world. That's the way I figure also.

He said he has some pull. I don't know who he's kidding, he has more than SOME pull. He's got incredible pull. He knows a man who's a big wig in the military. Max said he can put in a good word for me. We'll see what happens.

Zach

DECEMBER 1916

Dear Mom, Monday, December 25ᵗʰ, 1916

MERRY CHRISTMAS from New York City.

Hope you and the family had a nice Christmas. I can close my eyes and picture all the snow around the farm, and downtown Copper Harbor. Downtown Copper Harbor, I think that's funny. Here I am in Manhattan, New York on Christmas Day, with thousands of people all around me. Central Park is across the street with plenty of horse drawn carriages taking people for rides.

There are more carriages in the park than there are cars in Copper Harbor. I miss Copper Harbor when I think about it, so I try not to so much. Grandma always told me what goes around, comes around. I wonder if that's what she meant. I'll be 30 next February 14*th*, the day I got my middle name from, Valentine's Day. I never did thank you and Grandma for the name, so THANKS!

Sometimes a fella will kid me about it. I usually smile. One time I never told you about, Emil kidded me about it, and I hit him with a right hook on his nose. I don't think the bleeding stopped for two days. We were out behind one of the buildings by the dock. Emil started crying. I told him I was sorry. We were eight and he never teased me about my middle name again.

I sent you a note back on July 4*th*. I hope you got it. Then I realized I haven't written you an actual letter in a long time. I'm sorry, time seems to get away from me. You always know I love you, you are my mom, and I love you. One thing I learned over in Europe is everybody should have a mom like you. A lot of guys don't, that's a shame!!!

Max is an incredible man. I realize some folks don't always like him. They think he's not conservative enough. They think he's too generous. I know he can be, but he's not foolish. He's got a great heart. He got my friend Vernon, the Maitre-D from the Lusitania, a job at one of his places on an island near Georgia. He moved Vernon's whole family there and doubled his pay. How nice is that? Max is a good man.

I did a lot of work on Wilson's re-election campaign, and he was re-elected last month. If anybody from Copper Harbor ever wants to run for office, have them get in touch with me. I could help Emil run for dog catcher – no – I'd have the dogs chase him. I'm glad his boycott of your store, a year ago, never got off the ground.

I sure had a good time with Grandma, sitting at Grandpa's grave when I was home for Annie's birthday. I hope I get a chance to do it many more times. I miss Grandma's kisses a lot. When I was living at home, sometimes they'd annoy me, now I miss them. You can tell her what I said. Grandma must be happy to have Annie around. I'm sure now she kisses her a lot. Lucky Annie.

I mentioned I wanted to serve the USA in the war going on in Europe in my last note to you. At least I hope I mentioned it. Well, Max is almost certain it won't be long before we join England and France in the fight. Both of those countries are running low on money and soldiers. He also thinks the military will start using the draft, to get more men to fight.

Max said it would be better for me to join before I got drafted. Then I'd get a better job. It made sense to me. Max is almost as concerned about my safety as you are, so that should give you some peace of mind. Max says the draft will start next Spring. Every man between 21 and 31 will be liable for military service. I think Pete and Michael will be farther down the line because they have families.

Max talked to a fella he knows in the military who can get me set up for entering the service. The guy knows President Wilson fairly well, and since I worked on Wilson's re-election campaign, I've got a good shot at something nice. I'm hoping to get involved with the French war effort. I'm amazed at everything that's gone on in my life since I left Marquette. I hope you're OK with it.

I have to report to General Pershing, next month on the 22nd. He's going to lead the forces going into France. Max says he's an incredible leader, and it should be good for me. I know Max is worried. I like his positive attitude though. I'm beginning to relate to it.

I hope this letter finds all of you in fine health, warm, happy, and loving each other. I hope Christmas was good, and the New Year, 1917 will be nice to you also. I hope you don't worry too much about me, and I'll try to send you notes when I get a chance. Thank you for everything you've done for me, and I'll see you later.

Never forget I LOVE you!
You're Loving Son,
Zacharia Valentine Zabrinski
P.S. Have faith in my Guardian Angel!!!!!

1917

FEBRUARY 1917

Wednesday 2/14

My 30th birthday at Fort Slocum, NY. I'm not sure if I should laugh or cry.

When the fellow who checked me in heard my middle name, he had a smirk on his face. He was about to say something when his sergeant told him to keep quiet. I found out later General Pershing had my middle name removed from things. Except for that piece of paper.

I like my middle name. So do some of the girls I've known, especially Sally, Michael's wife. Got to keep it to myself though. Things here are hectic. I'm not sure anybody knows what to do. We do a lot of exercises. Some rifle training, of which I seem to be the best, and some machine gun training.

I never shot a machine gun before. I actually had fun. I hope I never have to shoot at somebody. That's something that's starting to bother me, shoot someone. I don't know how I'll react if I have to. I mentioned it to my commander, he shrugged and said it wasn't hard to do. I think he's done it a few times.

One of the new fellas here is Arron. He's Jewish and from New Jersey. He and I seem to hit it off. I get a kick out of his accent, and he mine. He calls me the hick from on top of the world.

He told me shooting somebody isn't so hard. I asked him how he knew, and he said he read about it in some western magazines. Then he started laughing, he was kidding me. I think it's why we get along so well. He's got a fantastic sense of humor. To get a laugh out of him, I told him my middle name, he doubled over. I'm not the least bit embarrassed about it. General Pershing didn't need to have it removed. I'll try to get it back in the records. If I get any awards I want my full name on them.

General Pershing told me I'd be helping the French army in their 4th Bureau. It has something to do with transportation, communication, and supplies. The French call it the Direction de l'Arriere. Considering I started the Oldsmobile place back in Michigan, it sounded pretty neat to me. Maybe I'll get to drive a Cadillac. From what I've heard, they're supposed to be a marvelous car.

Pershing thinks I'll be skipping some of the training here and may go to France in the next month or so. He told me Max threatened to pull 500,000 dollars out of the war effort if anything happens to me. I told him to tell Max to go suck eggs. First time I saw the General laugh.

Zach

Friday - 2/16
I'm on my way to France Monday morning.
Zach

JULY 1917

Wednesday – 7/4
France is reeling. They've lost over a million soldiers so far. In April they were attacking the ridge at the Chemin des Dames. They lost 40,000 soldiers on the first day alone. After enough casualties, half of the soldiers quit. They refused to fight, they had enough.

The French brought in General Phillipe Petain, who calmed things down. He decided to wait for the Americans and their tanks. It's a damn good thing we got here. General Pershing sent a telegram to the States saying we need at least a million more men.

I was able to bring my new friend Arron with me. I told my boss that with his incredible mechanical aptitude, Arron would be a big help. He bought it, so now both Arron and I are in the 4th Bureau. Arron asked me what I meant about his mechanical aptitude. I reminded him about when he told me he helped his uncle change spark plugs in their old Ford. Good to have a sense of humor, and a friend.

We declared war on Germany back in April and started drafting guys in May. We're starting to see more American soldiers every day. It's been great for the French people's spirits.

Zach

OCTOBER 1917

Thursday – 10/25

I'm in love!

Laying here in my hospital bed, I just met the woman I'm going to marry. This must be exactly how my father felt when he met my mother. Her name's Adeline, and I think she's beautiful. She smiled at me and changed my bandages. She likes my middle name. She called me her Valentine from across the sea.

I was delivering some important papers up near Belgium when we came under attack. Running from my vehicle I tripped over some tree root and fell sideways. The doctor in the hospital said it was a miracle. He said a fraction of a second sooner and the bullet would have gone in the side of my head. A fraction of a second later and the bullet would have gone in the front of my head.

He said I was one lucky man. He said all I'll have is a long scar above my left eye, and a black and blue face for a while. He introduced me to Adeline, my nurse, the woman I'm going to marry. I'll thank him later; he can come to the wedding. I'm happier than I've ever been.

Now I know why I had to come to France.

Zach

Saturday – 10/27

Adeline brought me some coffee. Best coffee I ever had. She changed the bandages again. I don't think they needed changing. I think she wanted to be near me. At least I hope so. She has the sweetest smile. Mom will love it, and Pete will be stunned. I can hear him now, "A French gal from Paris, you've got to be kidding, you're a hick."

What if she won't move to the States? Who in their right mind would want to stay here? What if she says no? Tomorrow I'm going to try to kiss her.

Zach

Sunday – 10/28

She let me kiss her. She said she's 25 and never been kissed by an American. I think she liked it. I think she likes me. We talk a lot, small talk mostly. Who wants to talk about what's going on around here?

She lives in Paris with her parents. She finished her schooling to be a nurse. She's glad it happened now when she can do so much good. I've never been in love, but if this is love, I'm all in favor of it.

That's a fact!

Zach

Wednesday – 10/31

I get out of the hospital tomorrow. Doc thinks I'm fine, just keep an eye out for any infection. He winked when he said infection. He knows how I feel about Adeline. He said love can be an infection, he said it with a smile on his face. Adeline and I are going out to dinner in Paris on Saturday, she wants me to meet her parents.

Happy day!

Zach

NOVEMBER 1917

Sunday – 11/4

Great parents! Now I know why Adeline turned out so great.

It baffles me how I feel so comfortable when I'm with her. We've got the war going on, the battles are costing so many lives, so much destruction, but when I'm with her nothing seems to bother me. The folks back home I'm sure are worried silly, especially Mom. I don't think about any of that when I'm with Adeline.

Her father told me he's never seen her so happy. He speaks fine English, said he learned it many years ago. They seem to be a pretty well-off family. He and his wife both work for the government. They live in a part of Paris where they can walk everyplace.

I asked him about automobiles, and he laughed. He said the army had all of them. The people in Paris try not to sound too worried about the war, however I know they are. How could they not be? They're counting on us to get them through this mess. So am I.

When I left their place, Adeline taught me how the French kiss. I liked it. I liked it a lot. I think she likes me. I have to head back to the base tomorrow. I told Adeline I'd be back in 2 weeks. We have a date set for Sunday the 18th.

I'm excited.

Zach

Sunday – 11/18

I missed her. I'm not sure I've ever missed anybody this way before.

I think I could live in Paris. Once the war's over France would be a beautiful place to live. The countryside's a lot like Michigan. The pace of life here is much more comfortable than it is in New York City. New York's nothing but hustle and bustle. Central Park's always crowded, subways and the elevated lines are always a mess. People, people, and more people.

France isn't so bad.

Zach

Monday – 11/19

Adeline and I went out for an early meal today. I had to leave again for a few weeks, and I wanted to see her before I left. She cried, we kissed a few times, and I was gone.

Zach

DECEMBER 1917

Sunday – 12/16

Nice to be back with Adeline. She helps me forget all about the war, the lives lost, the damage being done, all that crap. We had a great time today walking around. She showed me places a stranger would never see. Down back alleys, stores which were still open, coffee shops. Maybe my Guardian Angel kept me from getting shot in the head, so I'd meet Adeline. I think I'm going to ask her to marry me.

I have to go back to the base tomorrow. Colonel says with Christmas and New Year's coming we have to keep the moral high. Apparently, Arron and I have to help with all the festivities. They'll be small, but we'll still have them. Now I won't be able to see Adeline until next year.

When I told Adeline I wouldn't be back till then, she asked if she could come with me. I had a hard time explaining why women weren't allowed. She understood, only she was pretty unhappy. I told her I loved her, we kissed for a long time, I said Au Revoir, and left.

I'm slowly learning a lot about the French. I like it!

Zach

Dear Mom, Christmas Day, 1917

I'm in love.

I met a nurse named Adeline while I was in the hospital for a few days. Don't worry, I got a small scratch on my forehead, no big deal. Anyway, the nurse who changed my bandage was Adeline. I fell for her the moment I saw her, as they say up north, hook, line, and sinker. You'll love her.

We've been out on a number of dates, and I spent a weekend at her parent's home in Paris meeting them. We walked all around Paris together, went to the best French restaurant in Paris. Laughed, hugged, and kissed.

The war is crazy. I spend most of my time delivering messages between the front lines and the officers who do the planning. A lot of the information has to go in person because the Germans have cracked most of our secret codes. I drive a 1916 Packard, it's a ball to drive. A lot more sophisticated than the Oldsmobiles, and a whole lot more money.

It's Christmas Day here at the quarters and my friend Arron and I had to help with the festivities, otherwise I'd be in Paris with Adeline. Arron and I are stuck here until New Year's Day. Then I'm taking him with me to Paris. I want Adeline and her folks to meet him. If Adeline agrees to marry me I'll ask Arron to be my best man. Wish me luck, although by the time you get this I may be married.

I told her about all of you, PAPA'S, Copper Harbor, Marquette, the docks, about everything. She thinks Michigan sounds beautiful. Her folks love France, we'll deal with where to live later. I think France is beautiful also, except with all the devastation I'm not sure I'd want to live here after the war.

Adeline doesn't know I'm going to ask her to marry me yet. Arron and I will head there first thing on New Year's Day, and I'll ask her that night. January 1st, 1918, sounds like a perfect plan to me. I can't wait for all of you to meet her. Maybe we could get married on my birthday, she did say I was her valentine from across the sea.

I hope all's going well with everybody back there. Hope you had a nice Christmas, and the New Year will treat you well. With any luck the war will be over before next Christmas, and Adeline and I will be back in Copper Harbor for Christmas Eve. I'm sure she's never seen as much snow as we get back home. She'll be amazed. I love her!

Love,

Zach

Sunday – 12/30

Christmas here at the quarters was pretty damn nice. We had 3 Christmas trees decorated with empty shells from machine guns. Popcorn strung on the thread used for stitching wounds, and we used empty mess kits for the stars. Sang a lot of Christmas songs, had plenty of liquor and wine.

The French make great wine. All in all it was something none of us will ever forget.

There were a few altercations. Some fellas are Chicago Cubs fans, and some are New York Yankee fans. Mix favorite teams with liquor and strange things can happen. I told them I liked Oldsmobiles, and everything got a little lighter, until one guy said he preferred Fords. We all started laughing and everything was okay again.

There were a few fellas who had some trouble being so far from home. A couple of guys cried. My friend Arron stepped in and was an incredible help in calming them down. He has a way about him. He's so soft spoken and calming it relaxes a person. So there he was, my Jewish friend from Jersey, calming down a couple of big Catholic guys from Kansas, on Christmas Eve, up here in the North of France. Quite a life!

I found out no matter where you're from everyone loves Christmas. Like me. There was no fighting today, between us and the Germans. We all took the day off. It was nice, makes a guy wonder why we listen to the people who want war. I think all of us common joes don't want war. We want to be left alone to enjoy our lives. That's what I think anyway.

Tomorrow's New Year's Eve. It ought to be a hoot. Arron and I will probably sleep till noon on New Year's Day. We'll leave here around 2 and be in Paris by 3. I've worked out a signal with Arron. When he, Adeline and I are at supper, he'll excuse himself from the table for a while, and I'll propose to her. He says he's more excited than me. I doubt it!

Zach

1918

JANUARY 1918

Wednesday – 1/2
She cried.
Zach

Saturday – 1/5
She cried. I had it all worked out, only she cried. Arron had gone outside. The candle on the table was lit, the red wine was poured. Everything was perfect, but, she cried! She said she loved me, and then she cried. She grabbed my hand and held it tight, and she cried some more. Then she said no. She stopped crying for a moment, and she said no.

We talked. We walked. We hugged. Arron didn't know what to do, so Adeline hugged him. I was lucky he was with me. It reminded me of the time up in Marquette when I got the long letter from Grandpa Jake telling me all about who he was, and Pete was there to help me through. I'm lucky to have such nice friends.

Adeline knows she loves me, that isn't the problem. The problem is the war. The British and French have been talking about the possibility of a war with Germany for almost 11 years. It's all Adeline has heard her father talk about. He works for the government and it's always on his mind. She said he has sleepless nights over the war. It frightens her. That's why she became a nurse. To help.

Adeline can't count the number of soldiers she's seen die. The young men who've died from France and England, and now from America. She's frightened. She's frightened for me. She's frightened everyday she goes to work. Not for herself, for the world. Adeline is scared. I didn't know what to say, so we hugged. All 3 of us hugged.

Adeline loves me, she doesn't want to lose me, and she doesn't want to get married. She asked me not to see her until my birthday next month. We kissed, all 3 of us cried, and I left.

Zach

Saturday – 1/19

Still 4 weeks until I can see Adeline. The war is helping me keep my mind off her. I've been driving the Packard as though it had wings. One of my commanders asked me if I'd like to learn how to fly. I mentioned maybe after the war is over, and I'm back in the states.

I can sort of understand Adeline's thinking. What if something happened to me after we were married? She'd have the last name Zabrinski, and she'd be a war widow. Not a good situation. What if I died and she was pregnant? That's what happened to my mother. No good either. What if I lost both legs from a grenade? She'd be stuck with me, and she's only 25. Another bad situation.

Bad situations . . . too many times.

Zach

FEBRUARY 1918

Saturday – 2/2

Less than 2 weeks until I head back to Adeline. Arron doesn't want to go with me this time. I asked 4 times. He said last time was enough.

It appears we're getting the upper hand in the war, however, there's still too much killing. I'm sure Adeline's being kept super busy in the hospital. She's a fantastic nurse. I know all the soldiers love her. I sure fell for her. Is that what it was? How do I know? When will I know? Will I ever know?

I remember back when I was setting up PAPA'S, I was so sure of myself. When I was on the Lusitania I was pretty sure of myself. When I was working for Max, I was more than sure of myself. When I came to France I was sure of myself. Why do I question myself now? Has Adeline opened up something inside of me? My heart?

Zach

Thursday – 2/14

My birthday. Adeline loves me. She's convinced of it, she told me so, but she doesn't think we should get married until the war's over. Somedays I wonder if it will ever be over. I felt better with her in my arms today than I've felt in months. I know I love her. I know it doesn't make any difference where we live.

I have 3 more days I can spend here in Paris with Adeline. We can walk, talk, eat, hug, and kiss. I'm happy. I don't have to return to my unit until the 18th. Paris in February, not the best place to be temperature wise. When I'm with Adeline, who cares, SHE warms my heart.

Zach

Monday – 2/18

God! Where were You?

At 19.00 hours on Saturday our offices on Algiers Street were bombed by 3 German bombers. The building was almost ruined. 2 officers and some enlisted men were killed. 14 other officers were injured. Some had to be hospitalized. That's where I should have been if I hadn't been frolicking around in Paris. Arron was one of the enlisted men. Maybe I could have saved him.

DAMN IT!!!!

Zach

Sunday – 2/24

Arron was buried today at the cemetery at Suresnes, in the military section, on the slopes of Mont-Valerien. He'll have a view of Paris forever. I'm going to miss him.

War is HELL.
Zach

Dear Mom,

We buried my good friend Arron today. It's been a hard week. It's tough.

Arron was a swell fella. He and I became blood brothers. He read about them in those western books he always read. He made each of us put a small cut on our wrists, then we had to hold them together, and we became Blood Brothers. I really liked it. I have a brother looking down on me. I'm one lucky fella. Arron and my Guardian Angel.

I'm sitting in a coffee shop in Paris with Adeline. She says Hi. Our plan is to get married here in Paris after the war's over. Later we'll have a celebration in New York, for Max and the gang. Then we'll come home to Copper Harbor for another HUGE celebration. No one knows when the war will be over, but that's our plan. We're excited!!

I'm doing fine, try not to worry too much about me. Adeline's a great nurse, so she takes good care of me. You're gonna love her. I know it.

Things here are complicated. I've mainly been working with the French, even though I'm from the States. I think it has something to do with Max's influence. The French have been great to work with. We're seeing more and more American soldiers coming in, so now they have me bouncing around between them both.

Adeline has taught me more about the French language than I ever could have imagined. Both of her parents are fluent in both, that also helps me. Ms. Bagley would be proud of me. Those were some mighty fine days in Copper Harbor, before I turned 18.

Love,
Zach
P.S. Adeline just blew you and Grandma a kiss!

JULY 1918

Thursday – 7/18

Haven't been good at writing in this lately. Mom told me it would remind me of the good and bad things that have happened. It seems to remind me of the bad things. I haven't been in the best frame of mind these past few months.

I've been to Paris a few times since my birthday. Spent some nice days with Adeline, only she's incredibly busy at the hospital. She cries a lot about all the death, wounds, amputations, blindness, shell shock, and now some are dying from a new virus that's going around. It's scary.

I've been here almost a year and a half. It sure does wear on a person. Bombs, artillery, gunfire, sirens, it never ends. At least that's how it feels. It's nice being with Adeline, only we're both fed up with the war. She's been experiencing it for so much longer than I have. She sees death every day. I don't know how she manages.

Somedays it's hard just getting up.

Zach

Dear Mom, July 18th, 1918

I hope things up in Copper Harbor are much nicer than they are here. This war seems like an eternity. I'm getting tired. You've probably wondered why I never have the return address on my letters to you. I'll try to explain.

Lots of times I'll be with a fella who gets a letter from back home. He'll be laughing and telling everybody all about the stuff going on back there. Sometimes he'll even hug some of us. Then about an hour later, I'll find him some place, crying his eyes out. I'll ask him what happened, and all he can say is "I MISS HOME!"

So I don't want any letters from home. A month ago, one guy I got pretty close with, got a letter from his girlfriend. She broke up with him and married one of his best buddies. An hour later he went out into the woods and shot himself in the head. I don't want letters from home!

I remember home the way I want to. You, Grandma, Annie, Pete, Frank, PAPA'S, all kinds of good stuff. I want to remember how it was before I left. The farm, horses, new cars, Grandpa's old shack out in the woods, planting and harvesting, those kinds of things. Grandma's kisses. That's what I want to remember.

I think I told you about my dear friend Arron who died, and how we became blood brothers. Well after we put our wrists together, he pulled out a dollar bill. We tore it in half, and he gave me his half and I gave him my half.

We vowed to get together on the first 4th of July after the war. We were going to put the 2 halves together again. Me and Arron, together.

We were going to meet at Lombardi's Pizza on Spring Street, back in Manhattan, at High Noon. It's a cowboy phrase, he liked westerns. When I get home I'm going to give both halves to his folks in Jersey and tell them what a swell guy he was, and how much I miss him.

Adeline's fine. Being up near the front line of the war, I don't get to see her as often as I used to. When we are together she cries a lot. The things she sees in the hospital must be terrible. I love her a lot, only it's hard to think about love sometimes. It'll be nicer when the war's over.

I hope you're getting my letters ok. I imagine it takes a long time. Maybe by the time you get this, the war will be over. I'll give Adeline a kiss from you, maybe it will stop her from crying. Please give Grandma and Annie a kiss and a hug from me. Tell everybody I love them, and I'll be home soon. Remember I have a Guardian Angel!!!

Love,
Your Son, Zach

DECEMBER 1918

Sunday – 12/22

No matter what I say. No matter how hard I try to convince her. No matter all the begging I do. I can't change her mind!!

Now she says NO!

Back on my birthday we had it all planned. We were, we are, in love. I know it! Adeline loves me and I love her. Why can't she live with that? The war has hardened her. She's seen too much death, too much pain, too much sorrow. She has to dedicate her life to nursing.

She thinks it must be the reason God created her. I asked why He didn't create her to marry me. She laughed, she said she loves me, she says she always will. She just won't marry me. She loves me too much.

I promised we'd have a great life together. She asked, how could we, when she's so afraid of death? She said everyday she'd be worried I would die. She said she'd never be able to get a night's sleep, without worrying for my life. She said if I went to the food store, she'd worry I'd be hit by an automobile and die. If I went hunting, she'd worry I'd be shot and die. If I went fishing, she'd worry about me drowning and dying. No matter what I did, she'd worry about me dying.

The DAMN WAR has her scared stiff. All she can think of is death. All she wants to do with her life is save people she doesn't know. She said if she doesn't know them, and they die, she's used to it. If I died, and we were married she'd be devastated. She couldn't go on. She says she'd also die.

I begged, I pleaded, I cried. I did everything a man could do.

She said if I truly loved her I'd understand. She said if I cared about her, I'd let her live her life the way she wants. She said if I loved her, I'd leave her.

I HATE THE G-- DAMN WAR !!!!

Zach

Mom, Christmas Day, 1918

The wedding is off.

Adeline wants to commit her life to being a nurse. She thinks being married to someone she loves would be too hard on her. She claims she'd worry about me every day and it would take her mind off of what she wants to do. She said if I loved her, I'd leave her. Does that make any sense to you?

I met with her father before I left. He told me Adeline has been acting strange lately. He wasn't sure why, just something different. He told me she joined the French Army as a nurse, so she could help France win the war. He blames himself.

I'm numb right now. The war has been difficult, it messes with the mind. There's no rhyme or reason to anything. The war's finally over, I'm free to go. Max has pulled some strings. He wants me back in New York as soon as possible.

Love!

Your Son with the broken heart,

Zach

P.S. Belated, Merry Christmas.

Tuesday – 12/31 New Year's Eve

I've lost my true love!

I made one last effort to get Adeline back. I stopped at her parents' home before leaving France. She's gone. Now I understand. I wish she would have told me. Her parents said she couldn't. They said she loved me too much. She didn't want me to suffer.

They told me that's why she wouldn't let me hold her, touch her, or kiss her, when I saw her last week. She knew she was dying. Adeline caught the damn virus that's been creating almost as much havoc as the war. She got it from her patients.

She told them, if they ever saw me again, to tell me how much she loved me. She wanted me to know she'd always be looking towards Paris for me. She said whenever I looked east, I should think of her. Her father said that's the way she wanted to be buried. Her mother wept.

I left them, and slowly walked the same cobblestone streets Adeline and I walked so many times. Stopped at the same French café. Walked until I couldn't think anymore. Walked until I stopped crying. I don't know what I'm going to do.

All I know is . . . I'll be alone.

Zach

1919

FEBRUARY 1919

Friday – 2/14

Am I grown up yet? Max certainly thinks so. He's extremely happy I got back from the war in almost the same shape I went over in. He likes to kid me about the 4-inch scar and the darker color in my left eye. I think it's a great battle reminder.

I think about Adeline every day, not all day, just every day.

When I close my eyes I see 2 things – her wonderful smile, and the gravesite she's buried at. Right on top of the hill, looking straight towards Paris. Once in a while I wonder if I should have stayed in France, to be near her. Strange I suppose, however I do wonder.

Max gave me a 10,000-dollar bonus when I got back. I tried to make him take it back, although he already had it in a new account under my name. Maybe I'm not forceful enough. Maybe being brought up for so long by Mom and Grandma made me soft. Huh? How could I be soft after all the things I've been through?

Max had me set up in a swanky apartment up near Central Park. Way up on the 10th floor, had a stunning view of the park, a door man, everything I could want. It took some discussions with Max. I had to explain how being in the war and experiencing everything I saw over there. I couldn't take all the glitz in the swanky apartment.

I got a small apartment on Spring Street right down the block from Lombardi's Pizza. I feel at home. Adeline would have loved the area, maybe that's why I'm more comfortable here. Max shrugs when he comes here. I think the only reason he comes is because of Lombardi's. He says it's the best in New York.

Max has been a godsend for me. I do believe God was with me that day when I went to the bank looking for a job. There's no other way to explain it. Me, a hick from Copper Harbor, landing a job with this guy, simply amazing. Max said on the 4th of July, this year, he's going to make an announcement. He's promoting me to V.P. in charge of Foreign Relations.

I asked what it meant, and he said it's a new position. He said with the war, the victory, and all the European Countries who were involved, he needs someone who can work with them. He thinks I'm the best candidate for the job because of my involvement over there. Then he winked and said, "If you can track a rabbit on concrete, you can do anything." I like Max.

I never talk about pay with Max, never have too, he's overly generous. He said he was about to turn 57 and will be retiring when he hits 60. He sold his mansion over on Long Island. He bought a nice home south of Naples Florida, right on the beach. He's having it totally remodeled so in 3 years it'll be ready for him.

I'd never tell him, but when he retires, so do I. Then I'll start looking for my father. I should have nearly 40,000-thousand dollars in the bank. I'll be a free man. The way I was when school was out, and Mom and Frank got married.

Zach

Dear Mom, Friday, February 14th, 1919
HAPPY VALENTINES DAY!
I guess you know what that means. I turned 32 today.
I got back from France OK. I think about Adeline every day. Not a day goes by when she's not on my mind somehow. I think our love was for eternity. I was devastated from losing her. I know you know what I mean.

The French soldiers used to say, "It is what it is!" I always got a kick out of that. I could be delivering information to them, or I could be in a fox hole with them or laying on a hospital bed next to one of them, and sure enough someone would say "It is what it is!" That's a pretty good attitude. I've got to try to develop it.

Remind me of that when I come and visit.

I plan on being in Copper Harbor on Sunday June 29th, and I'll stay almost 2 weeks until Thursday July 10th. I don't think I've been in Copper Harbor for the 4th of July since '05. Goodness, It's been 14 years. It'll take all those days to catch up on things. Annie will be 10 when I get home. I'm excited.

I've got a nice apartment, I'm healthy, have a great job, everything seems to be going along great. Only my heart is BROKEN!

Zach

JULY 1919

Dear Mom, Saturday 7/19/1919

What a grand time I had!!!

You, Frank, Grandma and Annie pulled all the rabbits out of the hat for my homecoming. I never would have imagined anything so incredibly festive. The decorated float from your store, with the Oldsmobile pulling it for the 4th of July parade. Me sitting on it with a banner welcoming all the soldiers back home. It blew my mind.

I'm glad all the other fellas who were in the war were up on the float. They deserved it more than me. My wound's just a scratch on my forehead, Jeramiah had both his legs amputated. It'll be a long time before the wounds from the war are healed. Some may never be.

I lost my true love Adeline and my friend Arron to the DAMN War. I'll never get completely over Adeline. Our love was for eternity.

If Annie takes after my mother with her cute dimples and curly black hair, well, as I said last time, my mother must have been a real knock-out. You and my mother must have been the cutest girls in town!! I had fun spending a few hours working in your store. The best part was pumping gas for the 5 cars which came through. They were all Oldsmobiles sold right in Houghton, well, all except the shabby old Ford.

Frank sure has come around with the whole car idea. I noticed out in the barn he's got a huge area set up for working on cars. The pit he dug out so he can stand in it and work on the bottom of cars was fantastic. Pete was blown away. He said he was going to do that at his shop in Iron Mt., only he's going to use concrete.

I know I'm proud of all the things I've accomplished, it's just, when I come home, sometimes I feel as though I haven't done anything. Pete and Samantha have 6 kids. Michael and Sally have 3. Cute little Annie's growing up so fast. You and Frank have turned the farmhouse and the old barn into this amazing place. Frank has his work shops, and you've got a beautiful flower garden. The yard looks like a park with the pine trees and flowers.

Sometimes it seems as though I'm spinning my wheels. I know when I told you that, you got mad at me. You reminded me of the accomplishments I've made, but sometimes I still feel lost. I can't get over thinking it has to do with my father and having no idea what he was like.

Oh well, as the French say, It is, what it is!

I didn't tell you when I was home because I wasn't sure it would happen. Max has created a new job for me here in New York. He calls it V.P. in Charge of Foreign Relations. He says with of all my experiences in the war I can deal with any of those foreign countries. He's talking about all the countries in Europe. Can you believe it?

I'm a hick from upper Michigan. I keep reminding him, but he doesn't believe me. He says I must have grown up in Detroit. He keeps telling me there's more to me than I realize. I hope he's right. For now I'll believe him. One thing about Max, he pays well. Really well.

Grandma was quieter, maybe more tired. She acted like she was ready to quit sometimes, and her hands shook more than I remember. She also mentioned to me how Grandpa was waiting for her. She said he comes to her in her dreams dressed in his wedding suit and kisses her. It was nice, it made me feel closer to both of them.

Zach

P.S. What the hell was wrong with Emil at the parade? Is he anti me or is he anti America?

1920

MARCH 1920

Dear Mom, Sunday, 3/7/1920

I thought my heart could never be broken again.

Missing Grandma is going to be hard. She was always my rock, even though sometimes she was so confused. She always knew what to say to me to calm me down. You know, if I wouldn't have been in Paris, I'd have been at Grandmas funeral.

On one hand I wish I would have been there with you, on the other hand, there was so much dying in the war, I'm not sure I would have handled it very well. After we hung up I sat crying, and thought about my wonderful Adeline, and Arron.

I was sad for all 3 of them. I know God's with them. He has to be. They were the best. Grandma's finally with Grandpa Jake. As I told you in my last letter, Grandpa had been coming to her in her dreams lately. Those must have been omens.

I hope you're handling it alright. I know you've been through so much yourself. It's good you have Frank and Annie so close. Don't ever forget you ALWAYS have me, even when I'm so far away. You're always in my heart.

Being the V.P. for Foreign Relations has been the most interesting thing I've done so far. I've met with some incredibly influential people from all across Europe. We meet right here in New York.

Max is usually in the meetings with me, but he always lets me handle most of the conversation. He had me go on that trip to Paris. I met with some banking executives from the National Bank of Paris. We're establishing a relationship with them. Max wanted my take on how they'll be to deal with.

I spent an afternoon at the cemetery where Adeline and Arron are buried. The weather was great. The sun was out and not a cloud in the sky. However it wasn't quite so pleasant as far as my emotions went. Adeline's facing right towards the Eiffel Tower. That's the way I want to be facing when I'm finished. We'll be together in spirit for eternity. That's a fact!

I'm fine, don't worry about me. Remember I have a powerful Guardian Angel. I get to church fairly often. I think Grandma would be happy if I went more often. Maybe now since she's in Heaven, she can push me a little. Maybe that's what she always meant by what goes around, comes around. Maybe now she can push me onward.

I LOVE you! My thoughts are always with you!
Zach

Monday – 3/8
Got to go to church more often!! Grandma's watching.
Zach

Sunday – 3/14
Nice church Max goes to, not too far, nice walk. Joined the church today. Meeting with British diplomat Reynolds tomorrow for lunch. Max is in Florida. He's spending lots of time there. Invited me in June, for 2 weeks.
Zach

Monday – 3/15
Meeting was interesting. Now I've got a lot of figures to get together for Reynolds. He seems like a fine fella, maybe too persnickety, but a nice enough guy. I think I can sway him to our way of thinking. We'll meet again on Thursday.
Zach

Thursday – 3/18
Did I say persnickety? We spent at least 7 hours going over all the figures, dates, and time frames. Who gets what and when? How and when

we get paid? Why this and why that? Is it black or is it white? Does the sun come up, or does the earth spin around it?

The last 2 things I threw in at the end of the meeting, with a grin on my face. We were getting down to such trivial things I had to toss those 2 in. Then I took him to a popular British pub on the lower east side.

He's on board. Wants to meet Max as soon as Max is back from Florida. We'll all meet next Tuesday.

Zach

Tuesday – 3/23

Max is thrilled. Reynolds, Mr. Persnickety, is satisfied. I'm tired.

Max says I did get a huge feather in my cap!

Zach

MAY 1920

Sunday – 5/16

I've got a huge luncheon presentation tomorrow at headquarters. There's going to be 25 gentlemen in 3-piece suits smoking cigars, and 10 women choking on smoke, being catty, and showing off their diamonds. And all eyes will be on me and my charts. These are all the wealthiest people Max knows, and I have to sway them to his way of thinking.

Max said he'll be sitting in the back; he doesn't enjoy big meetings. He thinks I do. I'd tell him to go suck eggs, but he wouldn't understand. I told him I was going to start the meeting by introducing myself as The Hick from Upper Michigan. He liked the idea, said it would break up the tension.

Max is looking for contributors and he feels I can charm some of them into accepting his plan. He wants to build a hospital over in France, somewhere near Paris. He says it's our responsibility. Since the war went on over there, and not on our soil, he thinks it's the least we can do. I'm completely behind him on this one.

We did have a huge dispute over him spending so much money on a boat he wanted to buy. He was going to spend 50,000 dollars. I talked him down to a 30,000 dollar boat. I thought it was an awful lot of money for a boat which only held 10 people. Sometimes he's like a kid in a candy store. The 50 million dollars he inherited is almost 70 million now, still he should be careful with it.

This hospital thing though, it's right up my alley. I was in one for 4 days in the war. My Adeline worked there and died in one. It wasn't the greatest place to be. It didn't have enough beds, and the operating room was antiquated. I'm not complaining too much, however they sure could use a new hospital.

He wants to raise 2.5 million right away, and another 2.5 million by July 4th, and he's counting on me.

YIKES.

Zach

Saturday – 5/29

I guess the meeting 2 weeks ago went better than Max hoped. So far he has the first 5 million dollars in the bank, and another 5 million dollars pledged by July 4th. 10 million total, double what he wanted. He's thrilled, so am I. I'm amazed, I surprised even myself. Grandma would have been proud of me, maybe she was helping me.

When I introduced myself as The Hick from Upper Michigan, everybody broke up with laughter, even Max. He said when I told everybody to take off their shoes and relax, he almost spit up. He was amazed when everybody took them off, even him. He said he'd never seen those people so at ease during a presentation.

I guess, according to Max they were so relaxed, that when I told them about my Adeline being a nurse there, and dying in the old hospital, he saw some of them crying. I didn't mean to use Adeline for that purpose. I wanted to clue them in on the conditions in the old hospital. Max said it was fine to talk about my wonderful Adeline. So I'll accept it.

I won't tell Max, but right after the meeting, one of his competitors tried to hire me. He offered to triple my pay. When I told him I didn't know how much I make, he choked. I know he didn't believe me; he knew I wasn't about to leave Max for anything.

I wouldn't! Not for anything!

Zach

JULY 1920

Dear Annie, Sunday, July 4th, 1920

I bet you miss Grandma. I know I sure do! She was one special lady. I remember being at a dance when some guy called her a pretty little lady. He sure did know Grandma. Now you can go out in the backyard and visit with her and Grandpa Jake. You can also visit Angelica.

Someday I'll have to tell you all about Angelica. She was a special lady also. The same as Grandma, Mom, and You. Being home last year for the Fourth of July was a real hoot. I had such a good time with everybody. When I close my eyes I can still see your bicycle all dressed up with red, white, and blue streamers. I used to do the same thing when I was your age.

Summer's fun in Copper Harbor, only I was never nuts about winter. I'm not in love with cold and snow. Here in New York, winter doesn't last nearly as long as in Copper Harbor. The apple trees here blossom almost 2 months before yours, and they keep their leaves longer. I enjoy New York.

I imagine by now you're turning into quite a young lady, like Mom. I wonder if you ever see my friend Pete's son Zak. I don't know if Pete ever told you, Zak is his first born son, and he named him after me. Pete wanted me to be his Godfather, but I was away on the ship Lusitania. I was probably in the middle of the Atlantic Ocean some place.

I hope you're having a swell summer. Make Frank take you fishing out by the river near Grandpa Jake's old cabin. I always used to get a kick out of going fishing with Grandpa. You can catch those fighting trout by the dozens. Mom can fry them up for all of you. Thinking about it makes my mouth water!!

Tell Frank I think he should start teaching you how to drive. He'll get a kick out of that. He'll probably tell me to mind my own business – if he says anything – tell him YOU are my own business. Be good, hug Mom, say your night prayers, and think about Grandma and me once in a while.

Much Love,

Your Big brother Zach.

NOVEMBER 1920

Sunday – 11/7

New York City! It's nice to be back home. I know my way around here. I know the language. Lombardi's Pizza, Central Park, Broadway plays, and Max. It's good to be home.

Madrid, Rome, London, and finally Paris. After 3 months on the water, I don't care if I ever get on an ocean liner again. Even if they do have those beautiful staterooms, and those scrumptious food buffets. If I ever do get on another one, it'll be to go one place and stay there for at least a month.

Europe's a mess. Some of the most beautiful buildings I've ever seen have been demolished. In some areas, whole sections of a town have been almost flattened. There were nights I had to drink. It wasn't so much I wanted to drink. I HAD to drink.

Some of the things I saw, I'll never be able to forget, maybe I shouldn't. Maybe we all should remember what happened, so it never happens again. Is it wishful thinking? I hope not. I hope my wonderful Adeline, and Arron, and the other millions of dedicated people who died, haven't died in vain. If so, God help us all!

I did bring Max millions of dollars of new business, and we also gave millions of people new hope. Without money, what can they do? Most of them are broke and demoralized. Anything we can do for them could be lifesaving.

Max wants me to take time off, he says I need a rest, and I should go to his house in Naples. He said he'll pull the remodelers out of the house for a month, and I should walk the beaches of Florida. I might take him up on it. He wants me back by Christmas. He has a surprise for me. That'll be interesting, maybe he wants me to go to Germany. NO THANKS! They killed Arron.

Zach

Sunday – 11/21

I'll leave tomorrow morning for sunny Florida. Sounded like too nice of a deal to pass up. Me, alone in Florida, away from this dreary weather. Maybe we should open an office down there. I know I'm good at starting new locations. It worked out pretty well in Marquette.

Zach

DECEMBER 1920

Dear Mom, Christmas Day, 1920

It's supposed to be snowing on Christmas. I'm stuck here in Florida, it's 70 degrees outside, and SUNNY!

I was supposed to be back in New York for Christmas, but something came up in Miami. A banker was embezzling a lot of money and Max got word of it. He sent me to see what was going on, so now I'm in Miami. His place in Naples is much nicer.

I suppose I shouldn't complain. I get paid either way, no matter where I am. His place over in Naples, right on the Gulf of Mexico is pretty glitzy, 3 stories, 6,000 square feet. He told me 4,000, he probably didn't want me to critique him. For reasons I'll never know, he does appreciate my opinion. Maybe it's something I inherited from my father.

I've got a year and a half until Max retires, then I will also. My plan is to figure out what happened to my father. How did he die? I know I've told you a hundred times, maybe I keep repeating myself, so I don't forget.

I can close my eyes and see the farmhouse, the yard, Frank's workshops, your store, the 3 of you around a Christmas tree, and falling snow. It's a beautiful sight. Wish I was there, but just for 3 days, then I'd rather be back here in sunny Florida.

I head back to New York on Monday. Should be there on Wednesday, in time for New Year's Eve, and the big ball that drops down at midnight. Max will be glad I'm back. I don't know why he gets nervous when I'm gone. Maybe it's because he and his wife never had kids.

I love you all. Hope Christmas was splendid, and you have a great New Year. I don't know when I'll write again. Max said he has a surprise for me, and it could mean more traveling. As the French say, "It is, what it is!"

Zach

1921

JANUARY 1921

Saturday – 1/8

Max wants to open an office in Europe. He wants me to be in charge of it. He said he didn't make me V.P. of Foreign Relations for nothing. He has it narrowed down to 2 cities, London, or Paris.

He'd like me to stay on 5 more years with him. He'll pay me a yearly salary of 40,000 dollars. He said there was a 200,000 dollar bonus, plus a 5 percent cut of the profits for me if I stay the 5 years. Max wants me to make the decision on which city.

He wants to know by the end of the month. I've got some thinking to do. I thought he was going to retire. What about my father?

Zach

Sunday – 1/30

I'm off to London the day after my birthday. Paris was too close to my Adeline. I never would have gotten any work done. Max put the bonus money into a bank account in my name, the 5 percent cut will come when I'm done. I can get them the day after my birthday in 1926. I'll be 39. I'll have plenty of time left to find out about my father.

I can't let Max down.

Zach

FEBRUARY 1921

Dear Mom, Sunday, February 13th, 1921
Tomorrow's my 34th birthday.

16 years ago you told me I may have offended Grandma and God. That's a day I'll never forget. On one hand it was the day part of me died, but on the other hand, maybe it's the day I was born. Interesting, hey? I prefer being 34. Hands down.

Max is throwing a huge birthday party for me tomorrow so I may not feel like writing after the party. Tuesday I leave for 5 years in London. Max is opening a new office over there and he wants me to get it up and running. Reminds me of Marquette. Wish me luck.

He believes, because he gave me the title V.P. of Foreign Relations, I can do this. I hope he's right. He's financially compensating me way beyond what I ever could have imagined. More than I'm worth for sure. I won't tell him. He has the resources to do it, so I'm fine with it.

I hope you had a great New Year's Eve. I imagine it was a white Christmas and all the pine trees out in front of the house were decorated nicely. Annie told me Frank likes to decorate them for Christmas. Grandpa would have been proud. He probably is proud; I know he planted most of them.

I'm glad I called on Christmas. After I wrote the letter, I got homesick and decided to call. Fortunately, you were all there and I could spend some time on the phone with each one of you. Maybe someday I'll be able to see you while I'm talking to you on the phone. Wouldn't it be neat.

Annie's beginning to sound more grownup than me. I should take her to London with me. Now, THAT'S a darn good idea. I have to be there 5 years. Maybe I could get her there for a month or so, some summer between school sessions. Maybe? I think it would be great for her. London with her big brother. I could take her to Paris. We could go to Adeline's gravesite.

I don't know if I'll have much time to write a lot or not. Max has me doing everything, pretty much the way I did in Marquette. Find an office, get a place to live, all kinds of stuff. He does know a banker in London who he wants me to contact, regarding potential employees. Max trusts my judgement, although he wants his banker friend to verify some of my more important hires.

I'm totally in favor of that. I'd prefer his friend do most of the hiring. I'll see what we work out. I'm pretty flexible and Max is pretty trusting, so I'm not worried about anything.

Max made me choose between London and Paris for the new location. I spent almost a month pondering between the 2 cities. I chose London, because of all the allies we had in the War, England was our closest. Plus I was afraid of being too close to Adeline. I thought I'd spend too much time at her grave.

Goodbye for now. Always remember I LOVE you all, and nothing could ever take the place of Copper Harbor. I'll keep you posted, probably not as much as you'd like, but that's just me.

Love. Love, Love,

Your Son,

Zach

Remember, I have a great Guardian Angel looking out for me!!!

8 YEARS LATER

1929

FEBRUARY 1929

FEBRUARY 27, 1929
MOM – (STOP) - FOUND DAD – (STOP) - HE'S ALIVE - (STOP)
- WILL WRITE MORE LATER – (STOP) ZACH
   ZACH

MARCH 1929

Friday – 3/1
Thanks to Captain Dow, I located my father. Dow was pretty sure Dad may be somewhere in Brazil, near the city of Salvador. He didn't know if Dad was alive, dead, or hiding from something. That's as much as he knew, or he'd tell me.

How many years I've searched for any information about him. Everyone was convinced he was dead. I believed them, and now I find out he's alive. I figured I'd find a gravesite at best. I'd talk to some locals, take some pictures, write some notes, and go home. Maybe I'd at least feel less lost.

When I heard he was alive my reaction was shock. Then I was confused; then I was upset. I don't know if I was more upset with him, or me, for waiting so long to start my search. Then I wondered if maybe I'd be better off if he were dead. If he were dead I could go back to New York and get on with my life.

Now, since I've found Dad, there's a lot of explaining to be done. His doctor's taking me to see him tomorrow.

Zach

Saturday – 3/2

I met him at his doctor's office right after lunch. He's 69, looks more like 80. He doesn't know if he should believe me or not. I told him some things about Copper Harbor he may remember. He seems to be in decent spirits, except I'm not sure he trusts me. He said his life has been pretty hard.

It's been 43 years since he's been in Copper Harbor. I have to leave him alone for a few days, he wants this information to sink in. He promised me he wouldn't leave his place; he wants me to come back Wednesday. I don't know if I can believe him or not. He left me once before. Can I trust him this time?

Zach

Dear Mom, Sunday March 3rd, 1929

Hope you received my telegram dated February 27.

I'm quite sure, if you did, it took you by complete surprise. I met Dad for the first time yesterday, and he's not sure who I am. He doesn't really believe me, although I guess I can't blame him. Why would he believe me? He looks pretty beat up; says he's had a rough life.

I'll write more after I get to know more about him. I know a fella named Captain Dow who gave me some helpful information about Dad, that's how I found him. It took some searching, but it was worth it. Got to go for now, will write more in a few weeks.

Love,

Zach

Wednesday – 3/6

I'm not sure what I expected. Was I expecting a hug?

Well, we talked. I told him I've been thinking about him ever since I was a kid. He never once thought about me. How could he? He didn't know I existed. He says all he knew is my mother died from the influenza, back in February 1887. The year I was born, 42 years ago.

He says she was the love of his life. The only woman he ever loved, a love for eternity. When Dad left Copper Harbor in June of 1886, he left his heart there. He bought the biggest diamond he could find and made his way back to Copper Harbor in July of 1887. He was going to propose to my mother.

He sent his 1st mate and his cook to shore, to make sure my mother was still there. When they came back and told him she had died from the virus, he was devastated. He never knew I was born. He never knew about me! He never even thought about me, and he's been on my mind as long as I can remember!

I rented a house near where he lives. It's right on the coast. I can hear the pounding waves and smell the saltwater. It feels like home.

I'll stay here a while.
Zach

Saturday – 3/9

He's beginning to smile when he sees me coming! When we walk together I feel as though I'm 18 again. It's a damn nice feeling.

Dad says after he heard my mother had died he lost it. He had his 1st mate take over the ship. He went into his quarters and stayed there for over a month. He says he drank himself to sleep every night.

When he finally realized what he was doing to himself, he dedicated his life to her. He sold the diamond and bought his own cargo ship. He named it Angelica. He worked the Atlantic Ocean until the German U-Boats started sinking ships. He said he'd had enough of life on the Atlantic.

Dad knew Captain Dow, he told Dad when he was done he was going down to Brazil. Dad sold his ship and moved to Brazil, back in late 1914, when I was still on the Lusitania. When I told him that he grinned and shook my hand. I told him a lot about myself, Grandma, Grandpa, Mom, Celeste, Frank, Annie, the farm.

Then I told him about Father Dominic's grand old plan. How I was supposedly brought up from Detroit, the product of an illegitimate birth. How I was told Celeste was my mother. How they told me the truth after I turned 18.

Then I told him how Mother died. I noticed tears streaming down his face, so I stopped talking.

It made me both happy and sad.
Zach

Saturday – 3/16

We did a lot of walking the beach this week. A lot of talking, some laughing, and some crying. Dad said he was born in France. In the city of St-Nazaire right on the Atlantic Ocean. He said it was a superior place to grow up, and a super place for exploring. It sounded similar to my childhood.

I finally understand my love of France.

He thinks I've been brave. He believes most fellas would have quit searching, and some may never have started. I asked him if he was brave. He says he couldn't remember.

I hugged him.

Zach

Sunday – 3/17

Dad and I went to church today. I don't know what denomination it was, but I do know God was there, and Dad was happy. Singing, dancing, and clapping was everywhere. A lot of Praise the Lord, and hugging. First time in a while I thought about Grandma. Made me smile.

I asked Dad if he ever thought about going back to Copper Harbor, but I already knew the answer. He likes where he's living, he loves the Ocean, the pounding waves, and the smell of saltwater. Why wouldn't he? He's a ship's captain at heart.

I'm his kid!

Zach

Saturday – 3/23

Dad was tired yesterday. He says he hasn't been this happy since he was with Angelica. He claims I remind him of her. That brought a lump in my throat, and I started crying. I thought I was too old to cry. He hugged me.

I think it's a damn good thing Father Dominic died a few years ago. I'm mad as hell at him for coming up with the stupid story about the influenza. If Dad would have known my mother died at childbirth, he would have come on shore to find me. No one knows what would have happened, but he would have known I was alive.

Gramps was right. It was a lot of BALONY!

Zach

APRIL 1929

Dear Mom, Monday, April 1st, 1929

My father's alive!

He's not doing so well, but he's alive. I imagine you have a lot of preconceived notions about him. After all, it's been 43 years since you saw him. Everybody thought he ran out on my mother.

It's been 24 years since my 18th birthday and the infamous birthday news. How many times, over the years, I told you I felt lost, and I didn't belong anyplace. Well, here I feel at home. I can go to sleep at night, and not wonder who I am. I'm finally beginning to know who I am. It's a pretty darn good feeling.

I realize from all of our conversations, and Grandpa's letter, that you and I were great for each other. I think it's amazing, and I'll always love you. You're my mom. I know all about my mother, and now I have a real DAD. I'm beginning to feel complete.

Now I can tell you about him. He did come back for my mother, and he had a huge diamond for her. She was the love of his life, his only true love. His love for eternity. He was told Mother died from the influenza which was going around. He knew nothing about me. Nothing whatsoever. Father Dominic's STUPID STORY kept my father from knowing about me!!

My father was devastated. He went into his captain's quarters and hid for a month. Same as Grandpa Jake did at the cabin. If anyone would have stood up for me, and told the truth, my father would have known about me. I don't have any idea what he may or may not have done. I do know he would have known I existed. And me, him. I have no idea what I'll do next. All I know, is I'm his kid and he knows me.

I love it!

Zach

Saturday – 4/6

Sent Mom a letter. I hope I didn't offend her too much. I know she didn't have anything to do with the stupid story of Father Dominic's. She told me she was hysterical after my mother died. She said it was Father Dominic and Grandma's idea.

I think it was Father Dominic all by himself. I think he felt if anyone knew my mother had a baby, and wasn't married, they'd think he was a failure. They'd all wonder what sort of a priest he was. Why couldn't he keep his flock controlled?

I'll give Father Dominic an F.

Zach

Monday – 4/8

Dad and I went fishing yesterday. He has a friend with a nice boat, so the 3 of us, plus Dads doctor spent the day on the water. It's incredibly nice to see Dad happy and laughing. His doctor says he's never seen my dad laugh before. I felt good. I might see if I can buy the house I rented.

Zach

Friday – 4/26

Closed on the house today. All Dads friends are helping him move in this weekend. He smiles a lot. Great to see! Talked with Max. He and his wife are coming down for a few weeks in July. He said he's never been to Brazil. He thinks he should open up a branch here. Good old Max, always up to something.

Things are looking up!

Zach

JULY 1929

Thursday – 7/4

Seems odd being in Brazil for the 4th of July.

I asked Dad if he ever gets homesick, he says he never had a home. He started working on ships when he was 16. He says times were different back in those days. He thinks we've got it pretty darn good these days. He says I might be spoiled, maybe I have it too good.

I reminded him about the banker up in Marquette who turned me down. Working on the Lusitania, putting dishes away, serving dinners, sharing a bunk room with 7 other guys who snore. Fighting with Emil, getting fired at the dock, the fight at the Pub in Liverpool. Searching for him all these years, thinking he was dead. Never dreaming he may be alive.

Then I told him about my Adeline. Then I cried. He couldn't stop me. He tried, but he couldn't.

He says he understands.

Zach

Dear Mom, 7/6/1929

I bought the house I was renting; the white sand beach stretches for miles in either direction. I can hear the waves and smell the saltwater, just the way I used to dream about it.

I'll never be able to explain how incredible it feels to be with Dad. How great it is to wake up feeling at home and at peace. I used to feel at home on the farm until I was 18, only I don't know if I ever felt at peace.

Dad's my size. He has brown hair. It's long, sort of weird, but he likes it and I'm getting used to it. Max would have had me to a barber a long time ago. Max and his wife are coming here sometime this fall. He wanted to get here this month, but he said things up in New York are getting a little tricky with the stock market.

Dad walks with a limp. He says anybody who spent as much time on a cargo ship as he has is lucky to still be walking. He cried when I told him how Mother died. He apologized to me so many times about not coming on shore. He never even knew I was born, why would he have come on shore?

I'll discuss that with Father Dominic someday. I sort of think Grandpa has already done it in Heaven, probably more than once. Grandpa told me in his letter he thought it was a crazy idea. So do I.

I hope all of you had a great 4th of July. I asked Dad if he ever wanted to go back to Copper Harbor. He didn't have to answer me. I could tell. I'll try to get back home sometime in the next few years, although I must admit, I do enjoy the ocean.

Love,
Zach

SEPTEMBER 1929

Saturday – 9/21

Talked with Max yesterday. His travel plans are on hold for a while.

Max warned me about the economy. He said even here it may get bad. A man he knows is predicting a crash is coming to the stock market. Max wired me 10,000 dollars. He said I should go to my bank and get cash. He said cash might be hard to get for a while.

I often wonder why I deserve a friend like Max. He's the same age as Dad, so he's 25 years older than me. Why has he cared so much about me? Whenever I ask him that, he always says it was because I told him I could track rabbits on concrete. He told me it was the most confident thing he ever heard anybody say.

I thought I was being cocky.

Zach

Monday – 9/23

Went to the bank today to get the 10,000. All they'd give me was 5,000. They credited the rest to my existing account. They apologized up and down, they said the London Stock Exchange crashed last Friday. They said everybody in the banking industry is cautious about taking too much out of their reserves.

Zach

Dear Mom, Saturday, September 28th, 1929

I hope Annie had a great 21st birthday. I'm sure you and Frank had a nice party planned. I imagine she may even be thinking about getting married. I'd come home for her wedding!

Dad's doing well, he's perked up a lot since I've been here. His doctor's amazed at the progress. I think living near the ocean is good for him. When I got here, he was back in the rainforest, where it was dark, humid, and dreary.

He said he was in the forest because the ocean reminded him of Angelica. I think now since I'm here he's glad to be back near the water. We walk on the beach almost every day. Dad smiles a lot, I like it. I'd love to get him back up into the States, only he always says NO. Maybe someday he'll agree.

We eat well, exercise a lot, well we walk a lot if it counts as exercise. Dad has lost 25 pounds since I found him. He's thrilled. He'll turn 70 on November 20th. He thinks he can live forever. He says it with a wink, after a few drinks. He sometimes talks like a sailor, he said he earned the right. I don't dispute him.

I do spend some time wondering what my next job will be. It's great being here with Dad but I do miss working with people. I think after the 1st of the year, I'll go into town and see if there's anything that interests me there. Maybe they have an automobile dealer in town. Or maybe selling yachts, or fishing boats. I guess I'll never know where my life is heading. Do any of us?

Love,
Zach

NOVEMBER 1929

Dear Mom, Sunday, November 17th, 1929

It sure was nice talking with all of you on the phone. Just because I'm gone so much doesn't mean I don't think about all of you. I don't think a day goes by when I'm not thinking about at least one of you, or, all of you.

Dad has started asking about you. He says he remembers how fantastic he felt about having you, Grandma, and Grandpa as his future family. Then he doesn't say anymore. Those are the times I think he starts remembering about my mother, and the tears usually start coming. Makes me sad.

It sounded as though Frank was worried about the economy. I talked with Max last Friday and he has no idea what's going on. He said there were some tough days in September. Then some folks, I think he meant him and some buddies, put money in, and things picked up a little.

Down here, where Dad and I are, things are going along fairly well. There seems to be some dissention in the bigger cities, but out here it's pretty laid back. As I said before, most of the folks around here make their living from the ocean, and that's not going anyplace.

It's relaxing. Still, I am getting antsy. The last time I was at the bank I inquired about any possible jobs. Dad says he'd be fine with me getting a job, but he wants me to stay living with him. I think he's concerned about his heart.

So Annie and Zak are getting married July 4th. I'm not as surprised as I thought I'd be. I know they make a cute couple, and they come from 2 great families. I'll try my best to get home for the wedding. It'll depend on Dad, and how he's feeling.

I'm doing fine. I still love the sound of the ocean, but I must say, on the mornings the water's smooth as glass, and the sun starts coming up, it's absolutely gorgeous. Dad never gets up that early to walk with me. He says he's seen the sun come up before.

I hope this letter finds you all in good health and spirits. Tell Frank not to worry too much about the economy. It always bounces back.

Love,

Zach

Thursday – 11/21

Dad turned 70 yesterday. We had his doctor and 6 of his friends over for a party. I think they were all still here when I went to bed at midnight. They were on the beach singing, drinking, and cussing. Fun to hear. I laid awake for half an hour laughing to myself. Quite a day!

Zach

Sunday – 11/24

Talked with Max today. He's going to church more often now. He sold his place in Florida before he even moved in. He said he got almost what he paid for it plus the remodeling costs. He's afraid to leave New York. He wants me back there, but I don't know if I'm up to it. I enjoy living by the ocean with Dad. I'm torn.

I had Max start the paperwork to transfer my 5 percent of PAPA'S to Annie for her wedding present. I think it'll be good for her to have some ownership. Max said it'll be done long before the wedding in July.

Zach

Saturday – 11/30

Dad mentioned maybe I should go back to New York. He knows I'm antsy. He says he can tell. He thinks I remind him of himself when he sold his cargo ship. He moved to Brazil, and it took him almost 5 years to relax, at least that's what he's telling me. I'm not sure if I can believe him, or if he thinks it's what I want to hear.

I wonder what it would take for him to come with me?

Zach

DECEMBER 1929

Dear Mom, Sunday, December 22nd, 1929

Merry Christmas to all of you, and Happy New Year.

You probably won't get this letter before Christmas, but at least this year I'm writing it before the 25th.

Here in Brazil, it's almost impossible to tell the difference between summer and winter. I miss the changing of the leaves between summer and winter. Green gets boring after a while. I'm not complaining, just telling the truth..

For Christmas we put up a tree about 4 feet tall. Dad hung some fishing tackle on it for ornaments, I laughed at it. This huge house seems too quiet sometimes. It's nothing like the farmhouse when Grandma and Grandpa were alive. Or the first year you had the store, and you bought all those fancy ornaments. Even the Christmas over in France, with the rifle bullets hanging on the tree looked better. Well maybe not.

Dad says New Year's Eve here is really something. He says we'll hear the banging of pots and pans, guns shooting, fire sirens going off, and a lot of shouting. He says he usually goes to bed by 10, and gets woken up at midnight, then can't get back to sleep. I'm going to keep him up this year.

Dad has good days, but then he'll have a bad day. His doctor said the bad days are nothing like they used to be. He attributes it to me. Made me feel good. One thing I enjoy is seeing Dad smile. He has a great smile, and his laugh, I can hear it all the way down on the beach.

Tomorrow, he, and I are going fishing with his buddy. We can get out a few miles from shore if the weather's good. Dad likes fishing, it takes his mind off of everything. Sometimes I don't think he even puts bait on his hook. I think he likes bobbing up and down on the blue water, drinking beer, and smelling the ocean. It's in his blood. He calls himself a blueblood.

I love you ALL and miss you All!!

Love,

Zach

1933

APRIL 1933

Dear Mom, Sunday, April 9ᵗʰ, 1933

Spring here in New Jersey is beautiful. It reminds me of July in Copper Harbor. It's nice to be back in the Good Old USA. I think even Dad's happy.

I know you were disappointed when I couldn't make Annie's wedding. I told you on the phone, Dad had gone through a relapse of something even his doctor wouldn't tell me about. All he'd tell me is it had something to do with the type of cargo Dad handled.

He's been much better since then, he even agreed to move to the States. He kept talking about how he spent most of his life on the Atlantic Ocean, so that was his only request. When I told him about a city named Atlantic City, right on the ocean, he was all in. We moved here the end of March. We're about 4 miles south of the city.

It took me over 3 years to convince Dad to move here but it was worth the wait. While I was in Brazil, I did come back to New York for 3 weeks every 4 months. Max has kept me on the payroll. I'd meet with his friends, business partners, potential clients, anybody he wanted me to meet. I enjoyed it, and he made it financially worthwhile!

I hope Annie enjoyed my wedding gift. I know she deserved it. She's one of the in-crowd now. I'm looking forward to seeing everyone again, it's been a long, long, time. I know it's my fault, however I was willing to spend the rest of my life trying to find out about my father. I'm thrilled he's ALIVE.

I go up to New York now for 3 days a week to work with Max. He has a little, he calls it little, it's almost 3,000 square feet, penthouse apartment, I stay in. It's absolutely loaded. Only the best for Max. I said it once before, God was on my side the day I met him.

I'll call in a few weeks.

Love

Zach

P.S. Dad said HI, and to tell you he likes being alone for a few days a week. He also says, since he's my father, he must be Annie's Uncle.

Saturday – 4/29

Max is glad my dad agreed to come to the States with me. Now he wants me to try to talk Dad into moving to the City. He said we could live in his apartment, plus he's willing to give Dad a nice chunk of spending money every week.

I wonder how Dad would like New York. I've seen the docks and the ships in the harbor, maybe he'd get a kick out of it. He always says the ocean's in his blood.

Tuesday night I was feeling low. I went to the local pub and met a young lady named Kathleen. She's twice the gal Pete's cousin Sally is, only she's half my age. For whatever reason, I invited her up to my apartment, or I should say, Max's apartment. I did something I've never done. Not even with my Adeline.

I hope God wasn't watching.

Zach

JULY 1933

Tuesday – July 4th

The 4th of July in New York City. I'm keeping Dad awake tonight for the fireworks, no falling asleep early for him today. He'll be amazed. From the apartment we can see in all 4 directions. Dad will be going from window to window all evening.

Max likes my dad. He says he finally figured out where I get my personality. I'm flattered. Dad gets a kick out of Max. He wonders why Max ever hired me. Smiling, I told him it's because I can track rabbits on concrete. Dad has no idea what I'm talking about. I told him to ask Max.

Dad's 73, getting forgetful, and living in a new city. I had something made that he could wear around his wrist. In the war, we all had to wear something around our neck. Dads has his name, our address, and the office phone number on it. It's gold, shiny, and manly. Dad likes it.

Zach

Monday – 7/17

Met Kathleen for supper Saturday night. She told me she's carrying my baby. She's going to keep it. She sounded happy. I don't know what the hell I'm going to do. We had supper back in May and then she had no idea she was expecting. I'm not sure if I should be happy or cry.

Zach

Wednesday – 7/26

Figured as much. Dad took the ferry to Staten Island, forgot he had to take it back to Manhattan, and started walking around looking for our place. Luckily, a cab driver spotted him looking lost. He saw Dads bracelet, went with him on the ferry back to Manhattan, got to our building and called the office.

I was out, so Max paid the cab driver handsomely. I mean handsomely. He said it was the least he could do for a dear friend. When I asked Dad what happened, all he said was he had fun.

Max has some extremely powerful friends in Naples, Florida. He said they owe him big time. I've sent Kathleen there for a while, at least until the baby comes. I gave her enough money to last quite a while and said I'd be there in spring.

I'm not sure how to handle all of this. Am I doing exactly what my dad did? Dad never knew my mother was expecting me. I know Kathleen's expecting my baby. I've got to try to get them back up here.

Zach

NOVEMBER 1933

Tuesday – 11/6

Dad turns 74 in 2 weeks. He feels great, but he has to catch his breath more often. He still thinks it's from all the different products he hauled. I sometimes think it's from the saltwater. Whatever it's from it is what it is. I'm happy we're together, it's been 4 years and 9 months.

Dad and I go to the same church Max belongs to, it's only a few blocks away. Dad likes it, he says he wants to be buried there. I smile at him; I'm getting good at that.

Zach

Friday – 11/17

Max is sending me up to Albany on Monday, Dads birthday, for the week. Apparently the governor's doing some inquiring into the stock market crash. Max wants me to represent him. He told me to have everybody take off their shoes and relax, the way I did at the meeting for the hospital. He also wants me to introduce myself as the Hick from Michigan. Not going to happen this time.

Then he wants me to, as he said, "Clobber them with the truth." Max put together a 15-page presentation explaining, in his opinion, why the market crashed. He puts an awful lot of the blame on the federal government and the Federal Reserve.

Max feels the government should have foreseen all the hundreds of thousands of what he calls Stags. The amateur speculators and investors who were borrowing money to buy stocks. Everyone thought they were going to become millionaires overnight.

Max blames the government for not putting some restrictions on things long before it got out of hand. I told Max this is over my head, but he insists, with his 15-page presentation, all I have to do is make people comfortable. He's confident it'll go well. I told him I wasn't wearing a 3-piece suit or smoking a stinky cigar.

He laughed.

Zach

Sunday – 11/26

What a meeting!

I gave a brief highlight about Max's 15 page presentation on Monday after the governor made his talk. I introduced myself, explained my relationship with Max, and I didn't have to do any of the things I've done before at one of my presentations. This meeting was all Max's baby.

When Tuesdays meeting opened up the first thing the speaker did was suggest a round of applause for Max's presentation, and how I presented it. They loved it. Some of them were bankers and folks from Wall Street, and some of them were government officials from the state. They all agreed the federal government should have done more.

The next 2 days were spent talking about things I could've cared less about. Since I get paid so well, I pretended to look interested. When the event was over I must have received 30 sealed letters for Max to read.

Max was thrilled. This morning after church Max gave me a check for 50,000 dollars. He gave Dad a check for 1,000 dollars, he said it was a birthday present.

Max is an interesting man.

Zach

1934

MARCH 1934

Saturday – 3/17

This was a hard week. I have a 2-month-old baby daughter, but she's never supposed to know I'm her father.

Kathleen reminded me of all the things I told her that infamous night. How I wasn't sure if I was the biproduct of an illicit, passionate, sexual encounter, or a Child of God. She said it was the last thing she wanted for our daughter. She asked me if I'd marry her, but she already knew the answer. We're not in love, my heart belongs to Adeline.

Kathleen thinks if I would have known for sure that my father had died before I was born, I wouldn't have spent so much of my life feeling lost, confused, and searching for myself. Kathleen's going to tell my daughter that I died before she was born. Kathleen already has my gravestone.

Kathleen says she likes it in Naples. She doesn't want to move back to cold, noisy, dirty New York. She'd like me to support her and our daughter. She believes I can afford it. She thinks if I can afford the penthouse apartment I can afford them.

She worked out a financial plan that suited her. It seems odd, working out a financial plan about my daughter, but what choice do I have? What sort of father would I be? I'm almost 50. I can't seem to settle down. I've felt lost since I turned 18. Who am I to be someone's father?

I told her I'd always keep tabs on how she was doing with OUR girl, and I wouldn't bother her. I promised they'd be taken care of. I'll always love my little girl. So will God.

He just won't let me see her.

Zach

AUGUST 1934

Dear Mom, Saturday, August 18th , 1934

Your visit was more than I ever could have imagined. The 3 of you, here for 10 days, was a dream come true. I've been living in and out of New York for 27 years, and you finally got here. I've been here longer than Annie's been alive. It constantly amazes me how fast the years go by.

I was watching, and the look on your face and Dads when you saw each other, was indescribable. You last saw each other 48 years ago. It looked as though it was just yesterday. I loved it. I'm sure my mother was pleased. I imagine Grandma was smiling also. I'm not so sure about Grandpa, or Father Dominic.

I'm glad you all got to spend a day with Max before you left. He's been great to me. I've been working for him for almost 20 years. It's been incredibly rewarding both mentally and financially. He gives me so much free reign. Sometimes maybe too much.

Max thought you guys offering to buy dinner was absolutely the best. He hopes you weren't too upset with him buying. It's a club he belongs to, and he has to spend so much money a month. He thought Frank buying ice cream later was priceless. He likes the 3 of you. He says he feels like part of our family now. He's a fine man. We should be honored.

Annie sure does enjoy talking about PAPA'S. She said she was totally awestruck with my wedding present for her. I told her I wanted her to feel a part of the in-crowd. She mentioned now when she cleans the bathrooms, she keeps reminding herself she owns 5 percent of the company. Then she can giggle to herself. I liked that.

Dad's starting to talk about possibly coming up to Copper Harbor next year. After meeting all of you he feels like family now. He really likes Frank. He thinks he knows his way around the land. He always says he knew his way around the water. He respects a guy who knows his way around.

Dad's starting to have trouble breathing. Max has a great doctor who checks Dad every month. The doctor said Dads lungs have some particles in them. They cause difficulty breathing, and one of these days he may need oxygen at night. He said it was nothing to worry about right now.

Dad and I are meeting Max tomorrow morning for church. Then out for a delicious breakfast, at this neat French restaurant I found a few blocks away. I love thinking about the French and Adeline.

Love to All,

Zach

1935

MAY 1935

Wednesday – 5/1

11 pm – Dad's not home. Walked around the area looking for him. No luck. Doorman said he saw Dad leave this morning around 10 but hadn't seen him since. Think I'll go sit in the lobby for a while.

Zach

Thursday – 5/2

Called Max first thing this morning, he's at a friend's place on Long Island, to see if Dad was with him by any chance. Nope. Now he's worried. Said he'd be back this afternoon. Walked all around the area again. Stopped at the police station to see if they had any ideas. They suggested checking local hospitals. Did that, but they had nothing.

Max got here around noon, he's almost as frantic as I am. Still nothing on Dad. I did find his bracelet with all his personal information; he must have forgotten to put it on after his shower yesterday.

Max is starting to contact friends.

Zach

Friday – 5/3

I'm getting an awful feeling in my gut. Max says to pray and keep my chin up. Tough to do. We've checked, double checked, and triple checked everyplace we think Dad could have gone. No sign of him anyplace. Max must have 50 people looking for Dad.

I'm not much help, all I do is think and worry. Did he run away? Did I upset him? Is he dead? Where the hell is he? Where the hell is God?

I can hardly sleep.

Zach

Saturday – 5/4

I'm going frantic. Max tries to keep me calm, but it's not working too well. I called Mom to see if by some chance Dad went to Copper Harbor, now she's worried sick. Probably not so smart on my part, but I'll try anything. It's been 3 days since anyone's seen Dad.

Max keeps telling me it'll be okay. He says Dad's a big boy, he can take care of himself. I'm not sure if he believes that or not, maybe he's just trying to keep me from having a nervous breakdown.

Zach

Sunday – 5/5

This is almost as hard as when I lost my Adeline, but at least then I always knew where she was. I could see her, talk with her, touch her, well all except that last day, but at least then I could see her.

I'm worried, scared, and helpless. Max is a Godsend right now. His doctor has me on some pills to relax, although I think they may be more powerful than that. I feel pretty groggy most of the time. Almost like this has become just a bad dream. No a nightmare.

Zach

Tuesday – 5/7

Max said I've slept most of the past few days. He had no choice but to keep the pills coming. He said I've been a little delirious. He's worried about me almost as much as for my Dad.

Zach

Friday – 5/10

8 pm. Dad's home. I'm groggy as hell. Max is all smiles. Said he'll explain it all tomorrow.

Zach

Saturday – 5/11

Not too groggy this morning. Max gave me 4 cups of coffee before lunch. Dad's not actually at the apartment yet, he's in the hospital for observation.

From what Max could gather, back on Wednesday the 1ˢᵗ , Dad was walking around Grand Central Station. No one has any idea why he was there, but there he was. He apparently suffered a very minor stroke and became confused.

When a station attendant found him walking around, Dad told him he had to get back to Atlantic City, where he lived with his son. Needless to say they put him on the train to home with his son.

At the station in Atlantic City he must have had another seizure, so they sent him to the hospital. He couldn't remember anything other than Brazil and a doctor friend. No city name, no friend's name, no doctor's name, just Brazil. They took a photo of Dad and made some flyers to post around town. They requested anyone who recognized him to contact the police.

Max said the cab driver who found Dad walking around Staten Island a couple of years ago, just happened to be in Atlantic City and saw one of the flyers. Dad was brought back to our hospital yesterday morning. He can't wait to see me.

Thank God!
Zach

Sunday – 5/12

Spent 5 hours with Dad today. Huge relief. He looked great, was all smiles, and apologized for any problems he caused. He said Max told him I was drugged up for a few days and asked if I enjoyed it. He asked it with a wink! Dad's back and I'm fine.

Zach

Tuesday – 5/14
Dad came home today. All I can say is THANK GOD!
Zach

JULY 1935

Dear Mom and Frank, Saturday, July 6th, 1935

Mom I'm sorry I called so early yesterday morning. I know I woke you both, but I couldn't wait any longer. My heart's broken!

As I said, I found Dad sitting in his favorite wooden rocker. He was watching the July 4th fireworks going up over near the Statue of Liberty. He loved that view, there was something about the Statue of Liberty that always mesmerized him.

He'd talk about all the immigrants who must have loved seeing Her standing so tall over the harbor. The Harbor of Freedom, as he always called it. He was an ocean man through and through. I don't think he ever would have been happy in Copper Harbor. Maybe everything worked out for the best.

Well, Max's doctor said it happened instantly. He said Dad never felt a thing. He said the happy look on Dads face means he was content sitting there in his rocker, watching the fireworks, and drinking his beer. The doctor said it'd be a blessing if we all went that way.

Dad had the picture we had taken of the whole family, when you were here last year, sitting right on the table next to the rocker. He showed it to the cleaning people last week. He must have explained who everybody was for half an hour. I'll say it again, it was worth every minute I spent searching for him.

Love,

Zach

Sunday – 7/7

Talked with Pete today. It's been a few months since we talked. He said he felt terrible about Dad but was happy because we had over 6 years together. He finally understands why I had to go looking for Dad.

It might be tricky, but I want to bury my father next to my mother. I believe they deserve it. I asked Pete to go to Copper Harbor Cemetery and see if I can get a family plot large enough for 14. I told him I couldn't ask Mom yet, and he shouldn't tell anyone, not even his Samantha.

He said he'd go up there first thing tomorrow morning. Pete's a good friend. 30 years ago we were a couple of young guys ready to set the world on fire. Maybe we didn't do so bad after all. He said he'd call me tomorrow night. I told him cost was no object, and the plot had to face east.

Zach

Monday – 7/8

Pete called this evening. He said the cemetery people told him I had an unusual request, however, if I paid the money up front, they could set aside a plot that large, and it'd be on a hill facing east.

I think Pete could tell I was pretty sad, he did some small talk and tried to get me to laugh. It worked and I thanked him. I told him this was one of the best things he's ever done for me. I think he got choked up.

Now I've got to talk with Mom and Frank.

Zach

Wednesday – 7/10

It wasn't as bad as I thought it'd be. Mom and Frank understand why I want my father and mother together. The hardest part was convincing Mom that when they sell the farm, nobody's going to want to buy a place with strangers buried there. Frank understood a lot easier than Mom.

I called Pete and told him what was going on. I told him I was coming home with Dad and asked if he'd help me with all the arrangements. He said he'd be more than happy too. He said we've always been best friends, even when he didn't hear from me for years.

I'm a lucky man.

Zach

Dear Kid, 2/14/1935

What a wonderful time I've been having. Thank you!

I thought I was going to die in the woods in Brazil. Now, here I am, in New York City, having a great life with my son. The son I never knew I had. Thanks – and when you read this, whenever it is, don't fret – smile instead, and beat Max at a game of cribbage!

I've saved most of the money Max has been giving me. I've been putting it in his bank under your name. He doesn't know anything about it.

I want you to divide what there is into 3 equal amounts. Send one to my friend the Doctor down in Brazil for use in his clinic. Send one to my niece Annie, tell her it's from her loving uncle Zacharia. Use the last one however you see fit, maybe go to Paris, and visit Adeline and Arron.

I loved your mother with all my heart, and now I've gotten to love you. I've been a lucky man.

Thanks,

Your Loving Father,

Zacharia Marceau

P.S. Happy Birthday, and Always Grin Whenever You Think About Me!

Friday – 7/12

Found Dads letter to me. It brought on way too many tears. He wrote it on my birthday last February. I know he wasn't feeling well, he must have had a premonition. I'll try grinning when I think of him . . . but it'll take a lot of years.

I leave tomorrow morning with Dads casket, and the 8-foot marble Guardian Angel Max found out on Long Island. I've got it all loaded in a new, dark blue, Ford Panel Delivery Van; this is going to be quite a trip. I think Dad would have gotten a kick out of it. I know he'll be happy being next to my mother.

Max says he's proud of me, he supports me 200 percent. He wanted to give me money for the cemetery, so I suggested he pay for the Angel. He was thrilled about it.

I told Pete I should be in Copper Harbor by Tuesday around noon, and I want to meet him at the cemetery. He said, "So, I'm meeting the Hick on Tuesday." I liked it, made me feel good inside. Same as the old days.

Zach

Wednesday – 7/31

It's done.

Over 30 years of searching for my father. Now he's at rest next to my mother. God be with them both. I ordered a headstone. It reads, Angelica and Zacharia - Together Again for Eternity - We were lost... Now we're found.

Zach

1941

JULY 1941

Dear Mom, Friday, July 4th, 1941

It seems most of the time I write to you, I start out by saying I'm sorry it's been so long since I've written. I think I'll quit saying it. It's just the way I am. I have no idea why, and I don't care anymore. I am what the world has made me.

I've done a lot of traveling in the past 6 years. I took some money Dad saved down to his old doctor in Brazil. He died 3 years ago, but his clinic's still going strong. Stronger now since they have Dads money. We built a new addition onto the existing clinic. It took a lot of sweat, callouses, and drinking. It turned out great.

I stayed there for 3 years. Most of the folks who knew Dad had died. I found a few beach bums who remembered him. I spent weekends with them. I looked pretty shabby when I left there, but I felt great.

From there I went to Paris and my Adeline. I stayed there 6 months. Every week I placed flowers on her grave. I would have stayed longer but apparently they're gearing up for another war with Germany. I'm thinking about having her moved to Copper Harbor. Both of her parents have died, and she has no siblings.

Max retired the year after Dad died. He moved to Miami Florida. I spent 6 months with him after Dads burial. When I left him, Max gave me more money than I could spend in 4 lifetimes. I've been at his place in Florida the past month. He says he's ready for his next journey. He looks forward to seeing Dad again.

Max calls it the Great Beyond. I think of all the people I knew who are in the Great Beyond. I hope he's right. It's a nice thought. I had an easier time imagining it when I was younger, sitting with Grandma, by Grandpa's grave. It's become harder to picture now.

I'll call you later this Fall. Maybe I'll even come home.

Love,

Zach

DECEMBER 1941

Sunday – 12/7

Pearl Harbor was attacked this morning by a Japanese squadron of bombers. It's as much as I know right now, but from what I've heard, those G-- Damn Japs are in for a fight!!

Zach

Monday – 12/8

Roosevelt declared war with Japan today, but I don't think this will stop with Japan.

Zach

Thursday – 12/11

Max died yesterday at 5:15 in the afternoon. He was in his office on the phone with President Roosevelt, his secretary said he was hollering. Doc thinks it was a heart attack, caused by what's going on in the world. I know the world situation was a huge bother to him.

He never wanted any war. He didn't need any profit from war. He hated the fact some people thought profit was his motivation. Max had more money than any person could ever spend. He was more than willing to give it away. All he ever wanted was to help folks. I'm truly going to miss him. That's a fact!

I heard both Germany and Italy declared war on us today.

Sleeping's been tough.

Zach

Thursday - 12/18

We sent Max to his Great Beyond yesterday. Why is death getting harder on me as I get older? I thought it would get easier.

For years, Max was more like a father to me than my father. I loved my father dearly, but Max was a part of me for so long. Since the first day at the bank back in 1915, almost everything I've done has been influenced or directed, by him. He was, or is, one in a million, make it a billion.

In his will he left the property in Miami to me, along with way too much money. He stipulated it went to Zacharia, the kid who could track rabbits on concrete. I don't need any money and I surely don't need a property in Miami. I'll turn his place into a retirement home.

I'll go home for Christmas. Didn't make it this past Fall. I could tell Max was getting worse. I didn't want to leave him.

Zach

Thursday – 12/25

Christmas in Copper Harbor. I know this should be great, only I feel as though I'm a stranger. It's Mom, Frank, and me, in this old farmhouse. Frank had it repainted in a light brown with chocolate trim. I don't care for it, but so what. I'm in my old bedroom, it feels strange now. Different then when I was 17.

Grandma's old room is a sewing room, and Mom stopped sewing 2 years ago. The workshop Frank had out in the barn is a space for junk now. The Oldsmobile Grandma bought back in 1905 just sits in a corner. Frank thinks it hasn't been started since the depression.

Frank turned 77 this year. He quit driving when he was 75. He says his eyesight's pretty bad. I mentioned about moving into town, but he said Annie takes good care of them right here. She comes every day or so with some food, and 2 of her kids to visit.

Annie told me she loves the old house. She says she'd love to live in it. She and Zak moved back to Copper Harbor right after Frank had his first heart attack. I never heard about it. Not till today. Probably my fault for being gone so much.

There's another war going on, and we're supposed to have a Merry Christmas.

I don't get it!

Zach

Wednesday – 12/31

I'm meeting the old gang this evening. Pete and his family, Annie and her family, and Michael and his family, which includes my onetime girlfriend Sally. We're going to celebrate New Year's Eve. This celebrating doesn't make any sense to me.

Zach

1942

FEBRUARY 1942

Dear Mom, Sunday, February 1ˢᵗ, 1942

I'm being sent over to Europe for a while. Max had stipulated in his will that I remain the V.P. of Foreign Relations. The interesting thing is none of his cohorts disagreed with him.

I guess with my involvement in the 1ˢᵗ War, and the 5 years I spent over there almost 20 years ago, they think I can help with this new war. I'm not crazy about the idea, however if it helps Max's old friends, I said OK.

I leave for London on Wednesday the 11ᵗʰ. I need a briefing before I go. They think it won't be for too long. One of The Guys figures 4 or 5 months, and I should be home. I told them they had no idea what Europeans can be like. When you throw in the Japs on top of it, well who knows what's going to happen.

Hope all is well with both of you. I had a grand time on New Year's Eve with the old gang. I only felt out of place for the first 2 hours. The new supper club's a good addition for Copper Harbor. The enclosed check is for you and Frank to take Annie and her family there for a Sunday brunch.

Whatever's left you can use to build the sun porch Frank was telling me about. He said he'd like a sun porch facing the big flower garden you put in. The check should cover the cost.

Love,

Zach

Monday – 2/23

London's a mess. Europe's in chaos. Hitler's demented. The Allies need our help. This ain't going to be 4 or 5 months. This is going to take a while.

Zach

Saturday – 2/28

A long while!!

Zach

1945

JULY 1945

Dear Mom, Thursday, July 12th, 1945

It was nice to hear your voice yesterday, but I was heartbroken when I heard about Frank. I'm so glad you had each other for 39 years. You know, if I would have been in the States, I would have been at the funeral.

It's nice Frank and you had a chance to sit on the sun porch, look out at the flower garden, and have your grandkids running around. You've had a fulfilling life at the farmhouse. Imagine what life would have been without Frank. No Annie, no grandkids.

What would our lives have been then? We can thank God for Frank. Things have worked out pretty nicely for both of us. I think my mother would be, or is, proud of us. I know I'm proud of you, Mom.

As I mentioned, life in Europe the past few years has been tough. Victory was incredibly painful, but also sweet at the same time. That's something General Eisenhower told me when I met him one day. I've worked with him a number of times over here. He's brilliant, and a nice guy. He said he loves hunting. I should invite him to Michigan after the war. Pete would get a kick out of that.

I finally got a chance to visit Adeline's grave. I'm working on getting her casket moved to the Copper Harbor Cemetery. The folks at the Suresnes Cemetery said it won't happen until sometime next year. They said I should contact them next July.

It looks like I should be heading back to the States next Monday, July 16th. I'll be based in New York City for a while. Some of The Guys at the office have something they want me to read. I call them The Guys because they don't want me to use their names. They're all pretty influential and don't want their names in public.

They say Max had written something for me to consider. Max didn't realize the war was going to last so long. Now they want me to look at what he wrote. I never knew what was going on in Max's brain. All I knew is it was always something to get my head spinning.

When I get back, I'll try to get some time off, so I can get up to Copper Harbor. I could use a getaway, and I'd love to see you and Annie again.

Love,
Zach

Sunday – 7/22

It's good to be back in New York. Got a nice one-bedroom apartment on the 4th floor, across the street from Central Park. Nothing ostentatious, just nice. It's comfortable, quiet, and quaint.

Tomorrow's the meeting with The Guys. They want me to be open minded. Nobody would give me a clue as to what we're going to discuss. All they'll tell me is Max had this idea, and they all agreed with him.

I'm supposed to shave, dress nice, be serious, and listen. The only part I can do for sure is listen. I've spent time in Brazil on the beach and building an addition. I toured bombed out Paris. Roamed around demolished London. Witnessed a liberated Nazi concentration camp. I'm not into shaving or dressing good right now.

I'll try my best to listen.
Zach

Saturday – 7/28

Max had some bird-brained ideas in his lifetime; however, this may have been his best. When he died, he left a note suggesting I run for governor of New York. He said I was more qualified than anyone else he knew, and he was fed up with the damn Democrats. He wanted a Republican as governor.

Max didn't know Dewey was going to win the election in 1942, as a Republican.

I had shaved, dressed nice, and listened to The Guys. Then I laughed. I laughed out loud. I don't think it went over too well; I was supposed to be serious. Well, we all had a long discussion about the whole idea. I told them I was more than flattered but I was a hick from Michigan. That got a chuckle.

They believe Max was right. They want me to consider running for some political office in the future. Maybe even President. I said I appreciated their confidence. I told them maybe I do have considerable experience, just not in politics. They said, "What the hell do you think you've been doing for Max the last 20-plus years? If not politics, what the hell was it?"

Left the meeting with my head spinning. A lot like it did after my 18th birthday.

Zach

Monday – 7/30

Leaving for Copper Harbor in the morning. I bought a beautiful maroon 1941 Packard One-Twenty convertible. It's only got 276 miles on it. The original owner didn't trust other drivers, so she never took it out. Pete will be amazed.

I may stay up there for a while, who knows. Been doing some reading from these journals, and I think I've been overly stressed the past 40 years. Maybe it's time to find some peace. Find out if I can Trust Him.

Mom said I may have offended Him and Grandma on my 18th birthday, and I was supposed to apologize. I did OK with Grandma. I'm not sure I did OK with Him. Copper Harbor may be a good place to start.

Zach

OCTOBER 1945

Saturday – 10/6

Copper Harbor – Fall of 1945. The war's over.

Annie's 37, Mom's 78, Pete, and I are both 58. Between Annie, Pete, and Michael there's a ton of little kids, Mom calls all of them her grandkids, running around. Things sure have changed around here. I can't remember everybody's name, but whenever any kids see me, they say, "There's Uncle Zach!"

It makes me think about my daughter. I wonder what she's like. She's probably beautiful, the same as her mother. I never should have made the promise to stay out of her life. I goofed.

Damn!

Zach

Saturday – 10/13

I'm home . . . for now. Back on top of the world. I'll call The Guys and tell them I'm staying here for 5 years, then I'll go back to New York, if they'll want me. That's my commitment to myself. I'm going to be Uncle Zach for 5 years.

Zach

Wednesday – 10/24

Signed the contract today. Bought a nice home on Lake Fanny Hooe. Will move in this weekend. It'll be easy, all I have was in the Packard. The house is easy walking distance to Copper Harbor. It's smaller than I wanted, but I'll put on a nice size addition. We've got to have room for some of those kids when they visit G-ma Celeste and Uncle Zach.

The lake's great for swimming, boating, and fishing. The kids all love it. I'm trying to talk Mom into moving in with me. Annie wants to buy the farmhouse. She says Zak's OK with it. He likes hunting, and fishing. The farmhouse still has the 20 acres with it, so he'd be happy there.

Mom's hesitant, although she does enjoy walking into town. She may be 78, but there's no stopping her. She can walk to her old store in 10 minutes, just to keep an eye on the new owners. I told her I'd put on an addition, and she could decorate it any way she wants. She likes that idea.

Zach

DECEMBER 1945

Tuesday – 12/25

Christmas in Copper Harbor.

I completely forgot how much snow we get up here on top of the world. I prefer Florida. We had a huge party at the farmhouse, there had to be at least 20 kids, plus a lot of adults. Mom and Annie had the place looking spectacular. I was okay for 6 hours, then I had to take my leave. Kids make a lot of racket. I enjoy being Uncle Zach, but only for half a day.

Pete reminded me it's been 39 years since we started the Oldsmobile shop in Marquette. When he and Michael bought out Michael's dad Todd, they swore they'd keep PAPA'S for their kids. They'd divvy it up equally, but now they're running into some problems.

Annie owns the 5 percent I gave her. Charles, the other fella I hired in Marquette, gave his 5 percent to his cousin's son Fredrick. Pete and Michael both own 45 percent each. They're both thinking about retiring in a couple of years. They have 12 different locations, and they sell 4 different lines of cars. Put in a nutshell, they think they're worth a lot of money. They should have known Max.

Pete wants my opinion on what I think they should do. He claims, from all of our conversations over the years, I should have the answers. He thinks if I could help the French, the English, Brazil, Germany, Italy, Wall Street, Max, The Guys, and whoever else, I should be able to help him, and Michael.

Rats.

Zach

Monday – 12/31

I've set up a meeting with Pete and Samantha, Michael and Sally, Annie and Zak, and Charles' cousins son Fredrick, for early April. We'll meet at the dealership in Houghton. It should give me some time to figure out this mess.

Tonight's New Year's Eve, 1946. No war going on. No last-minute critically important meeting to set up for Max. No big ball dropping at Times Square. Me, Mom, and Copper Harbor.

Pretty damn nice!

Zach

1946

JANUARY 1946

Saturday – 1/12

Talked with some of The Guys in New York on Monday. Told them my 5-year plan, explained my situation, and told them about the pack of kids up here. I told them about the house I bought, my mom, the family cemetery plot, all the different things that make me want to be here.

They listened. They said they understood. They said all those things were important in my life. Then they gave me their ideas. They want me to be ready to run for a political office in the next few years. They don't want me to disappear for 5-years. No way. No how.

We worked out a plan, or maybe they worked out a plan, I'm not sure. The plan is for me to get back to New York for 2 weeks every 2 months. They say it will keep me in the Loop, as they call it. It will keep my name out in front of some incredibly influential people. They told me it was a win-win situation for all, even the kids.

If they hadn't mentioned the kids, I may not have accepted their offer. It showed me they have hearts. Since Max died, I wasn't sure any of them had a heart. The mention of kids sure helped. I liked the idea. I just had to convince Mom. She said she was fine with the idea, as long as I bring back souvenirs.

I'll start going back in March.

Zach

Saturday – 1/26

Talked with a couple of The Guys about Pete and Michael's dilemma regarding wanting to get out of the business in a few years. They want me to bring as much information about PAPA'S as I can get out of Pete and Michael. They said they'd like to go over everything I bring, and they'll come up with a solution.

They insist I stay out of the whole thing. They say nothing nice can come out of me getting involved with family, friends, and business. I couldn't agree more, it was a relief to hear. I'll talk with Pete next month.

Zach

FEBRUARY 1946

Saturday – 2/16

Had a nice talk with Pete. He's amazed at everything I've done so far. I told him I think what he's done is far more important than anything I've accomplished. He poo-poos me, but I'm right. He has kids, I don't. I should say, none Kathleen will let me talk about.

He understands why I want to stay out of their business concerns. Pete's giving me everything he thinks I'll need to give The Guys when I go there next month.

He brought me up to date about Emil. While he was talking, all I could think about was the day I hit Emil over the head with the chair in the restaurant, and the time Grandma told him to go ask the old bastard. Pete couldn't understand why I was laughing so much. I'm not sure I even understand.

Pete said now Emil's in Chicago, working the docks. He got most of the dock workers on Lake Superior to join the union. Then his uncle, who owned the dock here in Copper Harbor, fired him. Then, mysteriously, his uncle up and disappeared. Sounds as though Emil's heavily involved with the union and possibly the mob.

Not surprising!

Zach

Friday – 2/22

Mom fell at the farmhouse, she tripped on a carpet. Doc says she twisted her ankle. I believe she hurt her hip. She says, "What do you know?" Spending time with the doc reminded me of my Adeline. I've been sort of melancholy the past couple of days. Good thing Mom's over at Annie's place.

I did love Adeline.

Zach

Thursday – 2/28

Leave for New York on Saturday. Told The Guys I should be in town by Monday, and I'd be ready for a meeting on Wednesday. There's some nice hotels on Spring Street, right near my first apartment, and there's Lombardi's Pizza right down the block. Reminds me of my buddy Arron.

Good memories.

Zach

MAY 1946

Sunday – 5/5

As I thought, Mom had fractured her left hip when she fell. She's been at Annie's since the end of February. Her doctor suggests she stay there another month or so. I think it's overkill, but again, what do I know.

Mom's been waiting all winter for the summer fun to begin. She bought a new speed boat for water skiing, plus a knock-out fishing boat. We'll put a raft out in 10 feet of water. She can't wait to watch the kids having fun. I told her I'm good for maybe 6 hours tops. As usual she smiles, the way Grandma used to.

The Guys in New York had me going from 7 in the morning until midnight every day. They said if I lived there the pace would be slower. I said the pace up in Copper Harbor's pretty slow just as it is. They continue to insist I stay in the loop. I never liked that term, the loop. Max wasn't too fond of it himself. He always thought he WAS the loop.

I've never had that problem.

Zach

Friday – 5/10

Met with Pete this morning. Told him The Guys in New York are confused about PAPA'S. There seems to be some discrepancy in how Michael's dad wrote up the paperwork when he sold to Michael and Pete. From what The Guys could figure out, after 20 years, if certain parts of the agreement weren't rewritten, sole ownership would revert to Michael.

The Guys said Todd did some maneuvering, nothing was illegal, just underhanded. They say Todd was a pretty damn good lawyer to figure out how to do what he did. Standing right now, Michael owns 100 percent of PAPA'S. Everyone else is an employee, including Pete.

Needless to say Pete's FURIOUS. He's not sure if he should talk to Michael about it, shoot him, or hire one of The Guys to represent him. The Guys didn't put an actual monetary value on PAPA'S. They wanted to wait and see what Pete wants to do. Their rough guess is somewhere between 15 and 20 million dollars. I didn't tell Pete the number, I think he would have blown a gasket. Pete wants my opinion.

I wish Max were around.

Zach

Friday – 5/17

Talked with Alexander today. He's one of The Guys. He suggests Pete first talk with Michael about PAPA'S. If Pete doesn't get anywhere with Michael, Pete could start a lawsuit against Todd. Alexander says even though Todd's deceased, since what he did was for his immediate families personal gain at the harm of the other involved parties, Pete may find a judge who would overturn the legalese Todd did.

Then, PAPA'S would revert back to Pete and Michael each owning 45 percent, Annie owning 5 percent, and Fredrick owning 5 percent. It means instead of owning 100 percent of PAPA'S, Michael would only own 45 percent of PAPA'S. 100 percent of 20 million is 20 million, pretty nice. 45 percent of 20 million is 9 million, an 11 million dollar difference. Quite a hit for Michael.

Zach

Monday – 5/20

I'll take Pete out to lunch, and we'll hash this over. I'm sure Max would have gone for the lawsuit. He would have said, "Pete, what you got to lose? Right now you don't own a damn thing."

Alexander said he had one of The Guys looking into my question, about Emil's grandfather going to Detroit and dying there. When I heard about Emil's uncle disappearing I started thinking about his grandfather again. At the time no one questioned anything, but I thought it was odd. He and his grandfather used to fight all the time, and then out of nowhere Grandpa goes to Detroit and dies. Always seemed fishy to me.

Zach

Tuesday – 5/21

Mom's doing better. Her hip seems to be healing, although she does use a walker to get around. She's coming out to my place until I go back to New York the middle of June. Annie gave a small sigh of relief when she heard that. Reminded me of the kind of thing Grandma would have done around Mom. I got a kick out of it.

Zach

Thursday – 5/23

Pete's pissed. He wants to meet for lunch next week.

Zach

Friday – 5/24

Mom's still at Annie's place. She misses going out and sitting by Grandma and Grandpa's graves. I took her over to the new cemetery plot, she likes it, but she says it's not the same. She wonders if anyone will come and visit her when she's there. I reminded her of all her 'grandkids,' as usual, she smiles. So much like Grandma.

I leave for New York in 2 weeks. It might be nice to be back there.

Zach

Tuesday – 5/28

Good old Pete. He must get his stubbornness from his uncle Paul. Over the weekend he went and talked with Michael. I don't blame him, still, he should have had me with him. Now it's a mess.

Pete said, at the first meeting Michael was understanding, and was almost willing to put everything back to normal. Michael wanted a few days to figure out what his father had done. He wanted to look over the paperwork and see if those guys in New York knew what they were talking about. He said his dad would never have done anything like that.

Then came the second meeting. Michael talked it over with Sally. They offered Pete 20 percent of the value of PAPA'S, in cash. 20 percent of 20 million dollars is 4 million dollars. 45 percent of 20 million dollars is 9 million dollars, a 5 million dollar difference. Quite a cut in money for Pete. They did offer to keep him on as president with full pay until he turns 60 next year. Pete said he almost strangled Michael.

Annie and Fredrick are out of luck. Michael would give them both 10,000 dollars and let them continue to work as long as they like. 5 percent of 20 million is a million. I think Zak would shoot Michael if they had to settle for 10,000.

Pete's head was ready to explode. He's convinced his cousin Sally, Bedroom Sally, as Pete started calling her, has Michael by his privates and is turning the screw. I can understand his comment about the bedroom. I've been there. Pete said he'll be damned if he lets PAPA'S get under her control. He'll let it sink first. He wants to come with me to New York next month and meet Alexander.

I'm proud of him.

Zach.

JUNE 1946

Sunday – 6/23

Pete spent 2 weeks with me in New York. He's not a big city guy. He likes Gratiot Avenue in Copper Harbor much more than Broadway. He didn't understand me back in second grade, and he still doesn't. We are best friends though.

The Guys think Pete, Annie, and Fredrick have a good shot at beating Michael in court, as long as it isn't in Upper Michigan. Todd was pretty influential up there. They want it to be in Lansing, where PAPA'S was founded. Alexander said he'd be more than happy to work with Pete.

The Guys are willing to do this for free because Pete's my best friend. Pete was surprised at how much they respect me and want to keep me in the loop. That's a term Pete wasn't familiar with. I told him it was new to me also. It's big city talk, not hick talk. Pete laughed about it.

Now Pete has some thinking to do. Pete said the money isn't all that matters. He says it's also about family pride. He and his uncle Paul started it, and he'll be damned if some bedroom floozy is going to take it away. He says if he loses PAPA'S, somehow he'll bust it up. I love his spunk. Max would have liked him.

If I weren't the one who hired Michael, I'd be upset with him. I liked Michael and his dad Todd. I'm confused as to why Todd did what he did. Maybe I should talk with Michael without Sally around.

Zach

Sunday – 6/30

Michael doesn't want to meet me. Pete called him and said they were going to court, and I was helping Pete. Pete called Todd a crook and told Michael he thinks this is all Sally's fault. Pete told Michael, he thinks Sally's using his thingamabob to influence his brain, then Michael hung up on him.

I told Pete I thought it wasn't a nice thing to say, after all, Sally's his cousin. Then Pete said, "What do you know, you don't have any money invested in PAPA'S, and so what if she's my cousin?" Then he hung up on me. Maybe I should go back to New York. Two wars, a great depression, working with Max on hundreds of important meetings, and I don't remember anybody ever hanging up on me.

Zach

AUGUST 1946

Friday – 8/23

Pete, Annie, and Fredrick, are taking Michael to court. Unfortunately, they have to go to court in Marquette. Their case will be heard by the local judge, another bad luck draw. The judge knew Todd. They used to play poker and golf together. The date's set for late October.

Alexander says it's OK. He thinks if the judge rules in favor of Michael, they'll have grounds for a mistrial. Then they can take it to Lansing. I like the idea; I'm beginning to have a great respect for Alexander. He never worked with Max, and I never worked with him before this. He's only 32 and one of the newest members of The Guys. Nice fella.

Zach

Sunday – 8/25

Mom's having an unforgettable summer. She's been staying at the lake house since I got back in late June. Her hip's much better, and she hardly uses the walker. Annie has a lot of kids here every day. Mom watches kids, sits in the sun, and makes everybody lunch. She goes along in the speedboat once in a while. The one she reminds everyone she bought.

All the kids love her. Grandma and Grandpa would be incredibly proud of Mom. I used to talk a lot with Grandma about God. It came so easy. It's not quite the same with Mom. I think she has a guilt feeling about my mother dying 59 years ago. I think it's still on her mind. Especially when she's with me for a long time. Someday I'll try talking with Annie about God.

Zach

Wednesday – 8/28

This whole thing with Michael has quite a few folks up here upset. With Michael being from Marquette and Pete and Paul being from here, the locals see it as a big city take over. Copper Harbor's threatening to take over the courthouse for the trial.

The town turned Paul's blacksmith shop into a museum before the war in 1940. They're threatening to take it apart and set it up in front of the courthouse a week before the trial. A couple of the guys in town say the judge was a cheater at poker and golf. They're threating to tell the Marquette paper.

Zach

Saturday – 8/31

Pete's talking with me again. I knew he couldn't stay mad long. Like the time we drove those 1904 Oldsmobiles up to Copper Harbor, he only called me Zacharia one day. He's a softy, but he's mad as hell.

He's mad at Sally, Michael, and half of Marquette. I tell him about all the terrible things I've seen in Europe. Cities being demolished, people left homeless and broke, both spiritually and financially.

Pete says, "Yeah, but those were caused by enemies. Michael and I were friends." I have no comeback for him.

Zach

NOVEMBER 1946

Saturday – 11/16

Like Alexander had hoped, the trial's being moved to Lansing sometime early next year. The judge in Marquette decided he wasn't the proper person to hear both arguments. I think the replica of Paul's blacksmith shop on the courthouse lawn for a week, and an anonymous article about people cheating at golf in the Marquette paper, may have swayed his thinking.

The lake house is now a winter wonderland. Mom's still here, and she loves it. She thinks the view of the lake in winter is as pretty as in summer. I remind her she doesn't have to go outside. As usual she smiles. She sure does look like Grandma when she does that.

Supposed to leave for New York in a couple of weeks. Mom will go to Annie's place till I get back. Annie and Zak bought the farmhouse. Now I can call it Annie's place. I can't believe I've owned this place for over a year.

It must be because Max isn't around to make me move. He had a knack for doing that.

This is comfortable.

Zach

DECEMBER 1946

Saturday – 12/7

The Guys wanted me to come to New York every other month for 2 weeks. I asked them if they've ever been in Copper Harbor, in winter, with 3 feet of snow. I explained what traveling was like in these conditions. That kept them quiet.

It seems, for whatever reason, The Guys think I have all the answers. A couple of them have said, since I was so close to Max, I must have gained an incredible insight into how things work. Things politically, financially, and personally. I told them I think they're crazy, but they laugh it off. They keep asking me to move back to New York. I told them I'd be back in March.

Weather permitting.

Zach

Wednesday – 12/25

Christmas Day in Copper Harbor, just like old times. Brings back memories.

Memories with Mom, Grandma, Grandpa, Pete, Ms. Bagley, the farmhouse, the hunting cabin, Old Black Eye.

Wonderful memories.

Zach

Sunday – 12/29

Went to church today. I went alone. It's been a long, long time. I thought a lot about PAPA'S. Both wars. The Lusitania. The depression. The

Guardian Angel I talk with. My mother Angelica, my Adeline, Max, The Guys, The Loop, God, and the night when He said "Trust Me."

I wonder if I ever let any of them down.

Zach

1947

APRIL 1947

Saturday – 4/5

I thought it was an April Fool's Day joke. I cracked up right in the meeting. It must have taken me 10 minutes, well maybe just a minute, to stop chuckling. It's a damn good thing most of them know me pretty well. They want me to move back to the city. Alexander talked to them, and they took a unanimous vote. They all want me back in New York.

Told them once again, I think they're all crazy. I don't know anything. They said I was trained by the best; how could I not know anything? They have a point there. I was trained by the best. They said how I've handled meetings was legendary. How I could get people to take their shoes off, and donate 5 million dollars after one meeting, will be talked about for a hundred years.

I told them after the PAPA'S trial, I'd consider their idea, and I reminded them about my 5 year plan.

The trial's set for Monday the 21st in Lansing.

Zach

Monday – 4/21

When I walked into the courtroom this morning, I felt a cold blast come over me. It may have been my imagination, but I know what I felt. Michael, Sally, and their lawyer were sitting on the left side. Michael gave me a look which sort of said HELP ME.

Sally, on the other hand, sat there in the lowest cut red dress I've ever seen. She's a knockout, even at 57. She was smiling at the judge. I'm beginning to wonder if she didn't have some influence on Michael's father. Todd became a widower around the time of all the changes. My thoughts went back to the night in her brother's bedroom. The night I sat straight up.

Pete, his wife Samantha, Annie, Zak, and Fredrick were sitting on the right side. Alexander was sitting on Pete's left side, with 2 of The Guys right behind him. Alexander looked like he knew something. I stopped by him to see how things were going, and all he said was, "Sally sure is a knockout, hey?"

I sat on the left side, behind Michael, a few rows back. I felt sorry for him. I've always liked him. I think he's been taken advantage of by Sally. I think Michael was happy when he saw me sitting there. Pete had a weird look, but I knew I could explain myself to him.

Alexander and The Guys meant business. The judge never even heard any testimony. All the judge said, after banging the gavel, was that he read everything over, and he was reverting the ownership back to what it was. Michael smiled and thanked him, then he shook my hand and hugged me. He was relieved.

Sally stormed out of the room. I think smoke was coming out of her ears. Pete shook my hand, hugged me, and asked what I did. Zak hugged me. Annie gave me a kiss on the cheek. It reminded me of Grandma. Fredrick said he owed me big time. I thanked him and told him how much I liked his uncle Charles.

When we were finished, we all went out for a relaxing enjoyable meal. I asked Alexander what in the world they did.

He said I owe them.

Zach

Saturday – 4/26

Mom wasn't doing so well this week. She's hoping this summer will be better. She loves the summer sun, says it takes away all her aches and pains. Looking back on things I think she's right. Mom was always at her best working outside. It never mattered with who. Grandpa, me, the horses, as long as she was outside.

I was told that was the difference between her and my mother. My mother was smaller, and daintier. That's why she died when I was born. I could live to be 100 and I'll always feel some responsibility for her death. I know it wasn't my fault, but I'll always feel that way.

That's a fact.

Zach

AUGUST 1947

Sunday – 8/24

Mom's in her glory, we had a huge 80th birthday party for her at the lake today. Mom had an absolute ball. I rented 3 outhouses for the crowd.

It's been a terrific 2 weeks. The temperatures been averaging 82. Kids have been everyplace, swimming, water skiing, fishing. Mom and I grilled out every day, sometimes twice a day. I've worked up to handling 8 hours of kids, screaming, laughing, and running around like chickens with their heads chopped off. I haven't seen Mom this happy since Frank's been gone.

That's another fact!

Zach

Sunday – 8/31

Leave for New York tomorrow morning. I haven't been there since April. They're asking me to stay for a while this time. At least they're not telling me. They're asking me. I like that much better.

Zach

NOVEMBER 1947

Dear Annie, Thanksgiving Day, 1947

Can't really say it was heartwarming talking with you today.

I tried my best to help you both understand why I've been in New York so long. The Guys need my help. It probably doesn't make sense to you and Mom, but it's the way it is. We're having trouble getting some of the money we loaned to some foreign countries for the war effort. I can't mention any names, however it amounts to billions of dollars. We can't afford to lose so much money.

I understand Mom's upset with me. Her hip's acting up again, and she needs a wheelchair. I feel terrible about it, however there's nothing I can do. Even if I were there, what could I do differently? I believe being 80 is hard on Mom. I think she gets frustrated easier.

As I mentioned on the phone, I can wire the money to help convert the summer porch Mom and Frank built into a year-round room. I can also afford to hire full time people to watch Mom round the clock, at your place. Or we could move Mom to the lake house, and I'd pay someone to watch her there, full time. I'm not crazy about that idea though.

Money's no problem for me, my time is. I know you hate to hear it, but it is what it is. Here in New York we have newer places called nursing homes for people in Mom's condition. I could have one built in Houghton. I could pay Zak to oversee the project.

I understand you can't imagine Mom anyplace else, but maybe she'd have more fun with people her own age. I've checked out some around here. The folks seem to enjoy being with their age group. They play cards, play games, have entertainment, and social time together. It could be nice for Mom.

I love Mom, but I'm needed here right now, plus there's nothing I could do differently if I were there. Except hold Mom's hand. I know that would be nice, but it can't be right now.

Happy belated birthday. When I talked with Mom a while ago, she said you had a great birthday party and enjoyed my gift. Great.

Again, I love you and Mom. I'll call in a week or so.

Love,

Your Big Brother,

Zacharia

DECEMBER 1947

Monday – 12/8

As I thought, there are no records in Detroit of Emil's grandfather Walter ever being admitted anyplace. Alexander said 2 of The Guys spent last week checking every hospital, every old age home, all the city death certificates, anything which could link Emil, or any of his relatives, to his grandfather Walter. Nothing. They found nothing.

Alexander said there's no evidence of foul play on Emil's part, and his grandfather never went to Detroit. They also did some background checking on Emil and his family, and they found some interesting stuff. Alexander said there were some fuzzy records in Houghton, regarding a young gal named Martha and a boy named Walter.

That got my attention.

Zach

Saturday – 12/13

Paris again! I asked why me? The Guys said why not you, you're good at getting money from people. I leave Monday. I hope it won't be for long, but I think I know better. It'll give me a chance to forget about Emil. Then again, will I ever be able to forget about him? Or his grandfather Walter, or his uncle, or the docks in Copper Harbor?

Maybe not!

Zach

Dear Mom, Christmas Day, 1947

I'm glad you were home when I called. I love hearing your voice. Always have, always will.

I know the time difference confused you for a while. It does me all the time. When I called you it was noon in Michigan, and 7 pm by me in Paris. We have an associate in Japan who's also trying to collect money. Well, by him it's already tomorrow. How's that for confusing?

Well I'm here, as I said, trying to collect on some past due payments. The big problem is nobody has any money. All of Europe's trying to rebuild. It hasn't been that long since the war ended, and it'll take a long time to rebuild. So, now everybody's looking for more money. Because I've been here so often over the past 30 years, The Guys sent me.

This time I'm working with President Truman, the Congress, and the Senate. The situation we find ourselves in is bigger than The Guys, or anyone who's still around from The Loop could handle. For some reason, The Guys think I can deal with it. Hope I'm up to the task.

We have the money to loan Europe to help with their rebuilding, but all the politicians want to get in their 2 cents worth. If they'd get out of my way, I could clear up this whole mess in a matter of weeks. I think I may be here for a few months.

I did get to the Suresnes Cemetery. I made all the arrangements to have my Adeline moved to the Copper Harbor Cemetery. It took some doing, a little hand holding, and some promises made, but Adeline should be in Copper Harbor by July 4ᵗʰ. I'll be home for her burial.

Enough small talk,

Now to address your questions –

1 - Yes I have enough money to pay for any help you and Annie need, either at the farmhouse or the lake house. YES, YES, YES!

2 – Yes, in New York I've been to nursing homes, and the folks were enjoying themselves. So would you.

3 – Yes, I'd be thrilled to build one in Houghton. It could be within walking distance to PAPA'S, and no it wouldn't break my bank account.

4 – Yes, I think about You and my mother every day.

5 – And finally – Yes I'll be home before July 4ᵗʰ, for Adeline's burial ceremony, and for this coming summer at the lake.

Love,

Your Son,

Zacharia

Wednesday – 12/31

New Year's Eve in Paris 1947.

There was the time, 30 years ago, when Paris was exciting. I asked Adeline to marry me. Arron and I had it all worked out. The table was set, the candle was lit, the wine was there, and she said NO. She cried, I cried, Arron cried. The DAMN war.

Looking back, I should have taken her away from the hospital. If she wouldn't have been in the hospital she never would have gotten the virus. We'd have gotten married. How different my life would have been. Was it a twist of fate? Was it destiny? Was God watching?

Does God even care?

Zach

1948

FEBRUARY 1948

Saturday – 2/14

Happy birthday. I'm 61 and stuck in Europe.

It's tough trying to get money from nothing. Between Truman, Congress, and the Senate we finally arrived at a workable solution.

We'll help our allies any way they'd like. In return they'll start repaying us by January 1st, 1950. I should be able to get out of here by the end of March.

Zach

Dear Mom, Saturday, February 14th, 1948

I turned 61 today. I guess, as I told Grandma 43 years ago, I'm growing. It used to be more fun. Now I feel it more. I'm real close to finishing up here in Europe. I should have been done last month, but that's how politics go sometimes. Everybody has to be heard, even if they don't know what they're talking about.

The weather here isn't a whole lot nicer than it is by you. They don't have as much snow here, but it still gets cold. It's a lot nicer in Florida. Maybe you and I should move there. We could go surfing. Try to picture that scene. You with your hip and me with my limp.

I talked with Pete yesterday, he said he and Samantha are getting ready to retire. He's not sure what to do with his stock in PAPA'S. He wants to discuss it with me when I get home this summer. He'd like to sell it to his son Zak and

Annie; he just doesn't want to create a problem with Michael. I asked him, why not?

Sometimes I get tired of being asked my opinion. Maybe I'm beginning to understand why Father Dominic came up with the crazy idea about my birth. None of you had to make a decision. He handled it, no questions asked. Maybe that was good. When I get home I should reread some of my early journal entries to see how I felt back then.

Nah! I'd probably get a headache.

Remember – I Love You.

Your Kid,

Zacharia

P.S. I should be back in Copper Harbor by June 13th. Zak will make sure the lake home is ready for us.

JULY 1948

Sunday – 7/4

IT'S FINISHED!!

Adeline and I will be together for all eternity. Side by side, and cheek to cheek. My Adeline and me. Now she's waiting for me. God willing, I'll get there.

If a burial ceremony can be beautiful, this was it. Mom, Annie, and her family. Pete and his family. A lot of our friends. Alexander and 2 of The Guys. Since Adeline was buried in a Military cemetery in France, the local VFW was here. The VFW played taps and did a 21 gun salute. Adeline died in service to the war as much as any soldier. Maybe more than most.

It was heartwarming and tear jerking at the same time. Adeline and my marker is within feet of my mother and father. Grandma, Grandpa, Mom, and Franks are on the other side of our 8-foot Guardian Angel, and Little Fawn's next to my mother.

Mom bawled. Annie cried. Pete hugged me, and Alexander was hugging everybody. I think Alexander likes it here in Copper Harbor. He had reserved the Copper Pot a' Gold restaurant downtown from 10 am till 3 pm. Everybody from the ceremony was invited for lunch. The day was as fine as

I could have wished for. I told Alexander I'd be back in New York the middle of September.

Zach

Saturday – 7/10

Went looking for Patrick, Emil's younger cousin who I had when I was teaching. I hadn't talked to him since after the Depression. I wanted to find out a couple more things about Emil and figured Patrick would know. I was pretty surprised, although I shouldn't have been, when Patrick didn't want to talk about Emil.

He didn't let me in his house, so we sat at a run-down old picnic table in his side yard. The table matched his house. He said his wife left him right after the war. She apparently fell for some returning GI and disappeared. I thought of Emil's grandfather and uncle.

He said he hadn't heard much about Emil. All he knows is Emil's a creep. He said Emil was back once or twice in the late 20's, but it always looked like he was with gangsters. Then he came back after the depression and tried to borrow some money. Patrick told me to look around, did it look as though he had any money to give someone. I shrugged and left.

I'd say my suspicions are confirmed; however I don't even knew what my suspicions are yet.

Zach

OCTOBER 1948

Sunday – 10/3

Got back to New York yesterday, I was 2 weeks late. Alexander said 2 of The Guys think I'm irresponsible. He said not to worry, the 2 guys are democrats. He thinks they'll be leaving soon. They're the 2 guys who looked into Emil's grandfathers disappearance.

Things around here are incredibly busy; we're all working on Dewey's presidential election. Most of the folks around here think he's a shoo-in to beat Truman. With my life, I don't think anything's a shoo-in. I met Truman in France a few times. I thought he was a pretty nice guy.

I respect him, only The Guys say he's a democrat, he's got to go. He seems to have been slipping in popularity and the republican Dewey has been gaining. Maybe it's because Dewey's from Michigan. Max always had a thing about democrats. I never understood why, and he never explained it.

Zach

Sunday – 10/31

The big election's Tuesday. Everybody knows Dewey's going to beat Truman. The Guys say Truman's a democrat, he's got to go. I say why?

Zach

NOVEMBER 1948

Thursday – 11/4

Truman won!

Everybody around here is flabbergasted. They all ask me, what happened? I keep telling them I think Truman's a nice guy. They don't understand. I told them they should get out of the city and into the country more often. Mingle with some democrats.

Zach

1949

MAY 1949

Friday – 5/6
Annie called a few minutes ago.
Mom died today.
Will write more tomorrow.
Zach

Saturday – 5/7
Annie said they had dropped off the kids at school and were driving to Houghton to check out the progress on the nursing home I was having built. The home is opening on September 1ˢᵗ, and Mom was going to be the first resident.

She said they were having an in-depth conversation about life in a nursing home. Mom was all excited about it, then she told Annie she was going to nap while they drove. Mom was looking forward to being with people similar to her, not a bunch of kids. She planned on moving in as soon as summer at the lake was over.

When Annie got to Houghton, she went right to the hospital, however there was nothing they could do. The doctor told her Mom fell asleep, and her heart just stopped. She died with a smile on her face. He said we should all thank God.

I thank Him because I had her.
Zach

Sunday – 5/8

Went to church today. Prayed to God for everybody. Don't know if it helps or not. Don't know much of anything right now. I'll leave for Copper Harbor tomorrow. The Guys said I have as much time as I need. I told Annie I was driving back. I want time to think.

Zach

Saturday – 5/21

What a wonderful service. Sunny and close to 70. I'm sure Mom was looking down happy. Reminded me of Paris. I thought about all the people I've known and lost. All the places I've been and left. All the things I've seen and not been able to forget. Too much thinking.

The cemetery plot's slowly filling up. Annie says it's a history of our family. I told her, easy for you to say, you're only 40.

Zach

Sunday – 5/29

Sold the lake house to Annie and Zak for 100 dollars. They can make better use of it than I can. They told me I'll always have first dibs on using it. I thanked them and said it wouldn't be the same. If I can't hear Mom laughing, and see her smile, I don't want to be there. That made Annie cry.

I said welcome to the club.

Zach

Monday – 5/30

Spent today with Pete, just him and me. We talked a lot about the old days, reminisced about everything. I told him I'd bought out Michael and his cousin Sally from PAPA'S. I gave Michael 110 percent of what it was worth. I've given all of it to Annie and Zak.

Everything was finished before Pete ever knew about it. There was nothing he could do, except say his cousin Sally's a tramp. I concurred. I would have offered to buy out Pete, and do the same thing, only he would have been insulted.

I suggested he contact his attorney to see if he and Samantha can somehow deed their ownership in PAPA'S to Zak and Annie. We both laughed about how PAPA'S was started so many years ago by a couple of hicks from Copper Harbor. What did we know? We didn't care, we had each other. Friendship! Nothing like it!

I'm heading back to New York tomorrow. I'll miss summer at the lake, but I'll REALLY miss Mom.

Zach

1950

JANUARY 1950

Dear Annie, Sunday, New Year's Day, 1950
How's everything back in Copper Harbor?
I understand you and Zak are now the sole owners of PAPA'S.
WOW! Congratulations!!!
Pete and I never could have dreamed up anything like this. My little sister and his son, owning PAPA'S.

Pete and I drove those brand new 1904 Oldsmobiles all the way from Marquette to Copper Harbor all because Grandma wanted to buy 2 of them. Pete's uncle Paul liked them, and the rest is history. WOW!

I know you wondered why I wasn't at the lake last summer. I told you on the phone more than once, with Mom gone, I didn't feel up to being there. Hope you somehow understand. I would have missed her laughter and smile way too much.

When I talked with Zak last month he said everyone had a great summer. He told me you had a street sign made which reads Celestial Court, in honor of Mom. That's one of the nicest things I've heard in a long time.

I may not be back in Copper Harbor for quite a while. The Guys have something they want me to think about. I have an idea what it is, I'm just not sure I'm up to it. Everybody has skeletons in their closet. Even me. They say none of my skeletons are a big deal. We'll see.

I miss Mom also, but I've experienced death a lot more than you have. You never get used to it; I hope. Grandma was a tremendous help for me. She told me more than once, I'll see you again in Heaven. I hope she's right about me. I know she's right about you!

Congratulations on the upcoming birth of your first grandchild. I almost fell on the floor when Zak told me. I didn't realize your kids had grown up so fast. I've been gone more than I thought. I'm sure Mom and Grandma are watching over you.

Grandma would be telling you about how the life cycle works. How we grow and have descendants to follow us, and how it all makes so much sense. She was so thrilled when she heard Mom was expecting you. She said her lineage was going to be carried on. I wonder, sometimes, about my lineage.

Love to all of you,
Your Big Brother,
Zacharia

1952

MARCH 1952

Saturday – 3/8

The Guys say I have to make my decision soon, time's running out. If I'm going to run as Eisenhower's VP, I have to decide by July 4th so they can make a big splash. Ike likes me, and I have the utmost respect for him.

We worked well together trying our best to help Europe re-build after the war. We must have met a dozen times. He likes to get things done, same as Max. He never met Max but wishes he would have. I know Max would be pushing me to run. He'd say damn the skeletons, beat the Democrats.

Ike's from Texas, I'm from Michigan. The Guys say it's a perfect combination. I'm honored and humbled, I'm just not sure I'm qualified. The Guys say I'm a shoo-in. I think back to that day in Marquette at the 4 M's Restaurant – if the shoe fits – and laugh.

Zach

Thursday – 3/13

Alexander claims Kathleen, and our daughter, who I'm not allowed to have contact with, are no problem. She told him as long as I send the money she doesn't care what I do. Apparently the 5 million I sent her 4 years ago keeps her happy.

Alexander showed me a picture of my daughter. She's beautiful, same as her mother. She's 18 now, and she graduated from school with straight A's.

Must be a trait from Kathleen, I seldom got an A, although with Ms. Bagley's help I did graduate from high school.

Alexander says The Guys can take care of any skeletons which may pop up. I'm not sure how Max would feel about all of this. I have a feeling he'd tell me to own up to anything. What's done is done. Suck it up and be a man. Beat the damn Democrats. The Guys tell me to forget about the past, we're living for now. Make a decision.

I wonder what God thinks.

Zach

Monday – 3/17

I've got a meeting with Ike and some bigwigs from the party this Friday. They say I can bring Alexander, but just Alexander. They were even hesitant about him coming. I said without him there'd be no meeting.

Zach

Thursday – 3/20

Alexander tried his best to get out of coming to the meeting tomorrow. He thinks I should follow the bigwigs advice. I told him if I followed anybody's advice I'd still be in Copper Harbor. That made him laugh, the same way Max used to make me laugh. I liked it.

Zach

Friday – 3/21

We had a great meeting. They loved Alexander. Now they understand why I do. I told them I'd be in contact with them next week.

Zach

Sunday – 3/23

I believe I had a conversation with God today.

Went to the same church Max and I use to go to. I sat in the same pew; I think in the same spot. It's been almost 45 years since we were there together. I felt clean. It probably sounds stupid, but I felt clean. I'm not sure how else to describe the feeling. It reminded me of some of my conversations with Grandma, or the night in Grandpa's cabin when God told me to Trust Him.

Maybe it was Grandma, or Dad, or Mom, or Max. Maybe they're all His representatives. I don't know. All I know is I had a silent conversation, with The Almighty. Call it what you want, it happened before the service began. I was sitting alone thinking about running with Ike. Wondering if I had the qualifications to be VP.

I was questioning myself, and everything I've done these past 45 years, when the thought If the shoe fits, PUT IT ON, came to mind.

I'll join Ike.

Zach

Wednesday – 3/26

Alexander and The Guys are happy. I'm nervous. Now the work begins.

Zach

MAY 1952

Saturday – 5/3

One of The Guys who's a democrat, leaked out word that I was running with Ike as his VP. Alexander's furious with the guy, but with the election coming up in November, he can't kick the SOB out of the group. Alexander says it'd ruin the way we're perceived by the public. It amazes me how much Alexander reminds me of me when I was younger.

It seems the word's spreading like wildfire. It put a damper on what they had planned for the Fourth of July. They were going to call it a Let's back Zach party. They had planned a couple hundred gatherings around the country. The Republican Party was going all out.

Eisenhower had announced in January he was running for president, so the Fourth of July would have been the perfect time for my announcement. They're still planning the parties, but they have to come up with a different slogan. Alexander's fuming. I think it's all funny, but that's me.

I'm the hick from Upper Michigan.

Zach

Friday – 5/9

Ike and Zach. They've got YOUR back, that's the new slogan. I said I loved it, but I'm just along for the ride. It seems, contrary to what Max always thought, the higher up in politics you get, the less control you have over anything. I'm not sure I'm happy about that part.

When we started PAPA'S I had control, well, all except for the banker in Marquette, who said I was too young. Even then, I had the choice to quit and move on. Running as Ike's VP, Alexander says all my choices have to be cleared by The Committee. Now I've got The Guys and The Committee to deal with.

I liked working with Michael and Charles 46 years ago.

Zach

Tuesday – 5/13

Just my luck, now Emil's in New York. He said the dockworkers' union wants to meet with me. I thought about telling him to go suck eggs, but decided to just brush him off, and walked away.

Zach

Monday – 5/19

Alexander's fantastic at mending fences. I'll meet the dockworkers union next Friday. Alexander mentioned I should think back to all the meetings I ran for Max. All the times I was so successful, raised so much money, kept everybody so relaxed and entertained. He says I should be my old self, but I'm kinda liking my new self.

Zach

Wednesday – 5/21

Alexander brought in some notes and minutes from a few meetings I ran for Max. He wants me to look them over.

Zach

Sunday – 5/25

Sat through both services in church today. Our minister came over when he was finished. He's gotten to know me well and he asked if there was anything he could do for me. I asked him to hard boil 2 dozen eggs. I said I may need them this coming week. Told him I was meeting some union guys.

Zach

Friday – 5/30

Ike and Zach. They've got YOUR back!

I took 6 of those signs with me to the meeting with the dock workers union today. Emil was in charge of the meeting. I can't stand him. He's a creep, but he's become a smart creep, I give him credit for that.

Those union guys will boo at anything. They even booed when I smiled. It's probably because I wouldn't shake hands with Emil. He still gives me the heebegeebes, always has, always will. Thanks to everything Alexander had given me, I remembered how I used to enjoy doing these meetings. I pulled this one off fairly well.

The union guys know Eisenhower's going to be a shoo-in. They know their guy doesn't have a chance. Eisenhower's a war hero, there's no stopping him. All they wanted was some concessions when the time comes. I told them no problem, their boss Emil and I come from the same hometown. We're peas in a pod. That's what I said, tongue in cheek.

Then I had each one of them peel one of the hardboiled eggs which I brought. Their hands are so massive some of them needed 2 eggs in order to get one peeled. By the time we were all done, I had most of them laughing. Then in unison, I had all of us shout out GO SUCK EGGS. I told them it was meant for all the anti-union people in the country. They cheered.

Emil knew better.

Zach

JUNE 1952

Monday – 6/2

Alexander had a different one of The Guys check into Walter's death in Detroit. He said he was never comfortable with the report from the first guys. The new guy found a death certificate for Walter from Monday, May 28th, 1906. He brought a copy back with him.

It stated Walter had died from a self-inflected gunshot wound to the right side of the head. His grandson Emil told the police his grandfather had been depressed for a few months. Emil said he found him in his hotel room dead right after supper, with the gun still in his right hand. He said they had separate rooms.

According to the report, his grandson was despondent, and it was hard to talk with him. He had his grandfather cremated on that Thursday, and he took the ashes home to Copper Harbor. The police wrote it off as a suicide.

Alexander showed me the report, and while reading it I turned pale. Alexander asked what happened. All I could say was Walter was left-handed.

Zach

Friday – 6/6

Emil called me today. He said the meeting I ran with the union guys was the best showmanship meeting he's ever seen. He called it a dog and pony show. I told him I thought it was more of an egg in your eye show. First time in 60 years I ever heard him laugh.

He knows Ike's going to win. He just doesn't want me running as VP. He said politics is scary. He said it can be a matter of life or death. He also said he doesn't want to bring up anything about his grandpa, my grandma, or our time together at the dock in Copper Harbor. I told him I didn't want to bring up the fact his grandpa was left-handed.

He hung up.

Zach

Sunday – 6/8

Alexander and I had a good talk today. We went over what happened at the union meeting last month, and my talk with Emil on Friday. I think Alexander's getting worried about my safety. I told him not to worry, Emil's a wacko.

That's what he's worried about.

Zach

Monday – 6/9

Emil called today. He wants to meet with me and mend fences. I suggested Thursday, 7 pm, at Lombardi's Pizza. I like the place. It's always crowded.

Zach

Thursday – 6/12

Emil was a half hour late. He was sweating. He said the subway broke down and he had to walk a mile to get there. I didn't believe him. Right after he came in, 2 of the biggest goons I've seen in a long time came in and sat down.

Emil and I talked about Copper Harbor, his grandpa Walter, my grandma Martha. The docks, the day I hit him on the head with the chair, PAPA'S, and Ms. Bagley. We reminisced for over an hour, had pizza and wine. We acted like friends. We were happy together.

Then he apologized. He apologized for everything. He said I was lucky to quit the docks. He wished he would have quit when I quit. He wished he would have taken over Ms. Bagley's job as schoolteacher. She had offered it to him. He said his uncle was an incredibly mean boss, and his grandfather was even meaner. He said he could never break the chains around him.

He apologized for being the way he was. He said I had no idea how much pressure's been on him since he turned 15. He said the docks were tough, and politics were tougher. He asked for my forgiveness for anything he might have done. He shook my hand, then he left. The 2 goons followed him, I sat there dumbfounded.

I wondered if it was safe to walk home.

Zach

Saturday – 6/21

They found Emil's body today, floating face down in the East River, near Pier 11. The news report said he must have accidently fallen in while checking out a shipment which had come in from Germany.

I DON'T BELIEVE A WORD OF IT.

As much as Emil and I fought over the years, I feel compassion for him. He is, after all, from Copper Harbor. His cousin Patrick is broke, he has no siblings, and both of his parents are dead, so I'm having him buried in the Copper Harbor Cemetery. Near my family plot.

Zach

Friday – 6/27

Alexander's vivid. He wants both of The Guys who originally went to look into Walter's death thrown in jail. He believes if this information would have come out back when they looked into it, Emil would still be alive. I agree with him. But if Emil were alive, would someone be coming after me?

Alexander said he's excommunicated the 2 guys from the group. I guess now that the word's out, nobody trusts them anymore. This whole deal's getting under my skin. Emil's been on my mind all week. I'm not sure Emil shot his grandfather, Walter had hundreds of enemies. Now with Emil dead, I'll never know.

Zach

Sunday – 6/29

Went back to church today. It's been over a month. I thanked our minister for the hardboiled eggs. I didn't tell him how I used them; it might have been too much for him. I'm not sure he'd like the phrase go suck eggs. He's a great fellow, but he's also a minister.

The big celebration parties planned for the Fourth of July are 5 days away. I've lost all interest in them. I'm not crazy about politics. I don't think Max was either, he never ran for anything.

Smart man.

Zach

JULY 1952

Wednesday – 7/2

I've backed out of the race as Eisenhower's VP.

Alexander's furious. He says he understands, but he's furious. I can tell. I've been in his shoes more than once. Sometimes I'd work on something for weeks so Max could make a presentation. Then, at the last minute, Max would back out of it. All the organizing for nothing. I used to get so damn mad at Max, but I never told him. Same as Alexander's doing now.

The reason I backed out came from something Max told me a long, long time ago. He always thought the family bond was so important. Something to never mess with. It got me thinking about Kathleen and our daughter. What if our relationship got out in the open, obviously, nothing's sacred in politics.

If my daughter found out I was alive, and she was the biproduct of an illicit, passionate, sexual, encounter, it could cause the same turmoil in her life that it caused in my life. I'd never allow anything like that to affect her. I may not be able to see her, but I do love her. I've thrown my support to a fella I've known off and on for a while.

Zach

Friday – July Fourth, 1952

All the festivities went on without a hitch. The campaign slogan is simply - I Like Ike. He'll get Nixon behind him later this month. Alexander's going to be Ike's campaign manager. Surprised the hell out of me. Probably shouldn't have.

I'm thrilled. I can rest. I can take some time off.

Zach

Dear Annie, Saturday, July 5th, 1952

Congratulations on the birth of your grandson Eric. I love the name. It implies strength, courage, compassion, and loyalty. Good choice for a guy with a Zabrinski family background. Grandpa would approve.

Things here in New York are the same as the last time I wrote. Which, knowing me, probably was a couple of years ago. I spent most of my growing years apologizing to Mom for being such a terrible letter writer, now I'll spend most of my final years apologizing to you for the same thing. I hope you don't mind too much.

I do talk with Pete every few months. We go back a long way, and we enjoy hearing each other's voice. He's your father-in-law, so he keeps me informed about you and Zak. He told me all about Eric. When he was born, how long he was, how much he weighed, and how he looks like him. Pete's thrilled to have a grandson. He said he'll spoil Eric rotten. I believe him.

After you called me, I could picture how things were going at the lake, with all the kids and activity. I miss those days. Life in Copper Harbor was great. I didn't realize it at the time. I always thought things were confusing back then. I had no idea what confusing was.

I've pulled out of The Guys. They had a project they wanted me to think about, but the whole deal went sour. It sounded interesting at the start, only so many people got involved and there was so much politics, I gave up on it. I did get to work with some fine people though.

Alexander LOVED Copper Harbor, and meeting all of you. Now he's working with Eisenhower on his presidential campaign. I guess I know some pretty high and mighty folks. Pretty nice for a hick from Copper Harbor. I've led a pretty nice life, thanks to Mom's teachings and Grandma and Grandpa's examples.

Thinking about Grandpa, I've got to tell you a funny story. I like to say "go suck eggs" every once in a while. I said that to some folks the other day in a meeting, and I had them all laughing. None of them ever heard it before, and I had to explain it to them. When I was 9, Grandpa and I sat out in the hen house one night, waiting for the critter who was breaking eggs and killing chickens.

Grandpa picked the night with a full moon so we could see better. Around 2 in the morning we saw a fox coming across the field. The fox snuck in the chicken house through a small crack in the back wall and was about to get the eggs, when Grandpa hollered GO SUCK EGGS. The fox froze and looked at us, then Grandpa let him have it with both barrels of his Remington double-barrel 12-gauge shotgun.

Well, I started crying from all the noise, the chickens went crazy, lights went on in the farmhouse, and the poor fox was blown to bits. Grandpa stood up, started laughing, and said, "Well, there's one sorry little critter." We had to fix the broken boards the next day. I did find the fox's tail. I hung it in my bedroom until Grandpa died when I was 15. I put it in his casket. I loved Grandpa!

Thinking back, life at the farmhouse was pretty darn nice. It changed when I turned 18. Someday I'll tell you about that. I'll be home again in early September. An acquaintance of mine, Emil, has died, and I want him buried in the Copper Harbor Cemetery. Someday I'll tell you about him also.

Have a GREAT summer, and I'll see you in September.

Much Love,

Your Big Brother,

Zacharia

NOVEMBER 1952

Saturday – 11/8

As expected, Eisenhower won. When all the votes were counted, it turned out to be a landslide.

Alexander's thrilled. The Guys are on cloud 9. The Committee isn't surprised at all. They can't understand how anybody could have voted for Stevenson in the first place. I'm relieved. Now I can finally get my time off. Happy days!

Zach

Dear Annie and Zak, Sunday, November 23rd, 1952

I'm glad you had a lot of folks at the cemetery for Emil's burial, it meant a lot to me. I'll read the letter Grandma wrote for me later. You said she gave it to you and told you to give it to me if Emil died before me. I have no idea why, but apparently it was her wish. Grandma. Go figure! I never could.

Eisenhower's election went off without a hitch. Alexander has a phenomenal job with Ike, he says he owes me. I told him to forget it. The

Committee isn't needed anymore. I'm finally free to do what I want. The problem is, I don't know what I want. Maybe I should ask God. I haven't talked with Him in quite a while.

Pete said you and Zak are doing a great job with PAPA'S. Pete said you've hired some experienced people to help run the place. He mentioned after the war, car sales skyrocketed, and you were in the perfect place to take advantage of the boom.

Grandma would be proud of how her buying those 2 1904 Oldsmobile curved dash automobiles all turned out. I can hear Grandma saying, "I don't want to buy any used Oldsmobiles, I want the new ones." We're mighty lucky to have some of her blood in our veins. Don't ever let your kids or your grandkids forget it.

I'm not sure where I'm off to. Right now I think I'll spend winter here in New York. I'm used to it. It feels comfortable, almost like my second home. Don't tell Pete what I said. Maybe someday you, Zak, and some of the kids could come out to visit. My treat.

I'll keep you posted. Probably not as much as you'd like, but, that's me.

Love,

Your Big Brother,

Zach

Thursday – 11/27

Grandma's letter to me.

Dear Zacharia, January 1st, 1908

I understand it's hard on you not knowing your birth mother or father. I'm proud of how you've handled it. I know what Father Dominic and I did might not have been ideal, but it was the best we could think of.

I'm writing this letter to you while my mind is still pretty good. I realize I've been slipping lately when you ask me certain questions. Mainly the ones about Emil's Grandpa Walter.

I hope you can follow this. It gets confusing even to me and I lived through it.

Walter forced himself on me one evening out in our barn. I was 16 and became with child. It wasn't hard to hide. I wore big dresses and stayed home.

My parents were destroyed. My father named the baby boy Carl and after 12 weeks he wrapped Carl in a blanket and put him on the church steps with a note which read, Adopt Me. It was 1864, and I was crushed.

Walter's father found out what Walter had done and beat him with a buggy whip. Then his father and mother took the baby boy Carl into their house and raised him. No one ever loved Carl, except me, but no one knew I was the mother, except Walter, his dad, and my folks. NO ONE knew anything, and I couldn't say anything. Walter's father threatened to kill both Walter and me if we said anything. I was 16 and scared. So were my parents. It was a terrible time in my life.

I married your Grandpa Jake when I was 19, and never told him anything. We had a wonderful life and had 2 beautiful baby twin girls, Angelica and Celeste, your mother and aunt. Maybe Jake had some idea, I don't know, but it could be a reason why he hated your father for getting your mother pregnant. Once he got to know you as a baby he loved you with his whole heart.

Walter and I never paid any attention to each other after that. He would start rumors about me once in a while, he never got anybody to believe him. He was a strange boy, everybody knew it. You'd ask me questions about him, and I tried my best to avoid them. Except for the one time in front of church when I told Emil to "Go ask the old bastard." That was fun! I know Celeste was shocked, but I watched you smile.

Now the interesting part –

Carl raped his 15-year old cousin out in their barn. What goes around, comes around, I guess. She became pregnant with a boy. They named him Emil. The boy you hate. The hatred goes back too far. Emil is the grandson of Walter and me. I know it sounds crazy. Emil is the product of his father Carl raping his cousin. Carl is the product of Walter forcing himself on me when I was 16.

You are the product of a loving relationship. I know your father would have come back for you if he could have. Something dreadful must have happened to him, otherwise I'm confident he would have been back. I liked your father and would have loved to have had him as a son-in-law. Before he left he said, "Bye Mom, I'll see you later." That's not a man who would run away. In my heart I know it.

Now for the touchy part –

Zacharia - You and Emil are second cousins. You should end the fighting.
With all my love,
Grandma Martha.

I need a drink.
Zach

1955

SEPTEMBER 1955

Sunday – 9/4

Alexander told me Eisenhower wants me to go down to the Suez Canal. It seems the British and French are having trouble with Egypt. The Brits and France have control of the canal; however Egypt wants to take control. Something about controlling the shipping of oil and petroleum.

I told Alexander I've had enough dealings with England and France to last 5 lifetimes. I'm passing, suggested Eisenhower go there. He's the big honcho now, he can get anything done. Or he could send Tricky Dick.

Alexander laughed.

Zach

Sunday – 9/25

My little sister Annie turned 47 today. I called her after supper. Nice to hear her voice. She wants me to come back home to Copper Harbor. I told her maybe in a few years. I've got a new plan.

Zach

Friday – 9/30

Tomorrow morning I'm off to Alaska and oil. Max would be proud of me!

Zach

1958

FEBRUARY 1958

Friday – 2/14

71 and growing, but today I feel OLD!

Have I lost control? Did I have control until the Eisenhower deal? If I lost control, what caused it? Or, is my brain just plain frozen? It's so damn cold here in Alaska, everything else is frozen. Why not my brain?

What have I done wrong? Maybe I shouldn't have tried doing it all on my own. Maybe I needed someone like Alexander. Someone I could trust.

Will next week be better?

Zach

Saturday – 2/22

Over 2 years, and still no oil. Running out of time, money, and energy. Damn it!

Zach

JULY 1958

Wednesday – 7/9

Alexander called today. I have no idea how he found me in Alaska, but I'm not surprised. He said Kathleen got in touch with him and told him to tell me I have a grandson. That's all she'd tell him, but she did ask for more money. She's going to spoil him; I wish I could. Alexander said she's concerned about me; she just never wants me to contact her. She really bugs me. Bugs the hell out of me!

Alexander and Kathleen formed a nice relationship years ago. She wants the best for me, the same as he does. Only she doesn't want me interfering with her life. She likes my money, just not me.

Alexander's with Ike, who easily won another term as president. When he asked how I was doing, all I could say was fine. Didn't want to tell him the truth.

Zach

Thursday – 7/10
She wants more money. Ain't that cute, more money. Maybe I can pull it out of my hat and send it to her. This all happened because she thought I was a worthwhile catch back in Manhattan. What a dope I was. Maybe still am.

Zach

Saturday – 7/12
I may have to pull the plug on the Double ZZ Oil Corporation. I thought it was a great idea. Oil wells. Half a dozen oil wells. All pumping liquid gold. It all started because of the request to go to the Suez Canal. It seemed the need for oil to make petroleum was a given. A worthwhile thing to invest in.

Alaska and its virgin territories is the perfect spot. At least to me and the Atlantic Richfield Oil Corporation. I guess they were smarter than me. They struck it rich, I should have stayed with them. They're pumping over a thousand barrels a day. I'm pumping a lot of hot air and dollar signs.

CRAP!

Zach

Dear Annie, Saturday, July 19th, 1958
Hope all is well with you, Zak, and the kids. It's been a long time since I last wrote to you or called Pete. I talked with Alexander the other day. He said

he keeps in contact with you every once in a while. I think it's great. I knew when he started working with me he was a keeper.

He probably told you about the fiasco when I was going to run as Eisenhower's VP back in '52. As I told you, it all went sour, and I wasn't sure what to do with the rest of my life. I was asked to go to Egypt in September '55 to find out what was going on with the Suez Canal. I turned down the offer.

What interested me though, was the importance of oil. It's become a hot commodity. I came up to Alaska and started looking into oil. I formed my own company. The Double ZZ Oil Corporation. It sounded great, but I did everything wrong. Right from the start, I did everything wrong. I guess I'm a great consultant, a damn good advisor, a decent partner, and on, and on, and on.

I think I'm an awful business owner.

Well, a huge chunk of my money went into drilling some holes in the ground, up here. They're some nice looking holes. They each have a huge structure, all pointing straight up to Heaven. As if God cares. They cost a fortune. However when they work, they're worth it. The trick is, they have to work. Mine don't work, but they sure are pretty.

I haven't told Alexander anything about my fiasco. I don't want to hear him laughing. Don't think he would, but I'm not taking any chance. I'm going to hang around up here in Alaska and lick my wounds for a while. It's beautiful country, cold and beautiful. I'll take some photos and bring them home with me.

Someday.

Love,

Zach

PS – if you say anything to Pete about me and my wells, be kind.

SEPTEMBER 1958

Thursday – 9/25

Annie's 50th birthday. Happy Birthday Annie! I'll call her Sunday.

Today's the day I leave Alaska. 3 years of blood, sweat, back breaking labor, and 80 percent of my money, in this remote place, is enough for me. Maybe if my holes in the ground would have been successful it'd be a different story. They weren't, so Goodbye Alaska.

I've leased my 6 oil wells to the Atlantic Richfield Oil Corporation for a dollar each per year. If they ever get them working, I'll get 20 percent of the profits. I won't hold my breath.

I'll figure out what I want to do when I'm back in the USA.

Zach

Sunday – 9/28

Annie begged me to come home. She sounded great, said she was happy, and they could use my help at PAPA'S. I think it was a guilt trip. Told her I love her, and think about her every day, which I do, but I'm not ready to come home. She said I shouldn't wait to come home until I was in a pine box. Laughed at that one.

Spending some time in Detroit. Going to find out the truth about Emil's grandfather. I don't believe Emil killed him back in '06.

Zach

NOVEMBER 1958

Sunday – 11/23

I start my new career first thing tomorrow morning. I'm 1 of 3 short order cooks at Gus's Pancake and Burger Joint. Gus couldn't turn me down when he heard I worked on the Lusitania in the dining area for 7 years. He wants me to bring some class to his joint. His words, not mine.

Been scouting out Detroit for a month, and his place is where a lot of cops come for a free meal. Gus is no dummy. I actually like him, but he could use deodorant once in a while.

There's an older retired cop named McDowell who stops by once or twice a week. He has to be close to 80. He should know something about what happened 52 years ago. Going to get to know him.

Zach

Thursday – 11/27

Thanksgiving day at Gus's. What an experience! They tell me I make the best Belgian Waffles anyone's ever tasted. Told them it's because I was engaged to a French Lady from Paris, not far from Belgium. I said I've got class, Gus said it's from the Lusitania training.

McDowell's coming in next Tuesday for one of my waffles.
Bingo!
Zach

DECEMBER 1958

Dear Annie, Thursday, December 25th, 1958
Merry Christmas from Detroit!
I'm as surprised as you are. Detroit at Christmas. I should start a list of all the places I've spent Christmas. I'd probably be amazed, well, maybe not. Hope all is well with you and the family, and hope your New Year is the best.

I decided to come here and try to clear Emil's name in the death of his grandfather. I spent many years hating Emil, and he me. We had plenty of arguments and fights over the years. I'm not even sure why, we just did. Strange isn't it? I never really knew him, and he never really knew me. We just hated each other.

Talked with Pete last month. He, as usual, thinks I'm crazy. He said you mentioned something to him about me and Alaska. All he knew is I think it's a beautiful area, and I'm bringing pictures when I come home. Thanks for not telling him about my holes in the ground. I've leased them to someone else, so I don't have to think about them.

I've got a great job here. Needed something to do to forget about my last venture. I'm working at a restaurant, similar to when I was on the Lusitania. I wonder if you have any of the stationary with the ship embossed on it. Those were some fine days I spent on the ship. It's a damn shame what happened to all the fine folks who were on it. Damn Germans.

Pete's absolutely thrilled with how you and Zak are running PAPA'S. He said he and Samantha plan on spending January through March in the Naples area. You and Zak must have worked out a nice financial plan for him. Maybe someday I'll get to Florida again.

Well, I've only been at the restaurant for a month, but tomorrow I have to open up. The owner, Gus, trusts me enough that he gave me the keys to the place. I only plan on being here until I clear Emil's name. However long it may take.
Love to all of you,
Your Big Brother,
Zacharia

Wednesday – 12/31

Happy New Year to myself.

McDowell and I are getting acquainted. I think he likes me. Maybe in a few months I can start asking some questions. He's 78, and he joined the force on his 21st birthday in 1901. He should know something. Otherwise my time at Gus's will have been just for the fun of it.

But I make great waffles.

Zach

1959

FEBRUARY 1959

Saturday – 2/14

Happy 72nd birthday to me.

Maybe all the stuff I told Grandma on my 18th birthday, about never being old again, was a bunch of hooey. Maybe I'm old. Old, and growing.

I had McDowell come in for 1 of my special waffles this morning. My treat, not Gus's. For a 78 year old guy, he sure can eat. He's a widower. He was married for 55 years, he says, "to the same wife." He's got a pretty good sense of humor, still, he's a cop through and through. A no-nonsense cop. This might be tougher than I thought.

Zach

Saturday – 2/28

McDowell came in for breakfast today. He looked down, maybe depressed. I asked what was up, and he said tomorrow would have been their 57th wedding anniversary. He had tears in his eyes. We talked about their wedding day, where they were married, how many kids they had, all kinds of stuff.

I asked him if he wanted me to go to church with him tomorrow. Maybe God can help us both. McDowell liked the idea. He said I'd meet some of his kids, and I wouldn't have to cook anything. They invited him to a party in the afternoon, and he wants me to come along.

Zach

JUNE 1959

Sunday – 6/7

Today's the 5th time I've been to church with McDowell. He comes across as a no-nonsense cop, but he does have an interesting sense of humor. We talk about the old days, the mob, the unions, how people just up and disappeared sometimes. Once in a while I wonder if McDowell was involved in any of that.

Haven't mentioned anything about Emil's grandfather yet. I'm taking this mighty slow. Don't want to goof anything up.

Zach

Monday – 6/22

McDowell has gotten to be a friend. I've met most of his kids, grandkids, and his 1st great-grandkid. I'm not sure what to do about him and Emil's grandfather. Maybe I'll bring it up on the 4th. That's a festive day.

Zach

JULY 1959

Saturday – 7/4

Spent today with McDowell and his family. His kids love me, and I'm getting fond of them. I haven't told him anything about my background yet. If he knew I almost ran as Eisenhower's VP, I think he'd pass out.

While we were watching the fireworks exploding, I mentioned I had a buddy from Upper Michigan whose grandfather died suspiciously in Detroit sometime in 1906. I figured with all the noise going on he might not pick up on it, and if he did, it would seem casual.

Zach

Tuesday – 7/7

He's a cop. Through and through. Day or night, he's a cop. McDowell came in this morning, had a waffle, and asked me what I remember about my buddy's grandfather. He said he still had connections and was owed a lot of favors. He wasn't as friendly today as usual.

Gave him Emil's grandfathers information. Walter F. Vindemuff, born in Hancock, Michigan around 1846. Died Detroit 1906, self-inflicted gunshot wound to the head. Then I told McDowell I thought it was a bogus report. I tried to play it down. Make it casual, like I wasn't overly concerned. He doesn't take this stuff lightly.

Zach

Friday – 7/31
I haven't seen McDowell for 3 weeks.
Zach

AUGUST 1959

Monday – 8/3
McDowell showed up at Gus's this morning with a packet for me. He wanted me to wait until I got home to open it. He thought it would be a smart idea for me to leave town, sooner than later. He said the brotherhood runs pretty deep. He likes me, but I don't wear the blue.

I thanked him, shook his hand, said I had no idea what he was talking about, and offered to make his favorite waffle. He said it wasn't a good idea to be seen together and left.

I made a pitcher of Moscow Mules, opened the packet, but I couldn't get past the first page.

Zach

Tuesday – 8/4
May Emil's soul rest in peace.

In the packet there were 4 pictures of Walter's dead body, and a 1 page hand-written note by McDowell. Walter was killed by a cop who was deep in debt from gambling and was controlled by union leaders. The union leaders were controlled by the mob bosses. The cop who killed Walter was found 3 weeks later floating face down in Lake St Clair.

The mob wanted Walter dead. He was deeply involved in the Haymarket Square Riot on May 4th, 1886, in Chicago. A labor protest which turned into a riot after someone threw a bomb at the police and 8 folks died. Walter managed to get out of Chicago and back to Upper Michigan.

When the mob found out Walter was becoming obnoxious, and outspoken, they decided it was time to get rid of him. I'm thinking back to the dance in town, when he grabbed Grandma, told her she was a pretty little lady, and Pete's uncle dragged him home. He was pretty obnoxious and outspoken that night, then he just disappeared.

There's also a note from McDowell, saying he and the cop who killed Walter, were partners when they both joined the force in 1901. In 1906, McDowell didn't know why his partner was killed, or why Walter was killed. He wrote, in those days you didn't question anything, still don't, and I shouldn't either. He wrote that Emil was completely innocent. He wrote he enjoyed knowing me, but I should probably make tracks.

Maybe I should try tracking that rabbit on concrete.

Zach

Wednesday – 8/5

Time to go to New York.

Zach

Saturday – 8/8

Bought a new white 1959 Cadillac Series 62 convertible. If I'm running from something, I may as well run in style, the hell with them all. Got to New York this morning. Called Alexander and we're meeting Monday. He sounded standoffish.

Maybe it's my imagination.

Zach

Monday – 8/10

Told Alexander about my time with McDowell. Said now I wanted to know why Emil died. I thought the Guys could help. Alexander said The Guys were powerful, but just in financial ways.

He said he'll look into why Emil died, but couldn't promise anything. He suggested I stay out of the limelight for a while just in case there was something fishy going on. I should lay low, sell the glitzy car, and he'll get in touch with me. I told him where I was staying.

Zach

Friday – 8/14

Haven't heard from Alexander yet, and every guy on every corner looks suspicious. New York isn't quite as much fun as it used to be. I'd leave, but I'm in this far, I may as well see it through. On the other hand, Copper Harbor sounds pretty nice right about now.

Went to Lombardi's Pizza for supper tonight. Even the waiter looked suspicious. Times used to be simpler.

Zach

Sunday – 8/23

Alexander was waiting outside of church this morning. Didn't even ask him how he knew I was there. He wouldn't tell me why Emil died. He told me it didn't make any difference why. Emil's dead, so Emil's dead.

Argued with him, and now we're meeting at Lombardi's Pizza Wednesday night at 7. He says he'll have a plan for me. The Guys are on my side. Some of them knew me back in the day. Back when I was on top.

His words, not mine.

Zach

Wednesday – 8/26

Alexander has a plan for me. Quite different than back in '46 when I did the planning. Grandma had her old saying, What goes around comes around. I'm leaving New York. The Guys think I should retire and live a calmer life. Alexander remembered how much I always talked about the

Atlantic Ocean, with the pounding waves and the smell of salt water. He's got a great memory.

He wants me to move to Cape Elizabeth, Maine, near Portland, so he can visit occasionally. It's about a 6 hour drive north of the city, and right on the Atlantic Ocean. He found a nice 2,000 square foot bungalow near the beach. The Guys already bought it for me. He said he still thinks the world of me, but I might be getting old. I should spend some time relaxing in Cape Elizabeth.

He understands why I wanted to find out about Walter and Emil, but he thinks the old Zacharia would have stayed out of it. I told him BULL SHIT! He didn't know me when I was in Europe for the 1st and 2nd World Wars. When I went to Europe to check it out for Max before the 1st war. When I went to Europe after both wars to help with financing. When I brought my father back from Brazil.

He smiled and said I was younger back then. He gave me 3 large envelopes, told me to open them later, then the pizza came. We shared some old stories, did some kidding around, laughed a lot, shook hands, and he left just before they closed the place for the night. The waiter said everything was taken care of and gave me a 100 dollar bottle of vintage red wine to take with me.

The way my mind was spinning, the wine took precedence over the envelopes.

Zach

Thursday – 8/27
Opened the envelopes today. One envelope was from Kathleen. It has photos of my daughter and my grandson. No names, no dates, no addresses, only photos. What a beautiful young woman, and handsome young baby boy. I guess, factoring in everything, I'm a pretty lucky guy, but I ain't that old. Yet!

Another envelope had all the info and keys to the beach bungalow. Along with pictures, directions, and the mortgage paid in full, plus a bank statement in my name, for The Portland National Bank, with a million dollars. The keys to a 1959 gray, plane-jane, Chevrolet 4 door Parkwood station wagon. It's parked in the parking lot on Spring and Broadway.

The last envelope was full of memorabilia from my days with Max. Flyers announcing the meetings I ran. Mementos from my days in Europe. So many things I'd forgotten about years ago. There was also a handwritten note. I know it was written by Alexander; I know his writing. It said Emil was an undercover informant for the FBI. He kept them posted on what the mob was doing. When the mob found out, the mob eliminated him. Emil died a hero.

My cousin Emil was a HERO.

Zach

Sunday – 8/30

Went to the same church Max and I used to go to. Sat in the same pew, near the same spot. Brought back some great memories. Also brought back some not so great. Thought about Emil and all the wasted time fighting. Maybe I am getting old. Maybe I am a little used up. I wonder if I'm going to wind up a recluse, the way my father was, when I found him. Maybe it wouldn't be so bad.

Maybe it's my time to hide out for a while. A long while.

Zach

7 YEARS LATER

1967

FEBRUARY 1967

Tuesday – 2/14

80 years and growing. I'm not feeling so old anymore. Life by the ocean has been nice to me. I can sit and listen to the waves, smell the salt water, walk a few miles on the beach. Think about my dad and smile. Pretty damn nice.

I used to wonder why Alexander wanted me up here in Maine. Was he putting the old horse out to pasture? Now I realize, Alexander wanted me to relax, and enjoy life for the few years he thinks I have left. I'll fool him, I'm going for a 100 years. 100 years and growing! That's a fact.

Annie and I talk once or twice every week. She sends me letters, and photos of all her kids and grandkids. I get back to Copper Harbor every summer for the month of July. They still have the place on Lake Fanny Hooe.

I talk with Pete every month. He's retired in Naples. His wife Samantha, Sammy as he always called her, died in '65. His kid Zak and Annie want him to move back home, but now Pete calls Copper Harbor the middle of no place. What goes around comes around. I guess. He says everybody up there's too young. I'm going to visit him in May, he says he misses me. The first thing I'm going to tell him is how I think our lives in Copper Harbor must have been so Supercalifragilisticexpialidocious. I saw Sound of Music last month and just had to write that word down to use on Pete. He'll love it!

Zach

5 YEARS LATER

1972

JUNE 1972

Sunday – 6/4
Annie called earlier.
Pete died last night.
I'm leaving for Copper Harbor as soon as possible.
Zach

Wednesday – 6/7
Monday I took the bus to Boston and caught the 1st flight to Detroit. Yesterday I got a shuttle flight to Marquette, and spent the night there, for old time's sake. This morning I had breakfast at The 4 M's restaurant. Still there, great waffles, just not as tasty as mine. Zak picked me up and we drove to Copper Harbor. The same route Pete and I took 67 years ago. Old memories!

Pete's death hit me hard, harder than most. Maybe Alexander's right, maybe I'm getting old. Pete and I go back 78 years. I've got every right to be sad. What does age have to do with anything when you lose your best friend? I feel as though a part of me also died. I'm going to miss Pete. Really am.

Apparently Pete wasn't feeling too well in March. He came back to Copper Harbor in early April. Said he didn't feel like he was operating on all 8 cylinders. He said he felt like some little foreign car, running on 4 cylinders. Annie says he sat around the house. On Saturday he had a headache, threw up once and went to bed early. That was it.

Goodbye Pete. Say HI to God.

Zach

Saturday – 6/10

I've been to a lot of funeral services since Grandpa died when I was 15. This one was the hardest. Even though sometimes we didn't see each other for years, we always had each other. Now I don't. Never again. No more thinking, I wonder what Pete's doing? Just memories from now on. Only memories.

I'm going to stay here for 2 weeks. Then it's back to Cape Elizabeth, my new home. I want to find out about my daughter and grandson. Someday I'll be gone. I want someone to remember me.

Zach

Friday – 6/23

Heading home tomorrow after lunch. Zak and Annie will drive me to Marquette. Then it's back to Boston. Alexander was here for Pete's funeral. It seems he's become one of the family. He helped keep PAPA'S in the family, so they've sort of adopted him.

Told him I wanted to find out about Kathleen, and my offspring. He shrugged and reminded me of my promise to Kathleen. He asked if I was getting senile in my old age. I told him to go suck eggs. He didn't laugh.

Don't think I ever told Annie about Kathleen. Don't think Alexander has either, but Annie has this look I've never seen before. I'm not sure if it's the look of a concerned sister about my health, or the look of someone who knows something about me but is afraid to say anything.

I'm looking forward to getting home.

Zach

Friday – 6/30

Good to be home.

Got a letter while I was gone. The Atlantic Richfield Oil Company's starting to send me 5,000 dollars a month. They went 100 feet deeper in each of my wells and they're pumping oil. This renews my self-confidence.

I'm driving to New York after the 4th of July, while my eyesight's still okay. I'm going to confront Alexander. I need to find out about Kathleen. The old '59 Chevy still runs well, shouldn't have any problem. Back in the day, Pete and I drove 1904 Oldsmobiles across Upper Michigan. What's the big deal?

I'll ask God for His help on Sunday.

Zach

JULY 1972

Monday – 7/10

Got 50 miles out of town when my front driver side tire blew out. Scared the hell out of me! The fella at the service station said they all had dry-rot. Never thought of that. A 13 year old car that looks brand new with 16,281 miles on it, and dry-rotted tires. I've got all the money I need, but I haven't bought a new car. Maybe I am slipping.

Zach

Thursday – 7/13

Traded the old Chevy in for a new burgundy Oldsmobile Ninety-Eight. The sales guy thought I was too old to buy a new car. Reminded me of when Grandma bought the 2 new Oldsmobiles 67 years ago. She was pretty old. When I told his manager I'd be paying in cash, we signed the deal. It's a beauty.

Did the same 50 miles this morning, and my hands started shaking. I started sweating. Now I'm afraid to drive far. 85 years old and I'm afraid to drive far. What the hell's going on!

Called Alexander this afternoon. He'll come up here this weekend, so we can talk. Can't tell him over the phone. He'd hang up on me.

Zach

Sunday – 7/16

I don't think I'm senile. Just because Alexander questions my judgement, doesn't mean I'm senile. Who the hell is he anyway? I taught him everything he knows.

I want to find out about Kathleen, my daughter, and grandson. Alexander says I can't. I promised I wouldn't many years ago, so I can't. He said I promised when I was of sound mind. I told him I could still track a rabbit on concrete. He wasn't very happy when he left this afternoon. He says he has to protect Kathleen and her family.

What about me?

Zach

Tuesday – 7/18

I called Alexander today, and asked if there was something fishy going on between him and Kathleen. He hung up on me. Maybe it was a nasty question. Am I getting senile?

Maybe I should see my doctor.

Zach

Monday – 7/31

Doc McIntyre says physically, for an 85 year old guy, I'm in the shape of a 70 year old. He was amazed at my condition. All the blood results are excellent, my reflexes are great, my vision's a little low, but not too bad.

He said I may have the start of dementia. He's not worried, however I should see him every 3 months. I've been thinking about Grandma a lot lately. I'm leaving for Copper Harbor on September 1st, for a month. I'll fly. I'll be there for Annie's 63rd birthday.

She's thrilled.

Zach

OCTOBER 1972

Sunday – 10/8

Copper Harbor for the month of September was perfect. Annie keeps asking me to come home. I tell her I have a home. It's right on the Atlantic Ocean. It's exactly what I've wanted ever since I can remember. It's a part of me, and part of my father. It's in our blood. Now she thinks I'm senile. Why don't they remember the old me?

I told her my doctor thinks I'm fine, I just need to see him every 3 months. That quieted her down. I know she loves me and wants the best for me, but I'm my own man. Always have been.

There's a gorgeous church in Cape Elizabeth I enjoy going to. The denomination never bothers me. I think God's in them all. I know some folks would disagree, but I have dementia. I can get away with it.

Zach

Tuesday – 10/31

Saw Doc McIntyre today. Everything's fine. He put me on a pill to help my memory. First time I've ever been on a pill. We talked about nursing homes. I should say he talked about them, I listened thoughtfully. Very thoughtfully!

I remembered how hard it was for Mom to listen to me talking about those places. She fought tooth and nail, at least for the first few months. It took Annie and me quite a time to convince her to accept living in one. Then she was all set, and she died. I sure do miss Mom, miss her and Grandma. Didn't know if I should have been more open to Doc McIntyre or not. Got to think that one over for a while.

I've got plenty of time.

Zach

4 YEARS LATER

1977

FEBRUARY 1977

Monday – 2/14

Happy 90th birthday to me!

Talked with Annie and Zak for an hour today. She wishes we could be together more often, only traveling in winter's harder on me than it used to be. Again, she begged me to come home. Again, I told her I was home. She cried. Women!

I love this place. It does get lonely sometimes, but I'm not leaving the Ocean. So I have a plan. I haven't told Annie anything about it.

Yet.

Zach

Tuesday – 2/15

The movers came today.

Sold the house last month. It's hard to maintain my own place. I figured if I could build one for Mom in Houghton. I could build one for me in Portland. Construction started 18 months ago. We're calling it the Portland Memorial Nursing Home. It's right across the street from the hospital.

The folks in Portland were thrilled when I offered to build it. Alexander helped me set up a corporation to run the place. I ain't so senile after all. It's a non-profit, self-sufficient entity. I paid the entire cost, with the stipulation I stay here as long as I live, at no cost, and in my own private wing. I can see the Atlantic Ocean from my window and sit on my balcony listening to the pounding waves.

Dad would've loved it here.

Zach

Friday – 2/18

Talked with Annie today. Told her all about the new place. I think she was mad at first. She wanted me to move to Houghton. She said if it was fine enough for Mom it should have been fine enough for me. I asked if there was an ocean nearby I could listen to, that shut her up. She can be cagey, but I suppose she loves me.

She said she hired someone to fly back to Copper Harbor with me in July. He's going to be, as Annie called it, my traveling companion. I said, what the hell does that mean, traveling companion? Annie's not sure I can make all the proper connections. CRAP! I told her I could find my way around Paris, London, or Liverpool if I had to. She just laughed.

She said if I wanted to see Copper Harbor again I had to listen to her. I'll be traveling with a companion. She damn well better pay him good.

AUGUST 1977

Monday – 8/15

Alexander comes up once a month. I've got 2 rooms in my wing for guests. He's around 63 now. I lose track. He says he's ready to quit The Guys. He thinks it's not as much fun as it used to be. It still sounds like fun to me, but I guess I've lost some of my edge. I probably couldn't even track a rabbit anymore. Max sure did enjoy that saying. Good old Max, I truly miss him.

Annie got me back to Copper Harbor in July for the month. I had my traveling companion. He was a nice enough fella. That's as much traveling as I care to do nowadays. Now I consider this my home. I love the place, after all I built it, and I have some fine friends here.

Well, all except for Chastity. I can't seem to keep her out of my wing. She's driving me nuts. She says she loves my ponytail, the other day she actually grabbed it. Damn near pulled me over. She says she loves me. Crazy lady, but she is kind of pretty.

Zach

Monday – 8/29

Talked with Annie on the phone today. I asked her how much did you pay that guy who kept thinking he had to hold my hand. She said – not enough. She thinks I wasn't grateful enough. I guess, maybe she's right. Next month when school starts she's coming out to visit me.

I know she'll try to talk me into moving back to Copper Harbor again. She's a pest that way, but I sure do love her. I imagine one of my luckier days was way back when Mom and Frank met. Without the 2 of them there'd be no Annie! Life just wouldn't be the same. I'm one lucky fella.

I imagine my next permanent stop will be the Copper Harbor Cemetery.

I'll finally be with My Adeline.

Zach

7 YEARS LATER

1985

FEBRUARY 1985

Thursday – 2/14

Happy birthday to me! Almost 100. Two more to go.

They sure do know how to throw a birthday party here. I think they're getting tired of me living so long. They keep giving me cake and ice cream, I'm getting fat. I think they want my wing. The hell with them, I'm going to 100. God willing.

I met a new kid today; his name is Randolph. He cleaned my bed-pan. Usually I don't use it, but I wanted to give him something to do. He says he's going to be a doctor, a damn good one. He's from Florida and said something about his buddy getting eaten by an alligator. Strange kid, but he isn't sassy, like some of the aides.

He asked me how it felt to be 98. I told him to mind his own business. I said I wasn't old, I was growing. He laughed. Dumb kid. Wants to be a doctor, got a lot to learn. I'll teach him. The way I taught Alexander. I like him though.

Maybe he'll be fun.

Zach

Saturday – 2/23

Asked for Randolph today. I wanted to take a walk outside. 40 degrees and sunny, way too nice to stay inside. The head nurse said it was too cold. I said BULL SHIT, I want Randolph. He came and we took a half mile walk. How nice to get outside with a human being. I've started calling him Dandy Randy. I know he hates it, but he tolerates it. Good for him.

Great day today.

Zach

Sunday – 2/24

Randy took me to church today. I reminded the folks here about who built the joint and said Randy's time at church with me counted toward his hours. They already knew it.

Annie and Zak are coming in May. After most of the snow up there on top of the world melts. The weather here is much nicer. I've got the Atlantic Ocean right by me.

It's got to be nicer.

Zach

MARCH 1985

Friday – 3/15

Spent some time with Randy today. The kid sure is a hard worker and he loves baseball. He explained about the alligator, this time it made sense to me. That's been getting harder to do lately.

Things don't make much sense to me anymore. Annie said I'm becoming more and more like Grandma. Maybe I'm getting too damn old. 2 more years and I can kick the bucket. I like 100.

That's a fact.

Zach

Sunday – 3/17

Alexander came for the weekend. I guess Randy went to Boston to visit some friends, so they missed each other. Alexander said he'd get to meet Randy someday. I think they'd like each other, but what do I know? I'm old.

Alexander said Kathleen may come visit me someday. I said now's a fine time, I'm 98, she took her dammed good natured time. He laughed. He does have a way about him. Max would have liked him. I like him MOST of the time.

That's another fact.

Zach

Sunday – 3/31

Randy and I went to church today. He usually goes to the Catholic Church here in Portland, but he agreed to go with me to the church on the hill back in Cape Elizabeth. We took my Old's Ninety-Eight. It's only 13 years old, but he called it a pig.

I said, what the hell do you know? I told him how I opened PAPA'S Oldsmobile Company in Marquette, Michigan way back in 1906. 52 years before he was even born. He was all ears. We went to lunch and talked for 3 hours after church. I liked it. He seems to be the only person with any sense around here.

That's also a fact.

Zach

APRIL 1985

Monday – 4/1

The staff here sure likes April Fool's Day jokes. We had a lot of fun.

I asked Randy if I could adopt him. I even had the staff draw up papers which looked official. He winked at me and said he knew it was a joke. He'd seen the papers on the counter. We had a hearty laugh.

Then he told me about his grandma Minnie, and how much he loved her. He said she was a grand old lady, who spoiled him terribly. He said his grandfather died in a hunting accident out in Montana, 4 months after they were married. He said Grandma Minnie never talked about him. She said it was too hard.

I understood.

Zach

Wednesday – 4/17

Doc McIntyre says my dementia's holding its own. I mentioned I think maybe it's because the nursing home has become more enjoyable. He agreed with me. My eyesight problem is called macular degeneration. It can't be fixed, but perhaps with another pill we can slow it down.

Another pill. What the hell's going on with me?

Doc McIntyre has met Randy a few times. Says he's a nice kid. Not the sharpest knife in the drawer, but a darn quick learner, and he has more motivation than any grad student he's ever seen. Nice report.

Zach

Sunday – 4/28

Alexander came up for the weekend. Once again Randy was in Boston. I want them to meet each other. Alexander says no problem. He'll work it out over the phone with Randy. Maybe next month. I told him about the April Fool's Day joke. He laughed.

He mentioned he told Kathleen I thought it was a little late to fix my screw-up. She laughed and said it's the funniest thing the old codger ever said. Why did I ever let her sucker me in? Was I senile way back then, or just horny?

I told Alexander that Annie and Zak were coming here sometime in May. He said he'd try to get back here at the same time. Sounded good to me. Maybe Randy can be here also.

I hope.

Zach

MAY 1985

Sunday – 5/12

Annie, Zak, Alexander, and Kathleen were all here today. All at the same time. This time Randy was off taking some tests in New York till Tuesday. I'm not sure why Alexander can't work it out with Randy. I've done all I can, now I don't care anymore. I get to spend time with Randy, that's what's important.

Alexander introduced Kathleen to Annie as an old friend from New York. Pretty savvy on his part, but I think Annie caught on. She's no dummy, I'm not sure about Zak. We did have a fine time. I'm a hell of a lot older than any of them, but I held my own.

I only fell asleep one time. Annie kicked me. Reminded me of something Grandma would have done. I liked it. She did hit my sore leg, but what the hell. Kathleen looked good. Made me feel better about my screwup years ago. It literally was a screwup on my part.

Annie and Zak are staying for 3 days, so they'll get to meet Randy tomorrow. Alexander and Kathleen left after supper. This place treats me pretty damn good. The meals, when I have guests, are on a par with any nice restaurant. The 3 of us sat on my balcony and listened to the pounding waves from the Atlantic. I loved it.

I may have dementia and be getting senile, but I know what I like.
Zach

Tuesday – 5/14
Annie met Randy today. They hit it off like peas in a pod. They both have noses which turn up a little, right on the tip. I kidded them about it. Randy said he never even knew it. Now he's proud of it. Annie blushed. I'm not sure she ever noticed it before. Maybe it's my imagination.

Hell, I'm senile.
Zach

Wednesday – 5/15
Annie and Zak left after lunch. They drove all the way. I was amazed. Annie said I'd done it a few times over the years. Sometimes I forget about those days. Now I have to fly. I'm due to go back to Copper Harbor this July. I hope Doc McIntyre gives me the OK.

Randy said he did extremely well on the tests. I thought, sure you did. We spent a couple of hours talking about New York. He didn't know I spent so many years living there. He sure has a lot to learn. Dumb kid. Just kidding, I like him a lot. If he wasn't here I may have croaked months ago.

Life's OK.
Zach

Sunday – 5/26

Randy and I went to church again today. This time I went with him to his place. God was there. I could feel Him. I'm sure of it. We took my Oldsmobile. He asked if he could buy it from me, since I don't drive anymore. He said it's a relic, but it's fun to drive.

I said kid, when I'm in the ground, you can have it. He started crying. He has a soft spot. It's a necessary thing for a doctor to have. A soft spot. Good thing. We stopped at one of those crazy drive-in hamburger joints for lunch. He thought the Oldsmobile fit in perfectly. The gal came out on roller skates. Crazy world.

I met with Doc McIntyre this past Friday. I've been seeing him every month. He comes here for all of us old people.

Zach

JUNE 1985

Saturday – 6/1

Slept in most of the morning. Randy's off this weekend, so I have the aides looking after me. Not quite the same. They're some great folks, just not as personal as he is. There is one of the gals who knows exactly how to get me to laugh though. I think she, or maybe her mom, worked at one of the delis I used to frequent in New York. Good old days. For sure.

Tomorrow we're going to have a bowling tournament. Plastic pins and rubber balls. Sounds dumb to me. The head gal says it's fun. We'll see. They do try to keep a person active around here, but I prefer my walks with Randy. Doc says it's helpful for my limp. I say it's terrific for my attitude.

I sleep too much.

Zach

Thursday – 6/13

Went for a long walk with Randy this morning. Did take my walking stick. My legs are still pretty strong, it's my eyes that have me concerned. How the hell could I even track a rabbit in the snow if I can't see?

Randy's coming with me to my church this Sunday. He likes how small it is. He thinks it's easier to talk with God in a small church. I thought it was pretty easy to talk with God anyplace. It's hearing Him that's tough. Now since I have dementia and I'm senile, I'm not sure He hears me anymore.

Hope so.

Zach

Friday – 6/28

Alexander was here today. He can be pretty damn confusing sometimes. He said he had something to tell me, but I could never tell anyone else. He thinks it'll make me happy, but I can't share the information with anyone. Not even Annie, or Randy, or Doc McIntyre. I can't even write about it in this stupid journal.

He made me put my right hand on a Bible and swear to God I'd never mention anything about it to anyone. I figured he killed somebody. Maybe Kathleen. That might make me happy. Nah! Then I figured he found out something about Max, or maybe The Guys. What the hell could they have done?

Well, he told me. It did make me happy. Very happy! I can't figure out why I have to keep it quiet though, it seems like fantastic news to me. Like the whole world should know. Alexander said The Guys agree, I have to keep it quiet. He said I was senile, and I'd probably screw everything up if I talk about it.

I used to be sharper.

Zach

Sunday – 6/30

Annie and Zak came to visit this weekend. Annie said the head nurse told her I was sleeping too much. Crap. Dad had a cat in Brazil who used to sleep at least 20 hours a day. So what if I sleep too much. It ain't any of my nurses business, besides, I told them I was inspecting my eyelids.

Now Annie's going to stay for a week. Zak's flying home tomorrow. Annie acts like an old mother hen. I remember them, from the time Grandpa shot the fox in the hen house. Boy that was something else. One of the good old days! For sure!

Annie says she worries about me. She'd like to get me back home. I keep telling her this is my home. This is the home Zacharia built. I built it for me, well, me and the city of Portland. I told her she can take me back to Copper Harbor in a pine box. Boy did she cry. She went to her guest room. I think she's still crying.

I am senile. Damn!

Zach

JULY 1985

Monday – 7/1

Annie and I had breakfast this morning. She told me I'd go back home in a much nicer box than a pine box. I told her she could send me back in my Oldsmobile, except I promised it to Dandy Randy. She smiled. I think it's as much as I can hope for right now.

Annie didn't cry too much today, but she did hold my hand a lot. Randy took both of us out for lunch. We went back to the place with the girls on roller skates. I had a chicken sandwich with pickles and mustard. Randy can make Annie laugh. They were comparing noses. I liked that.

I love Annie!

Zach

Tuesday – 7/2

Annie brought me flowers today. My room smells great. Annie, Randy, and I, went to the beach after lunch. I absolutely love the smell of salt water, and the pounding of the waves. I talked a lot about my father, and Mom, Annie's mother. I almost slipped up and talked about the stuff Alexander warned me about. I ain't that far gone yet, but I did want to say something. I sure did!

I've written a letter explaining everything Alexander talked about. I stuck it in the back of my journal. Mom always said keeping a journal was a good idea. I took her word for it. I've got a bunch of them. I'll give them to Annie when I turn 100. She likes to read.

Didn't eat much supper today, lunch pretty much filled me up. The 3 of us did empty a splendid bottle of red wine tonight. Randy said it was the best bottle he could find at the supermarket.

Annie and Randy. Life is good.

Zach

Wednesday – 7/3

Wasn't feeling well today. Must have been the wine, or maybe it's the sauerkraut I had with supper. Annie took me to see Doc McIntyre this afternoon. He said my vitals are OK. I wasn't happy, I always preferred GREAT.

Randy's excited. He reminded me tomorrow's July 4th. He knows I love the 4th of July. He said Portland has a stunning fireworks display, and a huge parade downtown. The 3 of us are going to watch it. He said he'd put out chairs along the route first thing tomorrow morning. What a kid he is. Reminds me of the old days back in Copper Harbor.

The hell with Alexander and my promise, I'm my own man, I know what's the right thing to do. Tomorrow, first thing in the morning, I'm spilling the beans. I'll talk with Randy and get it all off my chest. Tell the truth. God will be happy. Then next week I can go back home for the rest of the month and relax. I'd like to see My Adeline again. I miss her.

Truly another FACT!

Zach

Thursday July 4, 1985 - The day Zacharia stopped growing.

When I read yesterday's entry it brought tears to my eyes. I thought back to the first day I met Zacharia, at his ninety-eighth birthday party, when I was about to start my residency at the Portland Memorial Hospital. Then I remembered what all happened on that day thirty-three years ago, and it suddenly felt like yesterday. That's the day that changed my life forever.

I was in downtown Portland that morning, putting three lawn chairs along the parade route, where Annie, Zacharia, and I were going to sit. When I got to the nursing home, it was just after noon. There was an ambulance parked by the side door. No lights were flashing, so I didn't pay any attention to it. I should have.

When I got inside, the receptionist was crying. Zacharia had been going around the building looking for me. It seemed no one could calm him down. He was so excited about telling me something. The nurse in charge said he just had to tell me. No one could get him to slow down. They didn't know what to do.

Annie had gotten him out onto his balcony, but she couldn't get him to settle down. She told his nurse he was having chest pains. They figured it was because of his excitement. The afternoon before, Doc McIntyre told Annie that Zacharia's blood pressure was pretty high, and he seemed quite agitated. Annie had some new medication he started taking at breakfast.

Around eleven, his nurse called the paramedics, who were there within five minutes. Zacharia was alive when they got there. Annie said he got extremely fidgety when he saw the medics. He kept saying all he wanted to do was talk with Dandy Randy. He said he didn't want any medics! Then he died.

Zacharia was in the ambulance when I walked past it, and I had no idea.

I was beside myself. Blaming myself for not being there. Wondering why he wanted me. What could I have done for him? I finished my time at the nursing home, then I had to leave. Everything reminded me too much of him. I transferred to the Florida Hospital in Orlando, where I met my soon to be wife Rachael. I finished my residency there, and with my Grandmother Minnie's financial help, Rachael and I started a small, fun-filled medical clinic in Lehigh Acres, Florida.

Last month my practice was merged with the Adventist Health System of Florida. I turned sixty and was able to semi-retire and start reading Zacharia's journals. Reading them brought Zacharia back to life. He made Rachael and me more emotional, at times he made us cry. He made us more spiritual. We're lucky for that. God bless Zacharia Valentine Zabrinski.

Dr. Randolph Quincy Babcock

. . .

There's a sealed envelope stuck in the back of his last journal, and It's addressed to me.

On the front of the envelope it reads –

Dandy Randy - **<u>DO NOT OPEN</u>** *– Until You're 60.*

Dear Randy, Tuesday, July 2ⁿᵈ, 1985

I'm writing this letter today, so I don't screw up my promise to Alexander. If I don't write this down, I'll probably blow up on the inside, and say something in the next few days I might regret. I think Alexander would disown me.

So here goes . . .

I hope I make it to 100. I think it would be neat. The Hick from Michigan, 100 years and growing. I like it, but if I don't, so be it. I'm amazed I made it to 98. Who would have guessed?

If you're reading this, I know you made it to 60. Good for you! I hope you became a doctor. I know you have the personality to be a damn good one. I've enjoyed all our time together. I know Annie loves you. How could she not?

I always wanted Alexander to meet you, but for some reason he never put it together. I ask him why, and he never tells me. He must have a reason. Since you're 60, it means Alexander's gone, and his reasons have gone with him.

I've had a damn nice life . . . and now you're a part of it. That's a Fact!

Let me explain . . .

First off --- I Love You!!

I know I liked you when I first met you. I wasn't quite sure why, I just did. We had a chemistry between us. I enjoy calling you Dandy Randy. I get a kick out of it. You tolerate it very nicely. We make a good team. No... we make a fantastic team. Thank you.

Now the interesting part. The part Alexander made me promise not to talk about. I know, if I don't write this down, I'll blow it one of these days, and

Alexander will have me committed. Then I'll be kept from spending time with you. Not a smart idea.

I'm leaving all my journals for you to read. You'll find out why later. Annie says she also has some of my old letters. She'll give them to you when the time comes. I suspect it'll be when I go on to my next journey. When I come face to face with God. I know He exists. I've felt His presence a number of times in my lifetime. I'll be able to thank Him for the wonderful, wonderful guardian Angel He sent me. I can't tell you how many pickles His Angel has gotten me out of.

Now, since you've read about my life, there are some other things you need to know. Some things no one's ever told you . . .

Kathleen and Alexander have spent a great deal of time and money getting you here to the nursing home, so we'd meet each other. I had no idea who you were until they told me last month. They don't want you to know any of this until you're 60. I don't understand why, but I have to trust them.

I met your grandmother Kathleen, you call her Minnie, many years ago in New York. I told her some things about myself. She thought I'd been caught in a vicious circle of wondering who I was and where I came from. She was right. I was. She was beautiful. She reminded me of My Adeline. I found myself vulnerable. We became intimate, and she had a child.

Your grandmother, Kathleen, is a fine woman. She dealt with the situation she was in gracefully, although my money didn't hurt. According to Alexander, she raised our daughter to be a woman who never questioned where she came from, or where she belonged. He says your mother's a wonderful woman.

Randy – I'm your Grandfather.

God bless you and keep you safe, till we meet again.

Love,

That's truly a Fact!

Grandpa Zach

ABOUT THE AUTHOR

Jerry Ziemer was born in Stoughton, Wisconsin, and raised in Milwaukee. He spent his junior year of high school in Los Angeles, California, and his first year of retirement with his wife of fifty-six years, Julie, living near their oldest son and his family in Manhattan, New York. They have three children, Karen, Paul, and Chris, twelve grandchildren, and fourteen great-grandchildren.

Jerry Ziemer owned a sign company, Design Craft Signs, in Hales Corners, WI, for thirty-nine years. They turned their home in Hales Corners, into a bed and breakfast, The Lawson House, for eight years before retirement. They currently live on the southwest side of Milwaukee, in a cute little condo.

NOTE FROM THE AUTHOR

Word-of-mouth is crucial for any author to succeed. If you enjoyed *The Journals of Zacharia 1905-1985*, please leave a review online—anywhere you are able. Even if it's just a sentence or two. It would make all the difference and would be very much appreciated.

Thanks!
Jerry Ziemer

We hope you enjoyed reading this title from:

Subscribe to our mailing list – *The Rosevine* – and receive **FREE** books, daily deals, and stay current with news about upcoming releases and our hottest authors.
Scan the QR code below to sign up.

Already a subscriber? Please accept a sincere thank you for being a fan of Black Rose Writing authors.

View other Black Rose Writing titles at
www.blackrosewriting.com/books and use promo code
PRINT to receive a **20% discount** when purchasing.